HOSEA
reached out and
gripped Gomer's cold hand.
"I love you,"
he said tenderly.
His words entered her heart
and nestled there
like newborn babes.
She gazed up at him,
hoping, almost praying.
Maybe someday . . .
maybe someday
she could say the same thing
to him.

MARION WYSE

LIVING BOOKS
Tyndale House Publishers, Inc.
Wheaton, Illinois

To Dr. R. K. Harrison, with gratitude

The correct pronunciation of the names of major
characters in this book are as follows:

Gomer	Go - *mare*
Hosea	Ho - *shia*
Diblaim	Di - bla - *eem*
Shana	Sha - *na*

Hosea and Gomer was previously published under the
title *The Prophet and the Prostitute.*

First printing, *The Prophet and the Prostitute*, July 1979
First printing, *Hosea and Gomer,* March 1985
Library of Congress Catalog Card Number 84-51957
ISBN 0–8423–1496–2, Living Books edition
Copyright 1979 by Marion Wyse
Printed in the United States of America

CONTENTS

PART II PEKAHIAH

PART III TIGLATH-PILESER

HISTORICAL NOTE

Israel is old and yet ever young, both desert and fertile green, her people dreamers and yet practical. Thus it has been since Abraham came to that land; thus it still is. Egypt, Assyria, Babylon, Greece, Rome, England—all have added this tiny nation to their empires. Yet, it still defiantly shouts its independence to the world.

More often than fighting off the rest of the world, however, Israelites have fought among themselves. The greatest split in the country came after the death of Solomon, when southern Judea stayed with the true Temple-worship and the son of Solomon, but northern Israel rebelled against God and the weak king and went her separate way. The old religion of Canaan was revived in the north, although some semblance of the rites of Moses and Aaron was practiced by a few faithful.

The assassination of kings was a common thing in the north at this time. Trade was usually poor. But under the long-lived Jeroboam II a relative stability brought increasing wealth to the capital, Samaria. The bear of Assyria to the north was placated with tribute money, and relations with Judea were carefully friendly.

When Menahem took the throne in 752 B.C., when this story begins, he reaffirmed Israel's allegiance to Assyria and her king Tiglath-pileser and led his people even deeper into the dark and pleasurable worship of the Old Ones of Canaan.

Into this situation came a man sent from God, a prophet, sent to lead his people back to the true worship of the God of Moses. But the Israelites had no desire to worship any god who took away the pleasures of today.

PROLOGUE — 721 B.C.

The young soldier looked down and shuddered, carefully stepping around the ashes at his feet. Not many hours before, that heap of burnt flesh and clothing had been a woman, a woman who had run screaming from her home after his fellow soldiers had fired it, with her long hair and clothing flaring out like a living torch behind her. He had watched in fascinated horror as she fled down the street trying to reach the well. But she had tripped over a body and fallen with a sharp cry to the ground. No one had made a move to help her. The soldiers were busy with their killing and looting, and all her neighbors were dead.

The young soldier glanced down at the woman's remains again and walked on, vomit in his mouth. It was his first campaign.

Ahead of him, by the new ruins of the once magnificent double city gates, he saw the imposing figure of his commander, Renin. The general was supervising the swift dismantling of the surrounding walls, those massive double barriers that had held his army outside for almost three years. It had taken the cunning of the king's young son, Sargon, to finally scale these walls. A week of backbreaking work while several shifts of soldiers carried earth up the steep slope to the walls, a night spent piling it up into a small mound to top the gates—and the starving defenders of this hilltop fortress were doomed.

The young soldier shuddered again, remembering the hideous cries that had burst from the throats of the women his companions had found hidden away like rats in the foundation-cellars of the deserted palace. The enraged invaders had taken out their fury on the women, their husbands watching in helpless agony while they writhed away their lives impaled on the ends of spears. He himself had spent the better part of the day rounding up survivors, frightened women and children who had stared at him with empty eyes in blank, unbelieving faces.

Now the young soldier came up to his commander and saluted. "Master, the captives are ready on the west side of the hill."

Renin glanced at the youth quickly and, seeing his pallor, wondered how long it would be before he deserted. "How many?" he asked crisply.

A small clay tablet exchanged hands, on which the tally had been recorded. Renin stood and watched the young soldier bound away down the hill, his day's work finished. The general sighed. It had been many years since he had dared to tackle such a steep slope. He looked over at his teams of soldiers busy rolling the huge stones of the wall down into the valley and remembered the years he had lived in this city. Then those walls had been his assurance of protection. *Not so now,* he thought, *and never again.*

Just then he heard a commotion behind him and turned swiftly to see the cause. One never knew if an unnoticed enemy had escaped being seen, and was now intent upon murder. But he saw that it was only some noisy old man being dragged along by boisterous soldiers, and he relaxed. In a moment, the old captive had been dropped at Renin's feet, and the captain who had tossed him there reported, "We found this old crow hiding behind a statue of Tammuz in the square. He claimed sanctuary, so we've brought him to you, master, to decide what to do with him."

Renin glanced sourly down at the old man cowering at his feet. "The gods of this city of Samaria have been defeated in battle by our gods, Ashur and Ishtar. Even with Tammuz will a Samaritan not find safety, though Tammuz is the husband of our Ishtar, for he is not native to this place." The captain made a move toward his sword, but Renin lifted his hand and said, "No, leave him with me. I will question him."

Surprised, the Assyrian soldiers moved away, muttering under their breath. The old man would have made quite a noise before he died if the killing was done the right way, and they didn't appreciate their commander spoiling their fun.

The old man was shaking dreadfully with fear, and his toothless gums moved uncontrollably back and forth. Renin's lean dark face, by sharp contrast, was cold and firm, his black eyes grim and tired. "Old man, I have a question to put to you," he said in a low voice, waiting for his captive to look up. "If you satisfy me, you'll join the rest of the living on the west hill."

The Samaritan's eyes gleamed, and he nodded his bald head. "Aye, aye, whatever the master wishes," he offered, rubbing his dirty hands together.

Renin took a quick look around and saw that his soldiers had walked out of hearing distance. "Listen, then. There was a woman who came back here from Nineveh fourteen years ago with your holy man. I had made a promise to—to my first master, before he died, to look after her if I could. I tell you this to assist your memory, so that you'll answer if you can. I haven't seen this woman among the captives, and she was not a woman men would kill. Old man, know you the whereabouts of Gomer?"

"Gomer!" The old man spat out the name with such hatred that Renin involuntarily stepped backwards. *Gods!* the general thought, *he has a demon!* The captive was frothing at the mouth, brandishing his clenched fists above his head. "Gomer! You ask me, Zedediah, an honorable man, about the harlot of Samaria! So that's where she was all those years, with the heathen of Nineveh! I knew she was a traitor all along!"

Renin reached down quickly and struck the old man across the face. The officer was pale, his eyes burning. "Call her not such filth."

The old man shrank away. "I—I meant no harm, master—no harm!"

Renin controlled himself with an effort. "You knew her, then?"

"Aye, she—she was my neighbor while she grew up, a rebellious and evil girl. Nothing but contempt did she show me, an elder of the city!" Contempt was the only expression in Renin's eyes at the moment, but the old man did not have the courage to look up.

"Where is she now?"

"Master, I know not. She is gone, long gone—she and her whole brood, and that prophet who married her. They left three years ago, almost as if they knew you were coming. I've no idea where they went—south, perhaps. I heard that the husband had a friend in Jerusalem. You see? Traitors, all of them!"

The old man had risen to his knees in his rage, and hadn't noticed the return of the soldiers who had captured him. Seeing his general's face and misinterpreting the anger there, the captain drew his sword and plunged it through the old man's back. The captive crumpled without a sound.

So she was gone.

Renin stood beneath the stars, letting the night breeze blow away the dust and ashes from his shirt. The stones from the ruined wall lay about him in chaotic whiteness. The city lay in burning heaps behind his back. Below, in the valley, he could hear the shouts and laughter of the drunken soldiers as they celebrated their victory. The old king, Shalmaneser, had probably risen from his sickbed to join them, and Renin was certain that the crafty prince, Sargon, was leading in the fun of playing with the prettiest girls captured today.

But he, the general who had directed the assault, stood alone on the hilltop, his only company the memories he had never shared with anyone.

Could it really have been almost twenty years since he had last stood there? It had been a cruel hot day. The crowd—some of whom had undoubtedly been among the dead and captured today—had been jeering and throwing filth at himself and his companions in exile. He had suffered, not for his own pride, for he knew that the might of Assyria would repay them for that day's work, but because *she* had had to bear the degradation as well.

She had been beside him that day, and he almost wished she was with him now, wished that she had stayed so that he could have rescued her, so that he could have seen her just once more. She would be older now, probably a grandmother, but in his memory she was still youthful and lovely.

He had led her and his soldiers down this slope, away from her home, and she had not uttered a word. But her golden eyes had been full of grief. Would she be as grieved when she heard this news, now, as she had been then? He wanted to go to her and tell her what had happened, what he had been forced to do by his king. He wanted to search her out in the south and tell her, and bear her grief with her.

Almost she was there, her graceful body and innocent smiling face before him like a wraith in the moonlight, and his mouth parted in agony. So she had stood, the first time he saw her outside the palace gate. So she had been the last time she turned to him, in Nineveh. Always he had worshiped her, but always his masters had laid claim to her, and he was content merely to serve. Now where was she? Deserted? In a safe haven? Or dead? *Better to be dead,* he thought, *than to hear that her home is gone forever.*

Renin started down the slope, his feet finding the path unerringly, and again it was as if she were there beside him, the light fragrance of her perfume filling the air, the low cadence of her voice in his ear once more.

PART I
HOSEA

ONE

Ashes to Ashes

Samaria . . . The noise and color and dirt of the city filled her memory as she sat in that small room in Jerusalem. The sun that gently caressed her worn face and gray hair was that same sun that had struck gold in the depths of her eyes when she had played in the streets of Samaria. But those eyes were closed now against the glare, a glare that made today too real and yesterday but a dream.

Samaria . . . Could it really be just smoke and ashes now, her city, her home gone under the heavy tramp of Assyria's soldiers? But hadn't she known, since the day she had fled that fortified hilltop three years ago, that one day she would hear this news? Wasn't that why she and her family had left while there was still time, while Shalmaneser was occupied with subduing the northern cities? Yes, she'd known that defeat was coming for Israel and had escaped south to this home in an enemy country—and left one of their number in an unmarked grave east of the Jordan. Yes, she'd known—but sorrow coming is all the deeper for knowing of its coming.

Isaiah paced the small room restlessly, like a lion she had once seen in Nineveh, striding back and forth, a growl deep in his massive throat. He was expecting a messenger from the palace at any moment with a summons from the panic-stricken King Ahaz. Ahaz had sent troops to the support of Shalmaneser, but now was terrified for the safety of his own country. Would Jerusalem go the same way as Samaria? Would the Assyrian king go back to Nineveh to die, or continue his triumphant march down the Jordan? Ahaz would have all his soothsayers and diviners hard at work discovering the answer, and would grow so embittered with their varied responses that he would send for the man of God—and the man of God would come to him with the truth. So Isaiah paced about, praying desperately for guidance, while he glanced occasionally with pity at the woman by the window.

She had arrived at his doorway two and a half years ago, her eldest son supporting her, her youngest son clutching a bag of scrolls in his sturdy arms. "They were my father's," he had said with fierce pride.

Her daughter, a younger version of the woman who had once been a king's pride, had explained who they were, and Isaiah had welcomed them for his dead friend's sake. That night the woman had told her story far into the dawn hours, and he, a prince of Judea who laughed easily and hated tears, had wept with her.

Now there she sat, her back still straight, her small chin high, her eyes closed. Isaiah knew without asking that she was back in the past, in Samaria that was no more—praying, remembering, regretting.

T W O
On the Roof

She remembered how handsome and proud the homes of Samaria had been, how the sun had glinted from the polished stone to blind one's eyes. She could see it all from her workbench on her father's roof, all the houses stretching up beyond her home and growing ever more grand until the palace itself crowned the summit of the mountain.

Then she could turn and look over the city wall right beside her rooftop perch, into the ripe fields of the valley leading into the green hills and vanishing into the forest. Those hills were her horizon, and all within their circle was her world. It was all a part of her: the windy gales that swept down from the tiny Sea of Galilee to the north, the calling birds that dipped their wings above her as they flashed past to raid the fields below. And more than all the rest, the noise of the city was hers as well.

Right beside her home was the east gate, and all the traffic in and out of Samaria passed beneath her. Any time of the day she could lean over the waist-high wall that lined her roof and watch travelers from all over the world come to trade. Men with deep black skins from Ethiopia, men with yellowish tinges in their eyes from some country far to the east, men with lighter skins from the northlands around the Great Sea. Many they were, dressed in colorful robes, filling the air with their languages and laughter, leading their camel trains to the gate where they unloaded and headed for the market.

Once she had been a part of that busy market life, and it had been her joy to welcome her father's clients and take their goods in exchange for her mother's cloth. But all that was gone now, since the day she had run to her mother and whispered that her time for separateness had come, that she was a woman now. Her father had then decreed that she was too old to run about like a child, and the next day he had taken her sister Rachel with him to his booth.

Now the roof was her place, and she worked from dawn to dusk sorting and carding wool for her mother's loom, mixing dyes for the vast basins downstairs, laying out flax to dry. And during harvest she had to grind grain for their storeroom. The work in the market had been a pleasure, and she had smiled and laughed with the men who had stopped to finger her mother's linens and woolens, bright in their red and yellow dyes. True, there had been piles of plain bleached materials, but those were usually bought by the women for their work clothes. It was the men who bought the expensive, colorful cloths. For their wives, they said, and she had believed them, being a child of the Shabbat in a worshiping, Law-abiding household.

She remembered the times when her playmates had

run over to the booth on their way home from school, some who were sons of the city elders like her father, some sons of the valley farmers like her uncle. She had tossed her long hair and laughed with them, but her father had always ordered them off with frowns. Toward the time of her emergence into womanhood, he had been so fierce about their visits that they soon only regretfully waved to her from across the market square and went on home. She had missed them, but life had still been full and fun—until the day her father led her up to the roof.

Now she watched the crowds in the streets below and envied them. It was harvesttime, and the late caravans were hurrying to finish their business so that they could be out of these northern hills and into the deserts of the south before the rainy season came. She had piles of grain beside her waiting to be ground down into flour, and her arms were already aching with the work that had filled three bags. But the sun still had a way to go before it reached the western hills, and she knew her father would be angry if she didn't get another bag done. So she regretfully left her place at the wall and went back to squat before the millstone.

Round and round went her arms, smooth and rippling with strong muscles under the brown skin, and round and round went the thoughts in her bent head. Why was she here wearing herself out like a slave, while Rachel went with Father to the market and enjoyed herself? Surely they could afford to buy a slave. There were plenty for sale right across the square from Father's booth, captives from the Assyrian victories in Syria and Philistia. She had seen several strong girl captives who could have done this job much better than she, leaving her free to roam the hills looking for the flowers needed for the dyes, free to laugh and run in the meadows with her friends, free to go to market. But she also remembered the glower in her father's eyes when she had once suggested buying a slave. He had answered that he would have no lazy daughter in his house living off a stranger's sweat. She had been angry, being sure that it wasn't against the Law of Moses to own a slave, and it was usually the Law that governed her father's actions.

She was angry now at Rachel, who was still free to do all the things she had been taken from three years ago, and Rachel had just come into *her* womanhood too! Sweet Rachel, Father called her with his rare smile— little Rachel—*she* was always so obedient and modest, *she* was never scolded, *she* was always eager to do their father's wishes, *she* never complained, oh no!

The millstone went around faster and faster as her thoughts grew more vehement, and an angry tear splashed down on the busy ants who were carrying away some of the grain at her knees. She longed to hear the high boyish laugh of her cousin Dan, whom she had once chased across the fields. But when he came over these days he seemed to pay more attention to Rachel. Again it was Rachel, with her soft, gentle voice and her meek, black eyes, able to quiet boisterous Dan and soothe Father's harshness with a glance. She still called Father "Abba" as if she were a child.

The tireless, tiring rhythm of her thoughts went on and on, and her brows knit with weariness from the complaint inside her heart. Her unprotected head was growing dizzy in the heat of the afternoon sun. The dust from the busy street was filtering up to the roof and playing chase with the flies that buzzed around her head.

To banish her weariness, she brought her thoughts to the evening a year before when her father's brother had come up to visit from his small house in the valley. He had been a tiny round man, her uncle Dan, a funny man who loved to laugh and had passed on that laughter to his son. He was the complete opposite of his lean, intense brother. Her uncle had heard Father chastising her because she had darted out to greet him at his arrival, and so exposed herself to the view of the men of the city on their way to their nightly parties.

Dan had shaken his bald head in disbelief. "Diblaim, please! Be calm! What's that, Gomer? No, Dan couldn't come tonight; he had to tend to our ewes at the birthings. Brother, listen to me—why must you hide her away like this? First you deny her the marketplace, every woman's privilege, especially those who love to gossip. Then you shout at her when she runs out into the street to greet me! Can she help her attractiveness? You think little of our neighbors if you think she creates evil just by being seen!"

Gomer had run over to her uncle to hug him, and noticed with a sudden shock that she was a few inches taller than he. "Am I really attractive, Uncle?" she had asked, laughing, unaware of her flushed cheeks and shining eyes.

She remembered the amusement in his eyes as he answered her. "Have you no mirror, little one?" he asked as he looked up at her. She was just starting to laugh again when Father's harsh voice cut her off.

"She has no mirror—that is vanity, Dan, and I'll not have you encouraging her in it!" He motioned for his daughter to leave, and she did so reluctantly, going into the side room that she shared with Rachel. But she stood still just inside the door and left it open a crack to hear what they said, certain that it would be about her.

She heard her father's voice first, heavy and somewhat sad. "Can't you see that I must protect her from things she doesn't understand? You only have your son to worry about, so perhaps you don't see how a daughter must be taken care of in this city, in case—"

"This is protecting her, making her home a cage?" Dan was the only person alive who ever dared interrupt her father, and she had never heard his voice sound so bitter.

"Listen, Dan! Rachel needs no such . . . protection, because her goodness is her cloak. Every man in Samaria thinks of Jacob's Rachel when he sees her, and would no more harm her than the mother of the southern tribes. But Gomer! You haven't been with us in the market the few times she has gone with Shana in past years to buy food. I have seen the eyes of the men following her. I have seen the wickedness in their gaze. Oh, how Samaria must stink in God's nostrils! Would that he had sunk those men in Sheol before they laid their lustful eyes on my daughter!"

Gomer heard her father stumble over to a bench, and she knew the despairing anger that would be clouding his eyes as he thought of their people who slighted their God in so many ways. "You know Zedediah, my neighbor who holds Shabbat with us because he has no family of his own—he has told me about things that have been happening lately here in the street before our own home, while I've been at the market and Shana has been busy weaving. Zedediah tells me about the men and boys who gather here, and about games that no one else has mentioned to me because they know it would give me shame. Maybe to Gomer she is only playing as she used to in the fields; she is still a child. But what about those men and boys who chase her and laugh with her when she should be working? It's enough to make me call every man in Samaria to an accounting!"

Gomer was standing in the shadows behind the door, her eyes wide with astonished anger. Had she dared, she would have run out to the two men and screamed that Zedediah was a liar, a hypocrite. It was *he* who chased her when she went out the door each morning and headed for the steps at the side of the house leading to the roof. That skinny old excuse of a man who spent his days lurking in his doorway, waiting for her, trying to grab her as she darted into the alley between their two houses. Once he had caught her by the shoulder and grinned into her face, but she had torn away and run up the stairs, a nameless terror in her throat. Now he dared lie to her father and brand her a careless woman! It was no wonder her father always looked so pained when he saw her, and was always talking to her about the virtuous woman in the Proverbs of Solomon. She had thought he was teaching her how to be a good wife when the day should finally come. Now she realized, to her horror, that he had been trying to divert her supposed activities into their proper course. She had thought he was saying, "Learn," but he had been warning her, "Wait!"

Dan had been silent for a few moments, and when he spoke his voice had a curious sadness in it. "So you hide her away. Diblaim, my brother who believes every man who keeps Shabbat is as honest as you—do you *know* that Zedediah speaks the truth about Gomer? He is a known cheat in the market—no, let me finish! I'll never buy another donkey from him after what happened to the last one. 'Never had a heavy load on its back,' he says! The next day I prepare it for a short journey down the valley and as soon as I put a light pack on its back, its knees buckle and it falls down. Trust Zedediah! I'd sooner trust an Assyrian!"

Gomer forgot her anger in a wave of laughter as she remembered the rage of her uncle that day. *A tiny man should never get angry,* she thought. *He looks too funny!*

Her father had risen from his bench and was walking about again. "I cannot accept your doubts about Zedediah, Dan. He has been a good neighbor, and the donkey *I* bought from him has always stood up well. But I think often of Gomer and her faults, which I am sure marriage will cure. My daughters are being saved for the sons of believers, my brother, such as your own Dan. Trust me. I will find a husband for my Gomer soon, and I know what is best for her. Now let us leave this. Tell me about your new lambs."

Remembering this overheard conversation a year later, Gomer stopped in her work and gazed at the distant hills, blending now with the evening mist that was starting to rise from the river winding through the valley. Her uncle hadn't lived to make her father fulfill his promise, for he had died suddenly a month later of a swamp fever. She had never been able to tell him the truth, although she was sure he had known it. But the thought that her father would believe Zedediah over her was a continual ache in her young heart.

Gomer stood, stretched up her arms toward the scattered clouds overhead, and then relaxed. Yes, the rainy season was definitely on its way, and soon she would be a prisoner again inside the house, working beside her mother and listening to boring chatter about their relatives and friends. Until then, she was determined to enjoy what outside air she could. She had enough flour now for another bag, so she felt she had worked sufficiently for today. Brushing the dust from her dress with swift, hard strokes, she sauntered over to the edge of the roof and leaned on the top of the wall, gazing at the street below. A phrase from the conversation she had been remembering slipped into the front of her mind, something about the wickedness of the men of Samaria because they looked at her. Was that really true?

Certainly it was true that she had seen their eyes light up when she laughed with them. She had always thought it was because they found her words amusing. But that night she had, through her father's words, caught a glimpse of a world carefully hidden from her by her mother's simple explanations and her father's threatening silences after an indiscreet question. She found that hidden world entrancing by its very unknowableness, and wished that she had the freedom of the marketplace again to discover more about it. In that world were men, not boys like her old playmates: men who bought fragrant perfumes and bright cloths and smiled when they said their purchases were for their wives. She had loved the giddiness those perfumes had brought to her head on the few occasions she had been allowed to sniff at a bottle; she had loved the silken touch of the cloth the men held as they told how it had arrived at her father's table from the east. Now she had been cut off from that world for so long, and the shimmering lights and soft music she was sure it held made her ache more than ever to enter it.

Gomer ran her hand over the rough edge of the stone beneath her arms, watching the sunbeams glinting from the glassy edges of small pieces caught inside the rocks when they were formed. A lock of her hair fell over her shoulder and brushed her hand, and she smiled. She liked the way the sun brought out the buried golden lights in her hair as it fell in thick, shining waves below her waist. *Maybe it's my hair that makes the men smile.* She wondered and laughed. Silly men, to like her hair when no other girl she had ever seen had any like it! Rachel and their mother had black, dusky hair that curled over their shoulders like sheep's wool. Also, they were shorter, more to the regular height of Samaritan women, and she always felt awkwardly tall around them. Often she had wondered about the differences between herself and her sister and pestered her mother for an explanation, but Shana always pursed her lips and shook her head. Someday she would tell, but not yet— always it was someday.

She lifted her hand and gazed at it thoughtfully, her eyes sober. Yes, she was different, too different for the men of Samaria to like her at all. Her skin had a golden glow to it, a whiteness, while every other woman's in Samaria was a deep brown that went almost black during harvesttime. *Maybe I'm a child of the sun god,* she thought wistfully, remembering the stories she had heard told in the market by the white men from the north. *Maybe Mother found me when I was a baby and took me home. And if it's true, then Father isn't really my father at all, and I can do as I please!*

Well aware that she was being childish, Gomer couldn't restrain a wave to the sun and a delighted call:

"Hello, shining father!" Not receiving any other answer except a heat wave on the next breeze, she closed her eyes against the glare and slipped into her favorite day-dream, especially soothing to her well-being at the end of a hot day, when her arms were aching and her stomach cried out for food: She was the favored daughter of a king, someone like Menahem up in Samaria's palace, and slaves brought her ices and milk to cool her throat on a day such as this, and one stood behind her to fan away the persistent flies. . . . Or she was Rebekah, beloved wife of the patriarch Isaac, living in a spacious tent out in the open fields, free to walk and sing in the nearby hills. This dream was her most colorful and detailed, for Shana had brought her daughters up on the tales of old Israel, hoping to nurture in them the love for God that had burned in these heroes and their wives, trying to teach them to be women like Sarah, who had ruled her household wisely and guided her husband with wisdom.

Gomer had often wondered if her mother had day-dreamed when she was young. What must it be like to be tied to a man like Father for life, a man who believed equally in God and hard work and drab clothes, a man who demanded an accounting of every moment spent out of his sight? She thought of her mother, tired and gray after years of toil. She lifted her head to the sun she had saluted a few moments ago and vowed she would never live that life, that she would marry a man who was young and handsome and rich, a man who might believe just as fervently as her father in Israel's God, but who wouldn't be as harsh as that God seemed to demand.

Her daydreaming faded as Gomer heard calls from the street below. A caravan was assembling just outside the gates and would be leaving with the sunset. She ran to the side that overlooked the gate square, excitement rising within her as she thought of the places to which that caravan would carry her father's goods. Who knew? Maybe her future husband rode with this caravan and guided these camels. . . . Maybe he would take her to the land of the Ishmaelites, or the fabled land of Sheba far to the south.

She leaned over the wall, wondering if the world of reality below was at all like her dreams. But the fuss and the noise was as usual. Stubborn donkeys brayed and tugged away from the boys who held their ropes. The boys shouted at them in despair, calling on any gods who listened to save them from such unmanageable beasts. The camels ignored everyone and concentrated upon munching as many of the sparse blades of grass as were within reach around the well-trampled path. They had already drunk long and deep from the river a few yards away that tumbled down from its source over the mountain rocks, and they were ready for the long trek away from Gomer's world into the fascinating unknown.

This was the last caravan of the season, and she saw from the symbols woven into the camels' blankets that it was originally from Egypt. One picture had a bird's head on a man's body, another a looped cross under a blazing sun. Her father, when she had first seen such symbols in the marketplace and questioned him about them, had replied with disdain that these Egyptians believed their gods to be present in animals. Far from repelling her, the idea had sparked her lively imagination, and she had spent almost a week trying to get their own donkey, Nathan, to talk back to her.

Remembering her failure in this, and wondering if the men below talked to their animals, Gomer was so intent on watching the packing of the caravan that she didn't hear footsteps on the roof behind her. The voice in her ear a second later made her jump. "Gomer! What are you doing hanging over the wall? You know your father will beat you if he catches you like that!"

It was her mother, her eyes large with fear. Her hands were strong as she pulled her tall daughter away from the edge. But Gomer jerked away, her eyes flashing with rebellion. "I'm only having a rest, Imma! See? My work's all done. I've four bags of grain for you and a small pack for the widow Ischba."

"Yes, yes, thank you—but please, Gomer, you mustn't lean over the wall like that!" The mother's eyes were still afraid, for she hated it when her husband beat the girl with his hands. But being a woman of few and halting words in a crisis, she couldn't say anything about her fear to Gomer, and the girl wouldn't understand anyway. What could a mere girl know of her father's deep desire and need to have his family righteous in God's eyes, and his fears of punishment if they were not? Was not a father responsible for his family? So the Law said, and so Diblaim acted.

Gomer, in a mood to disobey, turned her back on Shana and looked over the edge again. She ignored her mother's soft plea to come down with her to prepare supper, and didn't hear the second call at all, for her eyes had been caught by the swift flash of a flowing blue robe. She followed the passage of the regal form that bore it through the weaving crowds below. He came into the open before the gate and turned, and when she saw his face her mind froze between one thought and another.

Who was he, that man down there? Her mother might have been 1,000 miles away for all the effect her call had upon ears that could hear only a pounding heart.

The man below her stood in the gates as if he owned the whole city. He stood there tall and arrogant, his flashing eyes missing nothing of the assembling of his caravan, his bearded chin held high as he spoke to his camel drivers. Gomer could tell that he was the owner by the deference paid to him by the others.

She leaned over the roof and gazed at him, sure he had walked right out of one of her dreams. She wished for him to look up and see her. She wanted to see him smile and walk around to the stairs and climb up to her. She took in his stance as he held himself like a desert king of the Ishmaelites, his white *kaffiyeh* wound around his head with a deep blue sash that matched his robe.

Suddenly she felt her mother grab at her arm again. "Gomer! Stop this waywardness and come down at once!"

Gomer whirled around and flung off the restraining hand, her face flushed from the turmoil she was feeling, her eyes filled with rage. She clenched her teeth and spoke low and distinctly. "Leave me be, Imma!" Shana stepped back in dismayed shock from the girl's fury, for the moment so much like her father's. "I'll come in a minute, when I please! Now leave me alone. I am a woman now, not a child!"

To Gomer's surprise, her mother scurried away. She didn't know how terrible she had looked in that moment of blind anger. But she wasted no time wondering. She turned back to the street, and her heart plunged.

He wasn't there! But wait—there were voices right below her, speaking with soft southern accents. She thought of Egypt, and immediately her daydream was all around her again. She felt the mysterious thrill which the thought of Egypt always brought with it . . . the memory of the land of unlimited sunshine where her people had once lived.

The clip-clop of a donkey's hooves on the now almost deserted street below caught her ears, and she stiffened. Yes, it was Nathan—she could tell by the hesitation in the fall of his hooves, for he had been lame since the time he had been run over by the king's chariot on the royal avenue. For that fact alone, Menahem was hated by Diblaim's family.

Father and Rachel were coming home after a busy day, and they would be hungry. She thought of her mother downstairs getting the meal ready all by herself, and she felt ashamed of her anger. Running over to the full bags, she knelt down and tied them together, then heaved them on her strong back as she arose. Almost doubled over with the weight, she was crossing over to the stairs when she heard her father's call from the front door.

"Gomer! Get down here at once and help your mother!"

Immediately all her eagerness left her, and the same helpless anger that always filled her when her father was present now threatened to smother her. She bit back a retorting shout that she was already hurrying, and glared down at the roof floor. The same thundering question filled her as it always did: Why, why, *why* did she have to call this man, one of the few men left in Samaria who observed Shabbat and called upon the one true God of Israel, why did she have to call this man her father? He worked her like a slave, she thought, and then he wondered why she didn't accord him the same love and instant obedience as Rachel did.

But the anger against her father slipped by in a few seconds, for she was remembering the man in the square below who had looked like a king. She started hastily again for the stairs. She descended swiftly, her long skirt bunched up at her waist so that she wouldn't trip, the bags heavy on her slender back. Reaching the bottom, she ran to the door and dropped the bags in the opening. None of her family were looking her way; so silently she darted past the doorway and ran to the corner of the house, her eyes wide and eager. Would he still be near the gate?

She reached the corner of the house and looked quickly around when suddenly her forehead crashed into someone's rigid spine. With a small gasp of pain she reeled backward, blinded by the collision, too stunned to cry out. She felt a strong hand grip her shoulder to steady her, and through the clearing haze she heard a low, husky voice. "My lady, my lady, are you all right? I am so sorry!"

She blinked her eyes a few times and managed a rueful laugh. "Yes, I—I think I'm all right, thank you." Then she looked up to see the person speaking—and looked right into two dark eyes that were watching her face with intensity, two luminous eyes under a white desert *kaffiyeh* that shaded his face from the sun.

Gomer, with her aching head and the sudden surge of power that had passed into her from the man's gaze, felt sure that she would faint. She blinked again and shook her head to get rid of the dizziness. She felt a sudden shyness in his presence. She glanced around, and the shyness nearly became panic.

Around her and the man from the caravan were his black camel drivers, with whom he had been speaking. Their gay red shifts glowed brightly against their ebony skins, and they were regarding with interest this foreign girl who had interrupted their conference with their leader. She flushed under their eyes as she had never done in the marketplace before the laughing men there; but she had never felt then as she did facing this man.

The grasp of the desert man's strong hand on her shoulder was paralyzing her, and she couldn't move away. But before she could wonder what to do, she felt a hard finger under her chin, lifting her head until she had no choice but to look into his eyes again.

They were so deep and dark that it was like staring into the depths of a mysterious cave, full of unknown and desirable treasures. His face seemed carved from smooth, brown stone and the shadows of his nose, forehead, and cheeks were sharp and sudden and magnificent, as a mountain is magnificent in its solid grandeur. The tilt of his head spoke of pride that was lofty and untouchable, the pride of a man free in a world enslaved. She forgot that she had seen fifteen harvests and felt like a small child before him. She wanted him to let her go so that she could run back inside, yet she never wanted to leave him. There was that in his kingly bearing that fired her heart, and before she realized what she was doing she had drawn imperceptibly closer and was smiling at him.

He smiled as well, a smile so knowing and sure that

she felt fear again, only a different sort of fear. His eyes started to glow and he said softly, "Just like the fawn of an antelope, you are——"

Gomer broke away from his grip and ran for the door, her heart pounding. But she stopped and looked back, unable to resist one more look at him. He was still standing there, his eyes brooding as he watched her. They exchanged a long look, and then she went inside and closed the door.

Diblaim came out of his workroom after entering the day's profits in his book and glanced around the kitchen. His wife was stirring a pot over the fireplace, and his beloved Rachel was tearing a loaf of bread into four pieces for their supper. Shana's hair was pulled back by a string and hung down her back in gray, greasy locks, her face streaked with sweat after a day spent between the loom and the cooking fire. There was little there to remind him of the girl he had wed. But when he looked at Rachel he saw that girl again, her glowing black hair flung back over her shoulders as she worked, her small round face puckered and intense over her tasks.

Diblaim's face, heavily bearded and browned, was usually lean and hard and his black eyes suspicious, but just now his look had softened as he watched these two women at work. Besides, it had been a good day since Senu-Amen showed up with his Egyptian goods. Both had been pleased with their trading, as always. He felt an inner warmth of contentment—until he chanced to glance at the table and saw his eldest daughter slicing onions. Her face was smooth and expressionless, although the tears streamed from her eyes. He could smell the pungent odor of the onions where he stood in the door. He frowned. There was a glow in her eyes that sat ill with that innocent face, and he wondered what she was thinking.

"Gomer!"

She looked up at him, shaking the tears from her face so that she could see. "Yes, Father?" She was secretly quailing inside, wondering if he had noticed how long it had taken her to obey his summons to help with supper. She had never been successful at lying to him.

"I see you did well in your grinding today." He glared at the shock in her eyes. Did she think he never noticed when she did a good job? "That's just as well, because I've asked your cousin Dan to bring in his shearings tomorrow and you will be carding it."

Gomer nodded meekly, her eyes downcast to hide the rebellion in them. *May Dan and his sheep fall into the pit of Sheol and never emerge,* she thought to herself. "Yes, Father."

Diblaim scowled but could say nothing, although his uneasiness about her grew. What was she up to now, this little fighter who hated work and discipline as much as once he had? He understood her moods and rebellions, and to curb her, to make her soul as meek and gentle as Rachel's, he was hard on her always, never letting up even when Shana begged him to show a little softness for her. But no! He didn't dare, for he wanted her to be made into a good daughter of Israel before he started looking for a husband for her, and he knew that had to be soon.

After supper, lying before the dying fire and listening drowsily to her father as he read in his deep, sonorous voice about the wanderings of Israel in the wilderness so long ago, Gomer found her thoughts slipping away into another dream. In it, those phantom figures who had for years courted her, the loveliest woman in the world, had crystallized into one man, the Egyptian. If the normality of her household had caused her to doubt that fleeting moment outside, the sore spot on her shoulder where he had held her dispelled such notions. No, he had been real, too real for her life here, and in her dream he was reaching out to her, calling her name in a low, endearing voice.

Shana watched her eldest girl from her bench in the corner, as she relaxed in the one quiet moment of her day. She knew her Gomer wasn't listening to the sacred Book. She knew it was dreams taking her miles away that brought a shine to the young face. She remembered the dreams of her own girlhood, and knew she couldn't discipline Gomer for her lack of attention. But she wished her husband would hurry and find a man for Gomer. The girl needed marriage.

Shana gazed soberly at the girl, aware of the picture she made in the firelight. Gomer's long rippling hair caught the gold from the embers and shone with a subdued radiance of its own. The girl's face was turned away from her mother toward the fire, but Shana could see in her mind's eye the smooth wide forehead, the large eyes that held mysteries and dreams in their golden depths and laughter in their warm brown sparkle, the high cheekbones that blended smoothly with her strong round chin, the large laughing mouth so red and the good strong teeth so white.

Shana sat there watching, and a tiny fear for her daughter brushed her eyes. *She is too lovely,* thought the mother, *too lovely in her proud, patrician way that makes me feel like a farmer's wife covered with dirt.*

*What plain man, serving and fearing God, would
want such a wife? Would he not live in fear of his
pagan neighbor, who would not follow the command
against coveting another man's wife? But she must
wed—we can't deny her the privilege of every
daughter of Israel to bear sons to serve God. Oh,
Gomer, Gomer, my daughter, God grant you the pa-
tience to wait until we find the right husband for you!*
Shana knew the power of dreams, and she knew her
daughter's stubbornness, and she was afraid.

Gomer also was thinking of marriage as she lay before the fire, but not as the protection or privilege her
mother craved for her. The only marriage she knew
intimately was her parents', for Uncle Dan's wife had
died in her only son's birthing. Gomer thought of a
husband as a prisoner thinks of his jailer, with fear and
loathing. She had no desire to spend the rest of her days
at the mercy of a man who worshiped God on the
Shabbat and worked himself and her to exhaustion every other day of the week. She couldn't imagine how
anyone could willingly go to such a life of drudgery, and
she shuddered at the thought that someday she might
be like her mother. Whenever she and Rachel had talked
about the matter, the younger girl had seemed eager to
get the yoke upon her back, especially if Gomer had
been teasing her about Dan's marked attentions.

Now a man had entered Gomer's life as well as Rachel's, but such a different type of man from the humble
valley shepherd! She wondered what it would be like to
be the wife of such a man, a wanderer with a caravan,
like Abraham of long ago. The face of the Egyptian was
before her again, and she smiled to herself, nuzzling her
nose into the crook of her elbow. To travel, to wear blues

and purples and yellows, to live at ease, with servants to do the heavy work while she supervised. . . . If only the man weren't an Egyptian, if only he were an Israelite and could come with honor to her father. . . .

The dreams wove themselves, with the ever-recurring question coming into them with a sigh: Will I ever see him again?

THREE
Senu-Amen

Rachel, on one of the few days Diblaim allowed her to stay home from the market, was busily folding the linen that her mother had finished just that morning. She hummed a quiet tune, and her eyes were sparkling as she bustled to and fro around the room like a tiny pigeon. There was always a bubble of joy struggling to burst inside of her, but this day it was being sternly subdued because she didn't wish to disturb her mother and sister, hard at work in the kitchen preparing for Shabbat that evening.

Just then, as she laid a bolt on the pile, Rachel heard a strangled yell come through the window. She dropped the bolt hastily and ran over to see what went on outside. Sticking her head out of the window as far as she could, she could see into the yard that fell quickly down the slope of the mountain.

Diblaim's ancestral home had been built right into the thick walls back in the days of Omri, and his forefathers had received permission from that builder-king to cut a window through the thick stone so that their workroom could be aired. Now Rachel, half of her plump body lying on the deep window ledge, was taking advantage of this foresight on the part of her family to watch whatever it was that caused that strange yell.

The women in the kitchen heard Rachel's laughter a moment later, and stared at each other in mystification. "What's Rachel up to now?" grinned Gomer, her eyes dancing at the prospect of a diversion.

Shana shook her head and frowned, but was curious herself. "Shall we go and see?" she suggested, rising to her feet.

Without waiting an instant, Gomer disappeared into the next room, her mother following more sedately. When Shana reached the window, all available space was taken up by her daughters, both of whom were laughing so hard that they didn't notice her until she pulled on their arms.

"Rachel! Naughty girl! Tell me—what's going on out there?" Rachel didn't seem to have heard her, so Shana pulled harder. "Is it the Assyrian soldiers at their games again?"

Gomer heard her mother, but Rachel was laughing too loudly to hear anyone but herself. The elder pulled herself back into the room to answer, her face red with mirth. "It's not the Assyrians, Imma. You know they don't know how to make people laugh! It's— oh, look out and see for yourself!" She grabbed her small sputtering mother and shoved her bodily into the window.

Shana held on to Rachel for support and when the girl realized who was beside her, she started laughing harder than before, tears running down her chubby cheeks.

"Imma! Look at the silly man! He can't be an Israelite, can he?"

"He's a northerner," said Gomer from behind. There was excitement in her voice. "I can tell by the color of his skin."

"What man? Where?" Shana was completely bewildered.

"Can't you see that camel, Imma?" Rachel pointed, and finally her mother picked out the cause of all the merriment.

Beside the road, just before the gate, was a camel with a strange-looking hump on its back, and the camel was jerking stiffly in uncomfortable motions. "My eyes are bad, you know that, Rachel! What, or who, is on that ugly animal out there?" Shana had always preferred donkeys.

Gomer interrupted again. "It's someone who's never been on a camel before in his life, Imma—and obviously asked for a ride. The owner probably didn't explain anything, and now look at him, trying to sit on it like it's a horse, and holding on to its hump from behind. He's going to get thrown, kicked, or bitten if he's not careful!"

Rachel disagreed. "No, Gomer, he's starting to catch on!"

Indeed, the man from the north, ignorant though he obviously was about camels, nevertheless could think quickly. Realizing his mistake in mounting just as the camel started to rise, he had hastily grabbed the hump in front and hung on for dear life. Now, higher above the ground than he had ever been in his life, he closed his eyes, said a quick prayer, and started to climb into the saddle. Sweating and groaning, aware of the show he was giving the amused townsfolk at the gate, the man muttered away to the camel in his own tongue, his legs spread-eagled across the animal's rump. Gradually he pulled himself up the hump until, triumphantly, he settled himself cross-legged in the saddle with a broad grin. The cheers from the people watching made him wave, very carefully clutching on to the saddle horn with his other hand.

The three women in Diblaim's household had enjoyed their brief respite, and now Shana turned back into the workroom with regret. Her daughters, however, stayed at the window for a moment longer. Rachel was plaiting her hair idly, humming a soft tune. Gomer leaned out again to wave to the farmers passing by into the valley. "Be careful, Gomer," warned the younger. "You know what Abba thinks when you do that."

"I don't care. They're my friends—at least, they were when I played with their sons in the meadows." Gomer remembered her lost childhood with regret, when she had been free to run out as she pleased. Now there were countless small tasks awaiting her return in the kitchen.

Rachel, however, had other things on her mind. She puckered her tiny, red mouth and glanced sideways at her sister. "I heard our parents talking about us last night after you were asleep."

"Really?" Gomer could not have sounded more disinterested, but her sister had seen her eyes light up. Both knew the topic continually under discussion these past few months.

"Yes, they were talking about husbands for us—again. Someday Abba is going to catch on that we can hear them when they're in the kitchen, and won't that be terrible? Then they'll only talk upstairs in their bedroom."

Gomer yawned. Rachel got the hint and went straight to the point, hugging herself. "Abba said that as soon as Dan has built up his flock enough to support me, I will be given to him as his wife!"

Gomer was too upset to let her sister be so happy. "But you're three years younger than me," she objected, her brown eyes flashing with petulance. "I've seen fifteen harvests come and go, and not a word about anyone asking for me!" Once again, Gomer wondered about her different looks, but didn't say anything out loud. Was she too strange for the men of Samaria?

"But Abba said—no, please listen!—he said that there's no one in Samaria he'd give you to because the sons of the believers don't come here for Shabbat as their fathers do. You know as well as I that as soon as they reach manhood they go and—and live terrible lives! Abba probably wouldn't let them in the door anyway—so he says—but he never tells me what they do. So he's thinking of taking a trip to Mount Gerizim for prayer, to see if any of the community there have sons that are fit for you."

Rachel wondered why such news made Gomer's eyes look black, and was sad that she hadn't made her happy. She turned back to folding the linen, but Gomer still frowned out at the surrounding hills, not seeing the gay yellows and oranges of harvesttime because of the turmoil in her heart. She couldn't say that she didn't want to marry a believer because no one would understand; no one could see the horror in her when she thought of the sternness of the men of God she knew.

It was in that moment that Gomer made up her mind that no matter what happened and what threats her father made, she would wait. For the Egyptian? For a man who was as yet unknown, but who would understand her? She didn't know, but she knew that she would refuse any man who had come at her father's bidding.

Gazing into the valley, watching the sheep amble aimlessly through the reaped fields, she vowed a small vow to herself that never, never would she wed a man unless he was all that a man should be to her. But what that meant, she wasn't too sure of herself as yet. She was still very young, and she knew no young men. Also, she had never really fought her father before.

Behind her, she heard Rachel burst into song, her high clear voice bringing the spirit of Shabbat into that dark, smelly workroom crammed with bolts of cloth, huge dye vats, and various-sized looms. Gomer felt the tenseness inside melt away under the tenderness of her sister's song. She closed her eyes and listened.

Bless Adonai, O my soul,
and all that is within me
bless his holy Name.
O bless our Adonai, O my soul,
and forget not all his kindnesses.

No one can sing like Rachel, thought Gomer, *no one*. A small tear slipped out from under her eyelid and caught on her long black lashes. Who else had the purity of heart and eagerness of soul to breathe such a loving tune to a God who seemed so harsh and demanding? The song of Rachel wove a fragile peace into that home and stilled Gomer in her rebellion.

Shana, kneeling before the fire in the kitchen, dropped her hands and smiled wistfully, remembering her own youth, when such a song had been the message of joy in her own heart. May it always remain the same for her sweet Rachel.

The song of Rachel hadn't changed, but many seasons had come and gone since that day when the northerner had tried to ride a camel. Many changes had come with the seasons. Dan had lost his small flock to a marauding lion, who had broken through a weak spot in the sheepfold and had slaughtered the helpless animals before the lad had arrived from his father's hut. Now his plans to marry Rachel had been set back at least five years, and he was working for neighbors until he had saved enough to start again, his payment being two lambs each spring from each farmer. But Rachel still smiled, knowing there would be no other girl for her cousin, knowing she could wait.

The changes had brought gray into the black beard of Diblaim, for the Assyrian soldiers were multiplying in the city. As one of a group of elders, he had warned the king of this and had been ignored. "The Assyrians are our beloved allies," Menahem had said in his haughty tone. "They protect us from Judah in the south and Philistia to the west." *But who will protect us from the Assyrians?* thought Diblaim as he and the others went away from the palace perplexed.

But one had to admit that the Assyrians were as friendly as their feelings of superiority would allow. The king's own son, Pekahiah, was serving in Nineveh as a captain under the great king himself, Tiglath-pileser. Each year the treaty between Israel and Assyria was read aloud in the marketplace, and it was worded as a treaty between equals.

So the fear in all was placated, and even Diblaim preferred to forget his misgivings. But the strands of gray in his hair betrayed his worry over his trade, and his wonderings of what he would do if war ever did break out between Israel and Judea. There had never been more caravans at the gates of Samaria than at present, there had never been more food in his home, and he wanted to keep it that way. He had even allowed his daughters to dye their dresses.

Rachel had declined the dye, preferring to remain in her unbleached linen for bereaved Dan's sake. But the father noticed that Gomer had taken advantage of his permission, and her dresses had blossomed out like springtime into soft greens, brilliant reds (at which he at first had glowered, until she reminded him pertly that the great King Saul had dressed the daughters of Israel in scarlet), and golds, all mixed with a cunning he hadn't known she possessed.

The results of her experiments with color looked so tasteful that he told her to spend more of her time on dyeing goods for him to sell, which she gladly did. Now his daughter's rich golds and blues and greens were in great demand with the nobility in the palace, and the king had sent his steward to compliment the merchant on his new dyes. Diblaim had walked proudly for quite a while after that, for everyone in the market knew about that visit. He completely forgot about his proposed trip to Mount Gerizim.

The seasons had brought more changes to Gomer than the colors of the dyes that soaked into her skin. She still often worked on the roof and descended at night for supper, but her gay laugh was rarely heard anymore. A new intentness was in her eyes, a new watchfulness, especially when a caravan was approaching the gates. She hardly ever spoke to anyone, even Rachel, and only gave brief answers when necessary. Her mind was obviously elsewhere.

But the donkey, little Nathan, could have told many a tale of how, in the evenings, Gomer would slip out to bring him a carrot and stay to caress his soft gray coat and whisper into his twitching ears the many things that lay in her heart. He knew all her dreams, did that wise old beast, and he would gaze at her out of his limpid brown eyes as if he shared her secret yearnings and sorrows. He never tried to kick or bite this nocturnal visitor to his tiny stable, but would solemnly chew at his carrot and listen to her, sometimes nuzzling her hand in sympathy.

After these visits, Gomer was able at least to go to bed and lie their silently in the darkness, but tears often crept down her face. Rachel lay beside her whispering prayers to her beloved Adonai, but Gomer never prayed anymore, except when the burden of tears grew too great and she needed the comfort of thinking that someone cared.

Her dreams were filled with impossiblities, and grew ever more colorful and forbidding as she grew older. It was coming up to the second harvest since she had bumped into the Egyptian, and his face had grown quite dim in her memory. But the forbidden thrill she had felt at the touch of his heathen hand was repeated and multiplied in her dreams, and she yearned for his return. She ached to leave this dull existence for the lands of the south, the north, the east—anywhere but where she was in dull, dirty Samaria!

Somehow she clung all that time to the hope that the caravan leader would return, and maybe take her away with him. She knew she would miss Samaria if she ever left it, but all that was left for her in the city was her own house anyway, for her father had forbidden her even the weekly trips to market with Shana for food. Now all she saw of Samaria was the day-long bustle at the gate. Her playmates still waved up to her on their way in and out, but they were men now with black fuzz on their cheeks and chins, almost strangers to her.

Zedediah still stood in his doorway and called to her as he always had, but she was swift of foot, and he never caught her. She still ignored him, and she loathed him even more each day, if that were possible.

There came a day like any other day, and the air on the mountain was clear and crisp with the coming of the rainy season. Soon the frost would coat the fields in the early morning, and maybe a light snowfall would make palaces out of every house in Samaria as the flakes coated the stones with whiteness.

Gomer sat on the roof, her busy hands stuffing bags with her day's labor at the millstone. Her face had lost the slight chubbiness of two years before, and the bones showed a noble molding of cheek and jaw. Her fair skin was brushed with the sun's golden rays, and her mouth was smooth and sad. Her eyes were somber and grave, in contrast to her gay yellow dress that was caught in folds to her slender waist by a deep brown sash. The tediousness of her days, the long grayness of her life was depressing the girl, so that she completely missed the crisp blueness of the sky and the high calls of the birds above her bent head.

The faraway calls of the reapers in the valley fields filtered through her thoughts, which were heavy. But suddenly a high shout from the valley broke into her ears, and she lifted her head from her work. She wondered with calm detachment if someone had found a thief in his patch, or if someone had missed the grain with his scythe and cut his leg instead.

Then she saw what they had seen, the long weaving caterpillar coming out of the hills—a caravan! Excitement drew her to her feet, and hope brought a flush to her cheeks. Every approaching caravan for the last two years had affected her like this, and in spite of every disappointment she still dreamed that someday the Egyptian would return.

The slow brown river of camels, brightened in an occasional spot by decorated blankets and a high-held standard, made its way along the paths between the fields, and finally reached the mountain road that ended at the city gates. Gomer had been watching with her hands clenched tightly on the stone edge of the roof, but now she ran over to the stairs and descended swiftly.

She flew into the front door, startling her mother, and ran to the workroom. "Rachel, a caravan!" Her sister dropped her armload and spun around to listen. "Quickly, Rachel, get the extra material Father left behind this morning while I saddle Nathan! You'll get to market today, blessed girl, but hurry!"

Diblaim, expecting no more customers from outside the city that season, had gone alone to the booth carrying the day's orders in a sack slung over his shoulder. Great was his surprise, therefore, when, relaxing after a sale to the goldsmith's wife, he saw his youngest daughter charging through the crowded square toward his booth, expertly weaving her way through buyers and sellers, with Nathan on a lead behind her coming at an unusually fast trot.

"Rachel!" Diblaim caught her to him in a hug and waited until she caught her breath. "Why this extra cloth, child? What are you doing here, my sweet dove?"

Rachel reached up on tiptoe to give her father a hasty kiss and then adjusted her head mantle, which was in danger of revealing her flushed face. "Abba, it's another caravan! Gomer saw it coming and helped me get Nathan ready to bring here. When I left home it had just reached the gates, so the leader should be here any moment now."

"My good daughter," smiled the merchant, his lined face brightened a moment as he looked at her fondly. "And you ran all the way here so that I wouldn't miss a sale. It's a good thing you did, too, for here they come."

The sudden appearance of foreigners with goods to trade raised the decibel level in the square to twice what it had been, as merchants of animals, gold and silver, jewelry, cloths, and spices tried to attract the attention of this new trade. But Diblaim stood silent, for he had recognized the leader and knew the man would make his way here to this booth soon enough. "Go home now, Rachel, and thank you for helping me. No, I won't need you here, and your mother will be getting supper ready."

"Will we have a guest tonight, Abba?" asked Rachel as she tied Nathan to the front post of the booth. Sometimes Diblaim brought his special customers to his house for a meal, if they were Israelite or Judean.

"Not tonight, little one. This man is an Egyptian." Diblaim firmly believed that his home would be contaminated if a pagan stepped inside, and he considered that he had fulfilled Moses' law of loving the stranger in the land if he traded with them. He watched his youngest as she went away, her plump form modestly covered with unbleached linen and her black hair hidden under the mantle.

Diblaim was one of those men who claimed that women's faces were a snare to men, and as a result Shana and Rachel wore their heads and faces covered when they emerged from their home. Gomer, of course, he never allowed out. There was that about the girl that couldn't be contained by modest dress, and he feared for her safety and virtue in the wicked streets of Samaria. He knew what went on in the homes of his people. He only had to stand in this market, day after day, and hear the bawdy stories and see the leering eyes to understand, with a sickened soul, how far Israel had departed from the Law of Moses and the ways of her fathers.

The father sighed deeply as he tidied his goods on the table, wishing for the thousandth time that he could leave Samaria, that he could take his family to the safety of Mount Gerizim, where a small colony of the faithful still lived and worshiped on that most holy of spots. But he was only skilled in the cloth trade, and he had married a weaver, not a farmer's daughter. So the city was as much his prison as his home.

A deep, well-known voice interrupted his gloomy thoughts. "Ah, my good friend and partner! It is good to see you after so long, Diblaim!"

Diblaim looked up and smiled, his black eyes lighting. "Senu-Amen!" The two men hugged each other with delight, their dark faces glowing. "It's two harvests since you've been here, my friend. Why so long away?"

The Egyptian shrugged and spread out his hands, laughingly imitating one of the Israelites' favorite gestures. "Who can go against the gods? My weavers in Ramses refused to work for months because the Nile flooded too much, and they had to help their families with their ruined crops and ruined homes. And so, alas, you see before you a ruined man!"

Diblaim shook his head, amused. "Ruined? Never, not you! You say something like that every time you come so that you'll get a better price from me, and it hasn't worked yet! Why do you still try?"

Senu-Amen stopped smiling and shook his head as well. "Because this time it is true, my friend. This will be my last trip up this way—forever."

Diblaim, now disturbed, sat down on the stool behind his table and motioned his friend to another. "But why? Your men seem well-laden."

The Egyptian held his proud head high, but sorrow was hidden deep in his dark eyes. "You must remember that I have been on the road for many months before I arrive in Samaria, Diblaim. These goods are the results of trading in Thebes, in Sheba, in Gaza, in Jerusalem—"

"Senu-Amen, forgive me, but how is Jerusalem?"

The Egyptian looked at his friend with smiling pity. "Every time I come it is the same question. Jerusalem is still golden under the midday sun, and her Temple is still full every day. But I heard rumors that the king's son is about to close it and forbid sacrifices."

"No! How can that be? The king, the good Uzziah—surely he will stop this blasphemy?"

"Haven't you heard about—but no, I am the only trader trusted to enter both Jersualem and Samaria, because I am the only one who is not a spy for some king or other. And of course, I haven't been here for two years. Forgive me, my friend, but it is sad news for you, I fear. Last year I heard that Uzziah apparently broke one of your priestly laws—I don't know which one—but your god struck him with the whitening disease and now he is condemned to live outside the gates, until it heals or he dies. His son Jotham reigns as regent, supposedly under his father's orders, but I doubt if the old warrior king knows what goes on in the city. He is completely cut off, and I hear that only one prince of the court, one Isaiah ben Amoz, visits the old king."

Diblaim lowered his head, his eyes closed so that the pagan trader couldn't see his anguish. "And God had so blessed that king. He must have done some terrible thing—do you remember at all the details?"

Senu-Amen shrugged. "Only that it was in the Temple, and the king made a sacrifice himself. Why a god strikes down a man with leprosy for burning an animal to please his nostrils with the savor, I don't know."

"It is our Law that only the priest in the Temple may make the sacrifice, so that it's done properly," explained the distressed Israelite, his shaking hand pulling at his beard. "The king must have blasphemed the priests in his pride, for he has had nothing but success since he became king as a boy. And now his son wants to close the Temple. O God, O my Adonai, how can such a thing be acceptable to you? When will you strike down the wicked and restore your people?"

The Egyptian sat in silence, respecting the other's grief. He himself had so many gods at home that he was quite content to let a hired priest do sacrifices for him. But he knew from the old tales told by the mothers of Egypt that the Israelites' god was a powerful god, and Senu-Amen was no fool. He wasn't about to utter any more opinions about this god in case he, too, should be stricken with the whitening disease.

After a few moments of inner prayer, Diblaim stood

up and bowed to his friend. "Come, let us get to our business, Senu-Amen." And so, for an hour or more the two acted like mortal enemies, screaming at each other and flailing their arms about as they haggled over the worth of this gold cloth, the value of this subtle Egyptian weave. Their voices drew a crowd of traders and towns-folk who always loved a good show, and a particularly shrewd deal on Diblaim's part was greeted with cheers. After all the desired exchanging was done, the two bowed to each other, and Diblaim started folding down his booth.

"Walk with me to the gate, Diblaim," requested the Egyptian. Now that the zest of trading was over, his eyes had dulled. "I won't be coming back up the path tomorrow, so I'll send one of my boys with that Persian silk you wanted."

The merchant paused in his packing and glanced up, frowning. "We didn't set a price on that."

Senu-Amen waved away that point. "It is my farewell gift to you, Diblaim."

Diblaim was touched. "Senu-Amen, I cannot let a friend leave so. I will come down myself tomorrow to bless your caravan and bid you farewell."

The Egyptian's eyes filled with unaccustomed tears, for he was a man who schooled his emotions and hid his passions. He knew this was an ancient Israelite custom rarely accorded to outsiders, and it told him how high he stood in the Israelite's regard.

In a moment the two were on their way out of the market, each wrapped in his thoughts and memories.

The Egyptian was remembering the first time he had come into this square, a timid lad ten years younger with no camel and only some homespun material of his sister's to sell. He had come this long way attached to a Persian caravan whose owner considered him sun-touched. He had heard that Jeroboam of Samaria loved to dress his women in Egyptian goods. Having no idea how to contact that king and afraid to go to the palace on his own, he had wandered about the square until he met Diblaim at his clothing stall. The older man had bought his material for twice the amount it was worth, paying him in silver, and told him to come back, because there were at that time no caravans from Egypt as the camel drivers were afraid of the enmity between Israel and Judea. A lad had dared go where more experienced men trembled, and it had paid off. With Diblaim's money he bought a camel and a guard and in the years that followed, as Jeroboam brought peace to the two warring countries, Senu-Amen had become a rich man. Diblaim's original investment had been returned many times over, for only he received Egyptian cloth to sell in Samaria.

But now the great flood had ruined the Egyptian, losing his best weavers to their families, and he had had to sell his wives to meet his accumulated debts, for he had lived high and well in the past years. This last trip had been more for the sake of his own soul than for any profit he might salvage. Once he reached Jerusalem again on the way back, he intended to sell his camels and slaves at the Ishmaelite market there, and then take his money and disappear into Persia. The rest of his creditors would search for him in vain.

Diblaim kept his peace as they walked, aware of his friend's distress, and only spoke once they reached his street. He tugged at Nathan's lead, for the donkey was regretting his earlier speed and making up for it by nosing at every blade of grass that showed through the cobblestones. "It has been a long and prosperous partnership, my friend, and I am unhappy to see that it must end. But you are still young; you will build again. Maybe in the camel market—"

Senu-Amen shook his head sadly. "No, Diblaim, I have no urge to keep traveling. There are too many dangers for a caravan leader: bandits, armies, the desert itself. I have been blessed by the gods, until last year, and now it is over. Although your king is at peace with Assyria, mine is not, and I am scarcely welcome. I take my life in my hands if I return again."

Diblaim nodded regretfully. He could see lean times ahead without his Egyptian goods to sell. He glanced up as they neared his home and saw the front door standing open to welcome him. He almost relented then in his stand about foreigners. But his resolve stiffened when he saw his eldest daughter in the doorway, her back to them as she gazed at the well in the gate square where Rachel was drawing their water for supper. Her hair hung unbound down her back and seemed to gleam with a light of its own where she stood in the shadow.

Diblaim missed the sudden catch of Senu-Amen's breath, so angry was he at Gomer. "Daughter! Get inside at once!" he barked. She turned a startled face on him, then saw the man at his side and froze. The father saw the look that sprang into her eyes and knew that Zedediah had spoken the truth, that all his years of care for her had been fruitless.

Gomer stood as still as a statue, but her heart was pounding so loudly in her ears that she missed her father's second sharp order to get inside. *He has come,* her heart sang. *He has returned with Father to ask for me!* The sudden glow on her face would have made a plain woman attractive; on her it was pure beauty.

Senu-Amen was remembering a day two years before when he had seen her eyes like that, large and bright like two stars piercing his soul and making his brain go wild. He had not known then who she was and had since forgotten her, but now the knowledge of her parentage burned inside. She was the daughter of a pious Israelite who would sooner feed her to the dogs than let him take her, as every nerve in him was screaming to do. The injustice of that thought hurt him terribly.

Diblaim was stunned that his daughter had twice ignored him and stood before his friend bareheaded like a common harlot. This wickedness and disobedience set his anger off like flint. "Gomer!" he shouted. "Do as I say!" He reached out and grabbed her hair. She cried out with the sudden pain, for she hadn't noticed his approach. She couldn't see the reflected hurt in the Egyptian's eyes at this treatment. All she felt was the tearing fire on her skull and the brutal kick that caught her leg, and then she was lying on the kitchen floor, her head a searing pain and her ears ringing from the slam of the door.

The two men stood outside, and Rachel scurried past them into the house, her water jar balanced on her hip. Diblaim waited until she was inside, and then turned to his friend. "I'm . . . sorry, Senu-Amen, that you should see my daughter acting thus. She . . . is very hard to control and seems to take delight in ignoring me. But come—I will bid you farewell for tonight at the gate and be down in the morning to bless your caravan." He led his friend on, too angry still to note the tightness on the lips of Senu-Amen. He had no clue to the sudden resolve that had entered the mind of the unbeliever.

On the floor, feeling the soft hands of Rachel helping her to her feet, hearing the broken murmuring of her mother's voice, Gomer knew a despair too bleak for words and that reached far deeper than her physical pains. He had come, he had shown with his beautiful black eyes that he wished to speak to her—and he was gone again at her father's command. She felt, indeed, her father's slave.

The next morning seemed, at least to Rachel and her mother, to be a normal one. Gomer sat before the fire and stirred the soup of lentils, wiping her perspiring forehead with her sleeve and keeping her skirt well away from flying sparks. Rachel was nibbling on a piece of carrot and sorting through the food supplies, for she and Shana were heading for market that morning to replenish the kitchen.

Diblaim came down the stairs from the bedroom he shared with his wife, a room occupying the whole second floor. He was wearing his finest cloak to go and bid farewell to his friend. He hadn't told his family about this, merely stating that he couldn't accompany them to market because he had some business affairs to which he must attend. He left right after breakfast, carrying a gift with him: a white fur robe from a country so far north that it was rumored the snow never left it. A few minutes later, his wife and Rachel left home as well, leaving Gomer alone inside. She had been commanded by her father not to go onto the roof that day, for he knew she could see the caravan from there, and he was running no risks of her being seen before Senu-Amen left. He was afraid and like all fearful men went to extremes to guard that which he held precious. He didn't realize that he was watching the wrong person.

Gomer had much work to do, and she stood in the doorway of the storeroom glaring at it. A pile of the flowers used in dyes lay on the huge stone in the corner. She went over to them and handled them listlessly. Once she would have looked with wonder at their colors, but now she could only pound at the stone they lay on with her fists. This stone was the one used to block their window in times of invasion or seige, but it was used as a table in times of peace. Generations of dye-makers in her father's family had worked their colors into the gray stone until now it stood as a permanent rainbow.

Unwilling to start work, Gomer wandered back into the warm, smoky kitchen and sank down onto a pile of linen Shana had just finished. She felt drowsy, and yawned. She wanted to sleep, for Rachel had awakened her that morning from a dream that she had been enjoying. There had been a camel, and its driver had been leaning down to her, and his face had become the face of her father's Egyptian client. He had been looking at her with his deep eyes, and his mouth had been smiling with some humor she didn't understand. Now he seemed to return to her eyes as she drowsed, and his smile was full of wonder and a fierce joy.

Gomer blinked and sat up straight, shock ridding her mind of sleep. He really *was* there, in the middle of the room, his cloak flung open and his *kaffiyeh* pulled back to show his face. She hadn't heard the door, or it had sounded like a part of her dream, and to suddenly have him there like a phantom of smoke stunned her.

Senu-Amen stood there a moment, drinking her in with his eyes, the girl who did to him what only a love-potion should do. Gomer sat on the soft linen gazing up at him, her lips parted in a question she had no need to ask.

He moved closer and pulled off his *kaffiyeh*, dropping it to the floor along with his cloak. "I had to come." His voice was low and husky, and she felt the magic of his spell weaving around her senses. She was trembling, but she felt no fear. She had always known that somehow, someday this would come to her, and she was glad.

The heavy darkness of his eyes was overpowering her as he moved closer ever so slowly. His hands reached down to touch her hair. She lifted her face to kiss his palm, and felt the impossible excitement inside as he smoothed her eyebrows with a gentle pressure.

The last ruddy glimmerings of the morning fire caught at the darkness of his eyes and made them suddenly like a fire themselves. He thought of nothing else, not his friend, not his caravan, not his honor. This girl at his feet had completely robbed him of all such considerations. He murmured gentle words to her, telling her that she would be his forever beyond the sands of the desert, that the gods would open all doors and speed them on their way, that all would be well.

Now she was smiling; her hand was lifting to his face. The world had shrunk to the small space still left between them.

"Lovely little fawn," he whispered. She closed her eyes. The world was no more.

The small, shifty eyes of Zedediah were for once stilled. They were fixed on one point, the closed door of his neighbor's house. Into that house he had seen a stranger enter a while ago, a man, and he knew that only Gomer was in there with him. He had watched the rest of her family leave, and the girl hadn't as yet passed his post to run up to the roof.

So the bent old man waited, his mouth drawn back on his few remaining teeth in a silent snarl of hatred, his eyes glittering with triumphant malice. At last she would be brought down from her haughtiness, and he would be the one to do it. As soon as Diblaim reentered the city gate, Zedediah would run and drag him inside and show him—what?

Zedediah licked his lips at that point, sure that he knew why the muffled and cloaked stranger had come, for he could think of nothing else that a man in his right senses would want with that girl. A born woman of the streets, that one, with northern heathen blood so obvious in her, a woman made only for men—but not any other man except himself!

The old man, his mind twisted with years of frustrated yearnings, now wanted only to see the object of his desires brought to the lowest. She would have none of his advances, and he knew better than to ask Diblaim for her—so no one would have her!

Zedediah shrank back into the shadow of his doorway and waited, well-hidden. Like his neighbor's house, his was built between the two massive walls of Samaria, the front and back walls being the city walls themselves. So his door was unnaturally thick, and he could hide as well as his fevered brain chose. He licked his lips again in anticipation, picturing the scene inside Diblaim's house now, and picturing what it would be when he brought the owner inside. He knew Diblaim would never think of going in on his own, but would head straight for market. Zedediah wanted the privilege of exposing Gomer—and of being the pious Israelite to throw the first stone at her outside the walls.

Just then the neighboring door opened and the stranger left quickly, once again well-muffled in his rich cloak. Zedediah frowned in anger. Why was Diblaim so slow? He left his doorway and stealthily followed the other. But by the time the old man had hobbled his way to the gates and peered around them, he was too late. His quarry had disappeared, and he could only see a caravan waiting at the bottom of the rocky slope. But up that slope was climbing a familiar figure, and Zedediah smiled evilly. After all, Diblaim had always believed him before.

Clutching his rich robe around his scrawny figure, Zedediah waited beneath the high arch of the gate.

F O U R

Rejection

She screamed like an animal, with terrible heart-rending screams of pure agony. Shana ran from the sound to her bed, her face melting with tears as she sobbed into the pillow. Rachel had been sent to her room and stood there now, trembling, not understanding what disgrace had come so suddenly to their house, praying desperately that God would wither her father's arm so that he would stop. But still the screams went on.

Gomer lay in a deep black darkness of agony, her fingernails dragging at the floor beneath her as she struggled to escape from the hell of pain that descended upon her with every breath. Yet the lash of fire that blazed across her back and shoulders never seemed to end. It ripped into her quivering flesh and drew out her hot blood so that it streamed to the floor. With every whirl of the whip she screamed, unable to think of anything but the pain.

Finally Diblaim lowered his arm and let the donkey

whip trail on the ground. He had counted twenty strokes and was panting with the strain, his eyes glazed as the sweat ran into them. He looked down and saw the trembling back of his daughter criss-crossed with welts and blood. *Those welts will heal,* he thought, *but never the pain of what she has done—never.* He set his face, knowing that if he could he would gather up the Law-abiding men of Samaria, have them drag Gomer outside to the ancient bloody stone that waited on the other side of the walls, and have her stoned to death as a harlot. But there were not enough men left who followed the old ways, and he knew he would be stopped by the elders if he tried it by himself.

As he glared down at her, to his outraged mind she seemed the living symbol of all that was blackness and wickedness, a mockery in God's eyes. He reached down and yanked her to her feet, heedless of the gasp of pain that escaped her clenched teeth. "To the roof with you, whore! To the roof, where other men keep their slaves—and now you'll join their ranks. Once you wanted a slave to do your work, but now you will be one!"

He pushed her ahead, unaware that she was nearly fainting with every step, and shoved her past Zedediah's baleful glare to the outside stairs. The old man had waited outside to join the party that would gather to stone the harlot, but no one had come, no one had been sent for. But he saw gleefully that she was half-naked, and that blood was still seeping from the wounds in her back. He had enjoyed her screams.

Gomer managed the stairs with difficulty and sank into the first pile of flaxen rushes to which she came. She huddled there, unable even to lift her head.

Diblaim stood over her like the avenging seraph that

had kept Adam out of the garden, slapping the whip on his thigh. "I will not ask how you could bring such dishonor to my house by enticing a heathen inside to lie with him in sin. It is enough that you have done so, and that this time I can believe Zedediah because I know who the man was—he was not at his camel to greet me when I descended. I have spared you before, waiting, sure that in the end God would prevail over your waywardness—and this is how you repay my mercy. So you will remain here, where no man can see you and your little games will not be noticed." His eyes were grim, his voice reminiscent of death. He looked on Gomer as if she were no longer his daughter, but a strange woman, an abomination which he must tolerate.

She heard his voice dimly through the waves of pain that still were threatening to bury her. She tried to speak, but no words came, only a moan. She wanted to say that it hadn't been like that at all—Zedediah still lies—he said he would return and wed me—he said he only left to find you and ask your blessing as a son should. But the husky voice that had filled her eager ears with promises was silent, and she knew now that he had never meant to return. He had known that her father would refuse, but he had wanted her to believe it with him for an hour, an hour snatched from the impossible.

Diblaim found his throat constricting, and he could say no more. She was no longer his daughter, this girl who had once dared to dress in scarlet like a whore. She would be his slave, but a strange nausea gripped him at the thought. *She has sinned,* he told himself sternly. *She must be punished.* He left her there and went slowly down the stairs.

Zedediah waited eagerly at the foot of the stairs, but

Diblaim walked past him as if he were blind, ignoring the spate of questions that the old man asked. He brushed him off like a troublesome fly and went to the gate. He looked down in the valley, and it was empty. So Senu-Amen was gone. He wasn't sure which had hurt more—his daughter's heinous sin, or his friend's treachery. Not that he blamed the man. Zedediah had told him often enough of the men Gomer had called to as she danced in the street before her father's door. This time she had been answered.

He heard vaguely the sound of weeping coming from his roof, and his mouth tightened even as his own eyes filled. *It is too late,* he thought, *too late to undo what you have done. Only repentance is left.*

Gomer had managed to drag herself over to the roof wall, and she, too, had seen that the caravan was gone. It was then that the tears had come like a gushing waterfall, the sobs shaking her body so that the stiffening wounds ached. She sat there for hours, her tears gradually drying, until the sun went down and the stars emerged from their daytime sleep.

Her thoughts gradually cleared, also, as the cool air soothed her fevered cheeks and she grew calmer. So he was gone. Her lover had taken her childhood dreams with him, and somehow she knew that he would never be back. And now her family, too, was gone as surely as if she had died, separated by the rooftop, living in another world.

But really it was I who left them, years ago, she mused, *left them to become a daughter of Canaan instead of Israel, for were not the stories of the Old Ones more to me than the stories of Abraham? Were they not more to my liking than my father's God? I left my family when I knew that I wanted more from this world than what their life had to offer me, when I wanted the laughter and freedom and revels I heard about but never saw. I didn't need any of them to discover the new world I entered today with the Egyptian . . . and I didn't need God.*

She turned her tear-streaked face to the deep mysterious sky that heard her thoughts and hid them. She sensed a large presence on the roof with her and was angry, for she knew it waited for her to decide something she thought she had decided long ago. "I don't need you! Leave me, leave me, God of my fathers who claims to be all things and in every place—leave me! What have you given me but pain and hardship? When have you shown me laughter? When did you show me love? I'll not repent of the joy I knew today, joy that you and my father despise and deplore!" She clenched her teeth as she muttered, half-delirious, and held her blood-soaked arms high over her head. "A man guided me today, a man you consider unclean, but I learned more from him about life and tenderness than you or anyone else has ever shown me!"

A sudden thought of Rachel crossed her mind, Rachel singing as she had years ago, pure joy lighting her face, a different sort of joy. But Gomer thrust the thought aside, for Rachel had never known the yearnings she knew. Rachel was a little sheep content with whatever was given her. "Leave me, God of my father," she said again, unaware that the tears had started to pour once more down her cheeks. "Leave me as my family has, as my lover has, as all joys and dreams have. Leave me with the pain and memory that are all that the days will hold for me. Only the rising sun each morning will remind me that I still exist."

But if the stars had had ears that night, if the night wind could have spoken, they would have passed on the echo of her weeping as it seeped upward into the music of the mountain air and climbed in a crescendo to the misty clouds above.

F I V E
Burial

Far to the north, hidden behind a mountain that deserved the name more than the mound on which Samaria was built, huddled the cold town of Dan. On the border between Israel and Syria, this town had often fought savagely for its right to exist and had just succeeded in turning back a detachment of Assyrian soldiers who had wanted to add this territory to their recent conquest of Syria. Nineveh had finally tired of the small and ineffectual rebellions of Damascus, and had sent its smallest army to quell the most recent. As another gesture of contempt, Tiglath-pileser had even allowed Rezin, the son of the slain Syrian king, to remain on the throne as his puppet. On hearing this news, Dan had fortified its already thick walls, and thus was ready for the Assyrians when they came. Now, weary and victorious, the people were celebrating.

The narrow streets of the ancient city were thronged that night with drunken men and women who, unaware of the slight drizzle of rain and the chilly air, were running about screaming with laughter, half-naked, their faces painted with gaudy colors. The men caught the women to them, not caring who they were, and dragged them into anyone's open door to start another orgy. The wine they drank was new; the games they played were old.

Ignored by them all, drowned by the crazy relieved merriment, a soft mourning dirge trailed behind a few people in sackcloth as they walked outside the city toward the burial ground. A man had died that day, the only defender to be killed by the Assyrians, and his son was burying him.

The son walked slowly behind the bier that his neighbors carried, his head low, his eyes blinded with useless tears. He was remembering the scene that morning when his father had pulled out his bow and arrows from their sheepskin covering and had started to cut another string.

"But, Abba, you haven't drawn that for nearly twenty years!"

"That's correct, son—since the day I met your mother and promised her never again to go into battle. But she has been dead twelve years, and this is different. I am defending my home." He had finished stringing the bow, and now stood up to test it. He was a short man, very thin, as if he didn't care to eat enough. His eyes were clear and brown, with the light of battle in them.

His son watched, unhappy. "Abba, please, stay here and let *me* take your bow. I'm young. I can run faster than you if they make a breach in the walls. I can see better than you to aim properly! You know your eyes are ruined after working so long as a scribe."

"Hosea, be silent." His father frowned sternly. "You

shame me, speaking like a woman filled with fear."

Hosea flushed angrily. "I'm not a woman, Abba! But if you'd only listen to me, you'll know I speak the truth. You know that when you go out into the sun you're blinded for nearly an hour!"

"And so will you be someday, my son," his father answered, returning to his usual mildness. "And someday you'll also know what it means to defend one's home, especially if, like me, you were gone from it for so many years."

"Samaria is home for me. That's where I was born, and would be now if that king, now dead, hadn't taken a dislike to you. But I'll go with you, Abba, and try to steer you in the right direction."

So father and son had gone together to the south wall and a few hours later, before Hosea's very eyes, his beloved father caught a stray arrow in the throat and died in writhing agony. Now his bloody, stiffened body was about to be put away forever in the family cave, and Hosea would be alone.

Many more memories flooded the son's heart as he walked, and he broke into quiet weeping. He remembered the joy he and his parents had known in their first home, that huge stone house in Samaria, filled with the delightful fragrance of his delicate mother's spices and perfumes, for her family were merchants in such goods. His father had spent the days working in the library at the palace, and his evenings playing with his son and hearing his lessons.

He remembered the painful day that his mother had died of the fever that had kept her in bed for weeks. He had missed her happy presence and her comforting arms and was inconsolable. But the mother from next door had come over every evening and silently held him so he could sleep. She had been small and plump and dark, that mother, smelling of bread and sheep's wool, and she had soothed him.

He remembered the days of sunshine when he had played with the girl next door and her rollicking cousin Dan—days that had been so rudely brought to a halt by the king's wrath.

His father had come home one day, white with unaccustomed anger, and had hastily packed their meager belongings into two heavy bags. "We are going away, Hosea," was all he had said to his wide-eyed son. He had then gone next door to buy his neighbor's donkey for the journey and the neighbor had returned with him, his eyes worried and his hands pulling at his long black beard.

"You'd best take the mountain road if you go north, Beeri, and not the plains road. Otherwise, Jeroboam will easily find you if he decides to give chase."

"Thanks for your help—and your donkey, Diblaim," answered the scribe, busy tying his bundles onto the donkey's back. "I don't think we'll ever be able to return, and I want you to know that no man has been a better friend to me than you, my schoolday companion. I'll miss our Shabbat meetings. Where we go, it's more than likely there are no believers left."

"Where will you go, my friend?" Diblaim laid a concerned hand on Beeri's shoulder. "Is it far?"

"Yes—to the border, in fact. I'm going back to my family home in Dan, where I was born." The packing was done, and Beeri motioned to Hosea to put on his sandals for the journey.

"Dan!" Diblaim was shaking his head gloomily, but he

managed a weak smile to the curious boy beside him. "It—it's such a heathen place to bring up this boy. Beeri, is there no other place you can pick? To go to Dan willingly, where that golden calf was set up by the first Jeroboam for our fathers to worship—that blasphemous city where I hear the orgies are worse than here."

The sound of those orgies was in Hosea's ears still. He didn't notice the stone before his feet, so angry was he at the thought of the heartlessness of the people for whom his father had died. He stumbled and looked up. They had reached the cave. The two men who had accompanied him rolled away the stone, and his father was placed inside.

On the way back to the gates, Hosea bade his father's friends a quiet good night and turned toward the fields and the hills. The moon hung low in the sky between the peaks of the northern mountains. He watched it slowly move. The day he and his father had arrived in Dan, footsore and weary, with the donkey dragging at its lead, seemed like another lifetime.

But the anger in Beeri had not dimmed with distance, and it had deepened into sorrow. This sorrow he had passed on to his son, who felt it now—a sorrow at the wicked ways of their people, a sorrow that saw evil and prayed against it and fought it whenever possible. It was this fighting that had enraged Jeroboam, when Beeri had stood up one day in council and read out, unasked, from the ancient scrolls he had been copying, all the Laws of Moses that the nation was currently breaking. He had demanded that the king set things right, and Jeroboam had roared that his scribe had one day to be out of Samaria if he didn't wish to see the inside of the palace prison. Beeri, willing enough to face such a sentence for himself to uphold his convictions, could not bring himself to endanger his eight-year-old son. So they had left.

Hosea remembered that Dan had seemed like a refuge in those days, although he was sternly admonished never to enter the temple in the square because evil was there also. Now the city that had sheltered them from Jeroboam, and that his father had died to defend, seemed dark and hollow to Hosea, a mere shell with no life inside. The noise and shouts and laughter that floated to him on the night air were for him the empty cries of empty lives, and in his soul he cursed them as evil. Again he knew his father's anger and sorrow, but didn't admit to himself that although he understood and agreed with the anger, he couldn't understand why sorrow was necessary.

The laughter from the city reminded him that he was alone, that the house would be empty, and suddenly the world seemed too small for the grief that overflowed inside him. *Abba, Abba, why did you go from me? Why, why?*

He sat down on a hilltop, unaware of the wet grass that soaked his clothes, and tried to pray. But the God of his childhood, the God whom his father had brought so close with his prayers and readings, was not there.

Hosea reached with yearning, and touched only the emptiness of his own heart. He remembered a psalm from one of Beeri's favorite scrolls, and he sobbed aloud in his agony, "Adonai, Adonai, why do you stand so far from me? Why is your face hidden in this time of need?" He remembered the terrible crying accusation of King David, and he stood up to reach his hands to the starry skies and cried out, "My God, my God, why have you so

forsaken me? Why are you so far from me? Why can't
you help me? Why can't you hear my cry?"

The words felt torn from his lips, and he stretched up
his arms with a bitter sob. Did God hear him, or was no
one there? Were the revelers back in Dan right, that God
didn't care, that the only thing to do was to bring offerings to the golden calf or the Old Ones of Canaan and
then go your merry way?

There was no answer from the sky, where the last
shreds of clouds were scuttling behind the eastern hills.
Hosea dropped his arms, beginning to feel unhappily
foolish, wondering what he had really expected. It was
only to such men as Abraham and Moses that God
spoke. Even the great David had only heard God
through the prophet Nathan. Who was he to expect to
hear God when he cried like a woman? His father had
said that only this morning—his beloved, smiling, studious, dead father.

Hosea found his way back to the city somehow in the
darkness, for the moon was gone and his eyes were
swollen. The people were still playing their games, but
the streets were empty now. They had gone inside; so
none witnessed the homecoming of the bereaved.

The early evening rain still glittered on the stones, the
early morning stars still glittered overhead, and the city
was a lovely sight, but Hosea noticed nothing. He came
to his house and closed the door behind him. A ghastly
loneliness came upon him as he did so, for now he
couldn't even hear the laughter.

S I X
Beyond the Torah

"Hosea, you've had long enough to mourn for your father." His old schoolmate stood in the door, a large bulky man who was used to bullying people. "Now come to my home tonight, and we'll help you get rid of your sorrows."

Hosea shook his head, staring down at the scroll he was copying. "No, Teran. It's good of you to offer, but I'd rather not."

"Why not? What's the matter with you, Hosea? When my mother died, my father spent only a week in sackcloth and ashes, not a month like you have. Now he's happily wed again and I'm expecting a brother any day! Come on—we're going to have all our old friends over, and the girls from the temple have promised to come as well. What more could a man want?" Teran's bushy brows were crumpled together in genuine bewilderment.

The mention of the temple girls made Hosea's throat

constrict with the now familiar anger. *These fools!* he thought. *They have no idea what they were really made for, or how wicked their lives are. And to assume that such women are fit to be the priestesses of a god! God in heaven must hide his holy face from them.* He shook his head again.

Teran shrugged, bowed, and left, slamming the door behind him. *Fool!* he thought with contempt, *fool to waste his days mourning, fool not to enjoy his youth and good health while he has them!* Then he saw ahead of him one of the girls who would be coming to his gathering that night, and he hailed her, Hosea immediately forgotten at the delightful sight of this treasure.

Every night since Beeri had died, Hosea had gone to his grave to pray, and these visits were not missed by the people of Dan. They whispered about the mad son of Beeri, who still prayed to the old God and expected, it seemed, to be answered. Hadn't he learned that the God of their fathers had long forgotten them? The few who still believed mocked Hosea as well, saying that all he had to do was bring a fatted calf to Mount Gerizim and all would be well. None tried to understand the misery that held him, or saw the searching in his soul for the lost comfort once found in prayers and worship. All had gone with Beeri into the outer darkness.

Hosea had seriously begun to wonder about God. His prayers seemed to be wasted, and the scrolls that once had made his heart sing were dead. The words of Moses concerning the doings of God now meant no more than the foolish words of Teran to his ears. He kept up his father's work, however, and as the months slipped by found a meager comfort in this contact with Beeri. The completed scrolls mounted up, and work came as well from merchants who wished family histories written out or dealings recorded.

Then one night, weeks after Teran's visit, he had a dream. It seemed that he walked outside the city walls, through the fields, and the darkness around him was heavy with fear. That fear entered him, and trembling he wondered why it was so. Then he saw the golden calf coming toward him, bawling at him to kneel and worship it and it would take away the fear. But he picked up a stone and flung it at the shining creature, and it ran away.

Then out of the mists came a man and a woman, and they were dancing around him, their shimmering clothes as molten gold and their eyes shining like jewels. The woman reached out to him with her slender black arms as she danced closer to him, and her low voice besought him to come with her and she would fill his life with fame and riches. The man mocked Hosea's sorrow as the townspeople had, and his strident voice called to him to be a hero, to seek renown in battle, and he promised youth forever.

Hosea covered his eyes with trembling hands to shut out the sight of them, but he still heard their calling voices. And the fear inside him grew, so that he cried out in despair, "God, what have I to do with these evil ones? Why are they here? And where are you, O my God? Where are you?"

The laughter of the shining ones grew louder, and they told him that God was no more, for they had defeated him in the hearts of his people. Only *they* were real, and he was a fool not to follow them. But still he called for his God.

No answer came and he said, "Then I will search until I find you again, O my God. I will search, and I won't listen to these liars, these false ones, for you alone are worthy of worship!" The cry in his dream woke him up.

Hosea sat up on his pallet, soaking with sweat, and knew what he had to do, now, before the dawn told him he was mad. "Moloch, Ashtaroth, Ba'al . . . ah, you false ones," he muttered as he rose and hunted for his small oil lamp. He lit it and started to pack some food. "You deceivers that entice my people away as you would entice me . . . But no, you'll not win me away. God may be far from me now, but once I knew him well, once as a child I trusted him. And someday, when I find him again, when I feel his Spirit within my soul again, I will be content."

When the sun rose, Dan was many miles behind him—Dan with its mockery and its emptiness. The hills of the Sea of Galilee were now near, in the south, breaking through the low bank of clouds that had drifted east overnight from the Great Sea.

SEVEN

Amoz

It was the rainy season, and the ground in the many small valleys was treacherous and swampy. But the hills of Jerusalem rose strong and firm through the mist, their earth still compact and hard. The trees that crowned the heights drank in new life from the wetness, and seemed to stretch ever higher into the clouds that fell around them. The greenery that ran up and down the slopes was rich and moist, untouched as yet by the white hand of frost. The man who was walking among those hills might well have believed himself back in Eden, on the far-off banks of the Euphrates.

Hosea was the lone man who saw this sight, if he did see it. He had just reached a tamarack tree and was sitting down, unaware of the dripping leaves overhead. He was lost in his own thoughts and sorrows, and had rarely raised his eyes from the sodden ground before his weary feet. The land he passed through might just as well have been barren desert for all the notice its beauty received from him.

Since the night he had left Dan, Hosea had kept to the same backroads over which he and Beeri had fled so many years ago, because he wished to avoid the cities and towns built over the main north-south trade route. His journey had been difficult, often dangerous. Many nights he had heard the low growl of lions hidden deep in the dense forests, although he had never seen them.

The bandits that haunted the wilds and hid in caves had watched him pass from their rocky vantage points, but had never molested him. He was obviously poor, for his cloak was patched and his small pack held the plainest of food. These bandits were not vindictive against their own people, but only against the rich who had robbed them of their fields, or against the Assyrians who had burnt their villages.

So Hosea had passed on his way unscathed, unaware of the many wild eyes of men and beasts that watched him. He still prayed with the sunrise and the sunset, although the emptiness of his soul received no nourishment. He had asked protection of the God of Israel, and received that protection without surprise. Hadn't the children of Israel in their wilderness wanderings received food for each day, and hadn't their clothing and sandals remained intact for forty years? Had not their enemies fled before them? When he thought about it, Hosea put his safe day's walk down to the watchfulness of his God. This gave him some hope, for if God watched over him, then surely he could, and would, be found.

Stopping at each farmer's hut he passed, giving the age-old greeting of peace, Hosea inquired politely into the inhabitants' pattern of worship. He went on each day more melancholy and depressed, for some gave scornful laughter, some gave wondering pity, and most gave a shrug of the shoulder as answer.

Once only in the long walk through the ever-smaller mountains of Israel did he find unabashed joy when he asked if the man of the house still worshiped the God of their fathers. He had been profusely welcomed. Those had been days to remember for the spiritually hungry man, as he listened to the farmer tell of his times of worship in the fields (there were no other men to form a Shabbat meeting) and of his painstaking perusal of the old leather scrolls he had hidden away in a chest. Hosea and the farmer had parted as brothers, giving each other a prayer for God's protection and peace.

But in the small villages, set up in the market squares, too often Hosea found ugly carvings of the figures he had seen in his dream—Moloch, Ashtaroth, and Ba'al. Their stone faces leered at him with contempt; their worshipers stared at this strange traveler who refused to leave an offering before the gods. The priests in the villages, the Levites who no longer followed their ancient order of worship handed down to them since Aaron, listened to his questions and laughed, gently urging him to listen to the voices of the land that were older and richer than the voice of Moses' God. The Levites still observed the holy days for, as they told him, they believed in placating *every* god. But the Feast of the First-fruits meant no more, and no less, than the Festival of the New Moon under Ashtaroth, Lady of all life, or the Festival of the New Year in the spring when Ba'al chose his Ashtaroth from among the village maidens.

Hosea said nothing when they gave these devious answers or when they laughed at his sincerity, but he would leave as soon as courtesy allowed. He never asked the names of these villages, and thus didn't realize that one day he stepped from Israel into hostile Judea. The ache in his heart still wanted easing; the tortured cries of his mind rose into the heavens each night. *My God, my God, have you deserted us at last? Have you finally left the people who left you so long ago? Is there no hope, my Adonai, is there no hope for us at all anymore? Where are your people, O my God? Where are the faithful who still call upon your unspeakable Name, whose prayers protect us from the evil in our land?*

He had bypassed Mount Gerizim on his way south, for his father had told him that the worshipers there lived in almost total ignorance of the outside world and were childish and superstitious in their fears. So Hosea had stayed away from that most sacred of places, the mountain where Israel had first cried out the blessings of her new covenant with God under Joshua's leading. He did this with regret, because he wanted companionship, he wanted to talk with those who still called upon the Name, he wanted the security of knowing he wasn't alone. But he also realized that their age-old answers would not silence his questions. So he went on his solitary way and still sought for God where he should have found him—in the hearts of his people.

Now Hosea was sitting under the dripping tamarack, unaware of how far inside Judea he was, unaware that just over the next hill was the shrine that brought all Israelites and Judeans to their knees in adoring worship: the glorious, golden Temple of Solomon, built to glorify the unspeakable Name of God. It shone in regal splendor over the gray housetops of Jerusalem on even the dullest of rainy days, and seemed to call to all beholders to enter and worship their Creator.

Hosea was sitting under a tree and had hardly any strength left in his legs to continue to the top of the hill. But he did stand up, to make the effort. He noticed that his robe hung heavily about his calves and reached down to wring it out. The people of the farms and villages he had spoken to had at least been courteous at first, for they knew from his robe that he was a scholar from the cities, a man such as their few rabbis who could read and write, who could discuss things of the mind. To his calling, therefore, they had given respect. It was later that they mocked.

Feeling dirty and unkempt, rubbing his aching side, Hosea started wearily up the slope, wondering when it all would end. Another day, another town—his exhausted brain reeled when he remembered the countless town gates he had passed through in his quest. *How much longer, O God,* he moaned inwardly, *until you show me where to find you and your peace once again?* He thought of the images of the other gods he had seen and the promises he had heard about their bounty, their awesome powers. *But none is like you,* he thought. *None of them came to my people and led us out of Egypt—only you. None of them helped us drive out the evil Canaanites, whose worship was bloody and whose rites were immoral—only you, the God who said his name was I AM.*

Hosea suddenly stopped, shuddering. *I have uttered the Holy, the Unspeakable,* he thought. He sank to his knees, covering his eyes, mud pressing around his robe. He waited in fear for what seemed an eternity, waiting for a sign that he had displeased God, waiting for the thunder of coming doom, waiting for he knew not what.

But no sound came, only the constant drip of the rain from the trees. The cheerful song of birds winging high overhead reached his fearful ears. The warblers were welcoming the sun, newly emerged from the gray clouds that raced in the swift wind above the earth.

Hosea rose again to his feet, staggering, his face bitter and his eyes bleak. Did God not even answer a blasphemy? Suddenly the whole time spent seeking seemed like a waste, a folly that a child would scorn. *No wonder they all mocked me,* he thought angrily as he started up the slope. He kicked a pebble aside with his foot, wishing he could kick aside his sorrow and questions just as easily.

He sighed, and his eyes grew wet. He had dreamed of more than this from life.

The sun quickly dried his robe as he strode up the path, and a light breeze blew his shoulder-length brown hair back from his broad forehead. His eyes searched the horizon as he climbed, and the surrounding hills seemed much shorter than the one he was on. *I'm getting very high,* he thought with surprise. *I wonder where I might be. And—I wonder what the people in this place will be like. I'm so tired. I hope someone will have an extra place for me to sleep this night. I'm tired of being outside under the stars. The days grow too cold to be living like a shepherd.*

His large brown eyes closed in weariness as he trudged along, his young beard framing a face grown lean with infrequent meals and inner suffering. He walked blindly, and once or twice he stumbled over a rock half-hidden in the soggy mud. His chin dropped to his chest, and his breathing was labored. He knew he couldn't go on much longer.

He had come to the summit of the hill, and he opened his tired eyes to see the level road ahead of him. His attention was caught by the sight of an old man sitting on the lid of a well at the side of the path just ahead, a dried-up thread of a man whose white hair moved softly in the breeze, whose bright lively eyes were watching him approach. The old man smiled, and his coarse white beard bobbed up and down on his scrawny, naked chest. "Ho, stranger!" he called, lifting his hand. "Are you thirsty? Come and drink, and bless our God for thinking to put a well here just for you!"

Hosea felt a startled thrill pass through him at those words, and he drew near. The knee-high grass at the side of the path grabbed at his robe with wet blades and he nearly tripped, so weak was he, but he reached the well. He took the bowl the old man handed him with a weary bow, and drank. He had never tasted such cool, sweet water and he savored each mouthful. The cool dribble soothed his aching throat, and he felt new strength course through his body.

Wiping his mouth with a dusty sleeve, Hosea handed back the bowl, and his bow now had more purpose in it. "Thank you, and may our God bless you as well for your kindness." His voice was trembling, and he knew the answer that would come this time to his questions. "It is very good indeed to hear someone call upon God as— as you just did, old man. It's been a long time . . ." He choked and fell silent, remembering the times he and his father had joyfully sung their blessing over a meal, laughing because God had been so good to them. The echo of that laughter was in his smile as he looked again at the old man on the well.

He may have looked old, but he didn't act his age. He leaped up from the well like a young goat and grabbed at Hosea's arm. "Yes, it is always good to praise his Name and remember his goodness to us!" His voice, though frail and trembling, was full of joy and reverence. "Welcome to Jerusalem, stranger. May I ask where you are from?"

Hosea stood very still. He said slowly, "Jerusalem? But—did you say *Jerusalem?*" His brain was spinning. A great exultation rose inside him, replacing the first spurt of fear at the thought that he was in Judea. Jerusalem! The Temple, the sacred Ark, the City of David!

The old man smiled, and a hundred wrinkles chased themselves across his face. "Yes, young stranger—Jerusalem! The home of all who seek to worship God! You've traveled far, I see. There are many miles of mud on the clothes you wear." His curiosity was like a child's, open and fearless. "Are you of Judah or Benjamin? Or are you a wandering Levite?"

Hosea hardly dared answer the question, for fear of the resulting contempt of a Judean for an Israelite, for Israel had forsaken the true God. He rubbed his eyes with one hand and walked a few paces along the path until the trees cleared and he could see down across the valley. Yes, there it was—the blessed Temple, built by the wise Solomon, its golden walls freshly washed by the rain and gleaming in the morning sun. His heart was thudding. Maybe this was God's answer; maybe there within those sacred walls he would find once more the security of God's constant presence and guidance.

He turned back to the old man, who still stood beside

the well, watching him with a curious tilt of his ancient head. Hosea forgot all about the danger that this man might be an ardent Judean. All he knew was that he was near the Temple, that maybe his long search was over. "It's the most beautiful sight in the world," he said softly, and his tired brown eyes had a new light in them. "I have come so far, and now I see it."

The old man came up beside him and peered long into his face. "Young man, you have not said where you come from, and I'm a nosy old man who likes to know the names of new people around Jerusalem. You spoke of God a moment ago as though it was a pleasure you seldom receive. I know that our land is not so full of believers as it should be, but then it's not that empty of them either! Now tell me, young man, where is your home?"

Hosea hesitated only a moment. After all, he could easily outrun the old man. "I am Hosea ben Beeri, born in Samaria, but lately of Dan."

The old man's eyes widened. "So a child of Israel comes to Jerusalem. And you have so far walked unscathed through my country?"

Hosea nodded, frowning a little in an attempt to remember the past few days of sameness. "I didn't even know I was in Judea until I met you. I haven't been into any of the villages I've passed lately, because—well, for a few days I've only wanted to be alone."

"Why?" For a new acquaintance, especially in hostile country, the old man was certainly being inquisitive. But Hosea found he couldn't be resentful against the first person to speak God's Name to him in so long a time. Yet, he was still wary about disclosing his purpose, wondering about its reception. "I—have many things to think about, and I needed to be alone to meditate—and pray."

The old man didn't laugh, and the twinkle went out of his eyes. "Yes," he said gravely, nodding his balding head, "yes, it's good for a man to be alone, and it's even better if in that loneliness he reaches out to God, for he always hears our prayers."

"Does he?" asked Hosea, and the bitterness of months of unsuccessful soul-searching and anguished prayer was in his tone.

"Oh, yes," answered the old man, his white eyebrows melting together in an intense frown. "You cannot doubt it, young man. Why, you are a scholar—look at your well-wrinkled robe, grown thin in the back where you sit all day. Don't you have a copy of the writings of Moses, then? Haven't you read about the care God took of our fathers in this very land? And the prayers of David and the Temple priests—were some not written in anxious prayer, and others in joyous praise?"

Hosea slowly walked back to the well, his weary feet still aching. He took off his sandals and looked at the holes worn in them, mute testimony of his long journey. Sitting down on the well's cold stone edge, he started brushing the dust off his clothes, wrinkling his nose in disgust at the filth. He'd been too long from water, he realized, and wondered if he dared enter the city and use the public pools.

The old man stood for a while where Hosea had left him near the trees, and Hosea noticed that his lips were moving silently. *He really is praying,* Hosea thought, and a wave of relief broke through the wall of bitterness that had been building up inside ever since his father's untimely death. When the old man finally did trot over and sit beside him, Hosea knew that he could be safely trusted with his story.

As the sun slowly climbed to its ascendancy above the Temple, Hosea and his new friend talked quietly. All the questions and doubts, all the uneasiness about his faith that the younger man had recently experienced— all came pouring out, and all was handled gently and deftly by the old man. "And so I search for the knowledge of God that my father had, that David had, that Moses and Abraham had so long ago. The Levites couldn't help me. Now I think that maybe at the Temple I will find God again."

"So you can't see the hand of God in your life, but you still must search for him," the old man mused, tugging his sparse beard.

"Yes, and I'll die before I cease my search!" Hosea jumped up from the well, fists clenched at his side, his eyes defiant as only a young man uncertain and in agony of soul can be defiant.

The old man chuckled, unimpressed, and reached over to pat Hosea's tense arm. "I believe you, my son—I believe you! You're quite near to death now, for a leaner man I've seldom seen even in beggars' row. When did you eat last?"

Hosea looked down at his pack, lying where he had tossed it in the deep grass beside the well. How long ago had he finished his last stale loaf of unleavened bread?

"I haven't yet told you my name, and I suppose it would be good if you knew it, Hosea," grinned the old man. "Then, as a good host, I shall invite you to my home to eat."

Hosea glanced over at the old man and took note of the worn loincloth which was his sole covering. "No—no need for that, although you are kind to the stranger in your land. I—I'm sure I can find somewhere—"

"Stop, Hosea!" cried the old man, who now was openly laughing. "You see my scanty dress and you say to yourself, 'He is so lacking in fat that a lion would scorn to kill him!' " The old man stood up, and his scrawny form assumed a new dignity as he bowed and then held his head high. "I am Amoz ben Judah, and my family name goes back in a straight unbroken line to the first prince of our house, the son of Jacob. The wealth that the first Judah accumulated with his caravans and sheepfolds has never left us, even during the Egyptian captivity, for there has always been gold in our chests. All the men of our family have dressed in purple, and it has been our duty and pleasure always to attend upon the king and serve him as captains in war."

Hosea didn't know what to say. He stood there feeling foolish, like an ignorant tramp who has been caught stealing sheep. Amoz could see exactly how he was feeling, and it amused him. "Come, young man," he said with a small chuckle, "it was a natural mistake to make. You can't see my cloak. It's hanging in the tree over there, drying off after this morning's rain. And I'm so short that to think of me as a prince is almost blasphemous! Now if you'd seen my son—but enough. I have an idea that you'll meet him as well, as God wills it. That's why I'm here at the well. I await my giant of a son."

"Where is he?" asked Hosea politely, privately wondering what meeting the son of this little old prince would accomplish.

Amoz gave him a sharp look, as if he could read the other's mind, and it made Hosea quite uncomfortable.

"My son is in the Plains of Moab right now, just across the Jordan, and . . . he is there for the same reason that you've been wandering without a home all these long months."

Hosea felt an eagerness inside. "So I am not alone in my seeking. Others, too, find the need to go out and look for God."

Amoz sat down again, frowning. "Yes, you young men are all alike. You can't sit still and see God at work around you. No, you have to go into unknown places and get into trouble before you see him protecting you. *Then* you believe. . . . But no, I do you an injustice. Some men need to seek him as you and my own son do. For you, the sacrifices and the prayers are not enough, and even the feasts bring little joy."

"The feasts haven't been celebrated properly in Israel for many years," Hosea answered sadly. "Some of our faithful families used to get together, especially for the Firstfruits, but they had to give up even that because the worshipers of the Old Ones would break in and desecrate the sacrifices. My father told me about this, and he hadn't seen any of the Levitical feasts celebrated since he was a young boy in Dan. The yearly sacrifice is still given on Mount Gerizim, but that's all. Except for those who meet in various homes to celebrate Shabbat, as we used to do in Samaria, the old worship of the God of our fathers is gone." The sorrow and anger were back in his voice.

Amoz shook his head slowly, tears welling from his half-closed eyes onto his sunken cheeks. "Ah, my God, how can you bear it?" he murmured, and his old eyes opened again to search the hilly horizon to the east, beyond which ran the Jordan. "It isn't as bad as that in

Judea, yet. Jotham hasn't closed the Temple—my son and I have managed to prevent that—but it's only a matter of time until it happens. The feast days are still celebrated here, but the crowds are much smaller than they were when Uzziah was young. Now he dies outside the walls in his private home, stricken from his blasphemy, and the worship of God dies just as slowly within the walls of Jerusalem. That's why my son is wandering and fasting in the wilderness. He seeks an answer to this falling away and feels that he must do something about it, but what that is he doesn't yet know. He has no clear call yet, Hosea, and neither do you. But for me to know that two of you thus seek, one from Israel and one here—maybe, maybe God is moving in a new way in our day."

The old man's voice was growing excited as he pursued this new idea. "Could it not be possible that God has decided that the writings of Moses aren't enough, and that he needs to send men now? But no, it's not for me to suggest such a thing to you, Hosea."

But Hosea had grasped Amoz's idea, seizing it with renewed hope and yearning. What if this old man was right, that God had guided him all along to this place so that he could hear of another who sought as he did, so that he could catch a glimpse of a hidden purpose so holy and awe-full that he wanted to cover his head with his cloak and sink down to the ground in trembling prayer!

But he couldn't let his mind dwell upon the idea. It was too large, and he was only a man, and afraid. Instead, he pushed it away with an outward motion of his hand, shaking his head with excited uncertainty.

He stood up again and sauntered over to the gap in

the trees. There it stood, tall and proud in its golden splendor as the noonday sun caught its upper beams and turned them into blinding flames. "Amoz," he said in hushed tones, "maybe I should go over there, not telling anyone who I am, of course. And maybe . . ." He left the thought unfinished.

Amoz was frowning again, running his fingers through the thin white strands of his beard. "I'm not sure that would be wise, Hosea," he said slowly, knowing instinctively that the young man would take his words as guidance from God. "My son goes to the wilderness because the Temple for him is barren of the presence of God. The priests have misused and almost rewritten the Laws of Moses, trying to bind us with their interpretations of what God gave us so long ago. Isaiah found those priests stifling and legalistic, and he was unable to worship God as he wished there, or to find the joy in singing that King David found. Indeed, even those who openly profess to follow other gods are now allowed inside, as long as they dress the right way and still wash before meals." Amoz's voice was heavy with scorn. "Yes, look well upon the Temple. She is indeed beautiful and the world will never see her like again. But some call the priestess of Ashtaroth lovelier still and dance in the high places all over Judea and Israel! Hosea, inside our bright and golden Temple is corruption and darkness. No, I sense that that is not the place where God will meet you. Yes, he will call to others when they worship him before the altar, but not you. You would be too resentful of the priests to be able to concentrate upon your prayers."

Amoz looked again to the east, as he had been doing occasionally as he spoke. Hosea suddenly wished that his father waited for *him* to return, waited and prayed that his son would find what he sought. *What faithfulness, that Amoz should climb this steep hill each day and sit here until darkness!* thought Hosea, marveling at the spirit of the old man. There was greatness here, and he hoped that the son was worthy of it. "Does your son spend much time in the wilderness?"

Amoz glanced back at him, grinning. "Yes—too much time for me, and for the king."

Hosea paled. "Does—does he still see Uzziah?"

Amoz raised his thin eyebrows. "Of course he does, Hosea. He is the king's closest friend now that all the other princes have taken after young Jotham. He doesn't violate the Levitic laws concerning leprosy, if that's what bothers you. He stays the prescribed distance, I think. Once he came home after three days' unexplained absence and I knew he'd been purifying himself, so I think he may sometimes in compassion come close when they talk. The disease has covered Uzziah's whole body with whiteness, Isaiah tells me, and he is wasting away in his grief and repentance. He doesn't ask God to remove the leprosy, because he thinks he should die a leper in penance for his blasphemy. But it's hard to be cut off from everyone while you're still young and vigorous. All Uzziah talks of now is death, Isaiah says, even though he could well live to be older than I."

"What—what does he look like? I've never seen a leper."

Amoz shrugged. "He's been covered with a white rash for two years now, otherwise he's the same as any man. He needn't die, only live apart from all other men. Some lepers recover, but that's unlikely in the king's case."

Hosea was beginning to feel an urgency inside, a hunger to get away from conversation again, even though the old man had been most helpful and kind. But he wanted to be alone. He bent over to pick up his pack and said, "It's good to know that your son is as hungry as I am for more than what we get from the scrolls and the sacrifices. Amoz, you've helped me, and I thank you."

Amoz waved away his gratitude. "Wait until God has spoken to you, young man, and then thank *him!*"

Hosea flushed at the implied rebuke. "Do you really think that God will actually—well, speak to me, as he did to Moses?"

Amoz looked away again and said somewhat reluctantly, "Isaiah says that he waits for the voice of God, because he so longs to enter the Temple and the palace and with the words of Adonai show those men their wickedness. He says that only the words of God can do this, and not his own. Yes, I know you're different. You have no urge to cleanse and revive your country, but from what you've told me, Israel is barren and needs new life. You found her so lacking that you had to come all the way to Jerusalem and talk to me before you found any direction! Now, why should God bring you here? And he did bring you, have no doubt about it. If you earnestly seek him, as you have done, he will guide you to the place where he will meet you. Hosea, why would you be brought to me, unless it was that I should send you the same way my son has gone?"

Amoz was looking straight at Hosea now, and his eyes had a fierce shining radiance in them. His short body quivered with excitement, and his hands were clasped as if in prayer. "Yes, I'm saying that you should go into the Plains of Moab, as Isaiah has, and you should listen in the emptiness of that wilderness for the voice of God. Isaiah has been going for years, so it may be that you will have a long time to wait as well. But I somehow think not."

Hosea was numb. He had no thoughts or words to answer what he had just heard. He stood there and watched as Amoz went over to the olive tree that held his sumptuous purple cloak in its stout branches. The old man lifted a pack from among the roots and brought it back to the well. "Food," he said simply, holding it out to Hosea. "I keep it here for Isaiah, for when he returns he is always ravenous, having eaten all he took at least a day before. Take it, Hosea, and go in peace. May Adonai protect you now, as he has done all your life."

Hosea took the goatskin pack. He tried to thank Amoz again, but his throat was unaccountably dry. Walking to where he had dropped his sandals, he slipped into them and then turned to the east. He saw the path running down the hill, the same path up which he had toiled barely an hour before, filled with despair and weariness. Now he would descend with a purpose, with new hope, with a place to go.

He looked again at the old man, who grinned at him. "Now I will have two sons to wait for instead of one," he said, a curious huskiness in his weak voice.

"God's peace be with you, Amoz. I shall return or die." Hosea turned and started down the hill.

EIGHT

The Wilderness of Moab

The Plains of Moab, running east from the sluggish brown snake of the Jordan River to reach all the way to the sudden upflung majesty of the mountains of Moab, hold beauty for the man who walks there, and terror.

In the seamless black of the night, the stars are close and throbbing with pale pulsating color. A man can stretch out his hand and cover the soft reds and savage yellow-whites of far-off suns and worlds. The cold chill of the desert breeze on his cheek will bring the thought that perhaps he has died, and the stars he sees are really the seraphim and cherubim of God moving about doing his business.

It was with these thoughts that Hosea spent his first night on the Plains after struggling across the silty Jordan. Hands under his head, he lay on the ground and marveled at the craftsmanship of the Creator. A new awe fell upon him as he considered the vastness of the night. How could the holy I AM of the universe stoop down and listen to the prayers of one such as he? How had he even dared to think that God would speak to him?

After hours of lying on his back among rocks and stubby grass, Hosea sat up, yawned, and stretched. He was too excited to sleep, too full of this new sense of at last being on the right path. The breeze that swept around him was becoming harsher, and he knew that the night must soon be over. Just then he saw a tiny thread of gray growing along the horizon, and the lumps that were faraway mountains became outlined against the sky. There was a change, too, in the silence that surrounded him, a tense and throbbing expectancy that stilled his thoughts and called him to attention. Over the unseen trees behind him that lined the last stretch of fertile soil this side of Jordan came the dying languid sigh of the night wind, as the slit of gray broadened into the deep blues and soft whites of a peacock's tail.

Suddenly, with no more warning than this, the sun rose, swimming in a deep sea of gold, and Hosea's heart bounded with joy in the music of that splendor. The sunbeams sped through the air and caressed his uplifted face with warmth. Dewdrops on the rocks also caught those beams and turned into tiny rainbows that shimmered in the cool air.

Hosea had just experienced the beauty of the wilderness, but as the hours passed he experienced the terror. The trees were gone, and only tiny scrub bushes clung tenaciously to the bits of soil between clumps of rocks, and there was now no escape from the heat of the sun. In the hills of Jerusalem Hosea had tasted a hint of frost in the air, but here in the Plains of Moab the sun still reigned supreme, sucking all moisture out of anything that moved. Only the occasional scurrying cloud hid the sun for a brief moment in its race westward over the Jordan.

Occasionally gazelles skipped among the rocks, on their way to the Jordan for a drink. Once a pack of wild jackals ran silently past him, their red tongues hanging out and yellow eyes glaring. Other than these animals, and the rare lizard who regarded him unblinkingly from a rock, he was alone.

Yet he didn't feel alone. A sense of being watched filled him, and once or twice he glanced over his shoulder to see if someone followed him. But he saw no one.

As the day wore on and his body grew sticky with sweat, his head started to swim from the fierce glare of the sun. If only he had come in another month, when the cool wet winds of the rainy season would pass over. . . .

The blazing heat was striking his face, and he realized that he was lying on the rocky slope of a small mound. He couldn't remember falling, and he realized hazily that he had been more tired than he thought. His bones felt like water; his robe was a heavy sack that held his limbs together. *Elijah went through this desert,* he thought. *Moses had a desert to cross as well. Isaiah lives here for days on end—and I faint before noon on my first day.*

Shame flooded him, and he forgot the miles he had traveled before he reached Jerusalem. *I am weak, weak and faithless, no man for any god to listen to.* Then he remembered that God had succored Elijah in *his* weakness, when he ran away from Jezebel and fainted for lack of food. So he looked for his pack, the one Amoz had given him, but it was gone. He must have dropped it as he wandered in his sun daze.

Close as panic was, he managed to fight it off. Hadn't God sent his angels to Elijah in the form of ravens, and fed him? God had raised him in his feebleness and sent him back to his people.

Hosea wondered where these thoughts were coming from, for he hadn't read about Elijah in years. And yet these thoughts filled his mind, bringing a strange peace and comfort with them, something very different than anything he had ever felt before.

Then the sense that someone was watching him became blinding certainty. He felt bowed down with weariness, but he raised his head and saw a man sitting on a large rock behind him.

The man was dressed simply, like a farmer. His face was in shadow, for he had his back to the sun that now slipped toward the horizon. Hosea had no time to wonder from whence he had come, for the man turned and looked at him and Hosea started to tremble. He felt like the smallest of desert ants before the hugeness of the presence of this One who sat before him. A second ago he had seemed just a man. Now Hosea knew his hand held the whole world.

The Man's eyes held Hosea's, and in them was all knowledge and joy and pain. Hosea could say nothing, think nothing. There was no strength in him.

The Man stood up and walked over to where Hosea still lay on his side and looked down at him. Panting, struggling, Hosea overcame his weakness and trembling, and pushed his body up so that he could kneel. But the trembling had reached deep inside until he thought that he would fall apart. His parched mouth opened, and on a sobbing sigh he breathed, "Adonai!"

The Man gazed down upon him with tenderness, as if

he saw and loved his child. Such an overwhelming love flowed into Hosea's starving heart from that gaze that he knew he must speak again, though he die. "Adonai . . ." he gasped, and fell down in a faint at the other's feet.

God had come to him at last.

NINE
By the Well

Old Amoz leaned his bare back against the smooth stones of the well, stones that had been old when David the conqueror first scaled these defended hills to defeat the Jebusites, who had built Jerusalem. The prince's bald head, with only a few wisps of white hair left over his ears, nodded in the afternoon sun as he drowsed. His blue-veined hand idly flapped at the flies buzzing around his nose. Awakened by an inconvenient itch, he reached down to scratch at his calloused heel and opened his eyes to see a lamb sitting in the grass a few feet away, eyeing him curiously. He grinned at it and called softly. It rose hesitantly, stepping toward him, wrinkling its tiny black nose for a sniff.

Just then a loud call came from the slopes behind the trees, and the animal stiffened. The call came again, and the lamb turned and whisked away in that direction. Amoz straightened up and peered around the well to see a shepherd scoop up the lamb and rejoin his small flock as it meandered toward the city. Amoz grinned again, recognizing the well-known limp of Zerah his cousin. Zerah, though a prince of Judah, had lost his wealth when bandits captured his caravan a few years before. Now he was enjoying himself immensely at a much simpler job that enabled him to spend long days and nights away from the tongue of his bitter wife. Amoz counted him a blessed man, although his own wife, now many years dead, had been a model of quietness and fortitude and had never given him cause to complain. Still, Zerah had sheep to watch each day, and Amoz only had a road.

"God's peace be with you, Amoz!" came a shrill voice. He jumped up and bowed to old Leah as she shuffled by on her way home from market. She had seven grandsons to feed now, poor woman, for her daughter and son-in-law had been banished to the leper colony. Only God knew how she managed to keep them all fed, with no other relatives in the city. Only the kind rich saw to it that she had work, for she was old and arthritic. She came once a week to clean Amoz's large house for him—after he had just cleaned it himself to spare her—and for this she received a lamb each time. He had promised her son-in-law, just before the wretched man left, that he would make sure none of the family starved, but the lamb was all the proud old woman would take. Old Leah had spent her whole life working hard, and she kept her sorrow to herself.

In the trees of the western slope played the children of the city, their echoing laughter proclaiming their delight over a little freedom from the duties and studies that filled each day. Their teacher, Rabbi Kathan, had once confided to Amoz—the two had been close friends since early boyhood—that he scarcely knew how to handle the young of today. How disrespectful they were, and how their indulgent parents spoiled them! Amoz had hidden a secret grin, remembering the frustration they two had caused their own rabbi so long ago, and had gravely agreed, offering his distraught friend his heartfelt laments.

"Abba! Abba! Are you there? Are you asleep again?" A great booming call from the eastern slope split the air. Amoz ran as fast as his old legs could carry him to the summit and shaded his eyes against the sun. Coming up the path toward him, their robes hanging with dirt but their faces shining with triumph, came Hosea and Isaiah.

"Still faithful, Abba?" called his son again, and in a moment the little father was lost in the massive embrace of his son. Laughing and weeping both at once, Amoz could say nothing, but his full heart cried out praise to his Adonai. They were both back, and how joyful their eyes were!

Putting his father down, Isaiah threw himself onto the thick bed of grass beside the well. He pulled off his sandals, bellowing, "Where's that bowl of yours, Abba? My feet are as thirsty as my throat!" His laughing black eyes met his father's, and the two were still for a moment, savoring the joy of the other's presence. Hosea looked from one to the other and then turned away, a lump in his throat because his own father was not there.

Isaiah stood up, his thirst quenched, and looked down at the other two. He towered over them, his once colorful robe bleached gray by the sun, his arms and legs covered with dust and mud. Yet there was an air of command and nobility about him, and Hosea had no need to wonder if this man was the prince he claimed to be. But there was humility in the midst of his grandeur, for he had a way of listening eagerly to whatever anyone said that had made Hosea trust him from the start.

Amoz touched his son's sleeve, looking up with love at the leonine head bent down to him, the square laughing face framed by the sun-bleached brown hair. "Yes, Abba?" boomed the son, and Amoz winced as the bass voice hit his tender eardrums.

"Quietly, quietly, my son," he pleaded. "You aren't at the palace trying to scare your enemies. You're here with friends! I've food waiting for you; so let's sit about the well and eat while we talk. Then you—you can tell me what's happened, and how you two found each other."

A few minutes later, the three men were laughing around the well, their mouths full of tender apricots. A Levite, passing on his way from the Temple to the next village, had noticed that they neglected to wash before eating, and his lips were tight as he wrote it down to tell to the high priest next time he saw him. The house of Amoz would one day break the laws one too many times.

Unaware of this censure, the three at the well talked as they ate, so eager were they to share the events of the past week. Hosea told of his meeting with the Man in the desert, and Amoz could hardly contain himself. "The Angel of Adonai who is Adonai himself, blessed be he!" he exclaimed. "He hasn't been seen in the land of our fathers for hundreds of years, since the time of the judges! Yes, God is doing a new thing in his land, for his people. His mercy has brought him to you, Hosea, so that you can tell others as you have told us. In mercy he comes, when our land deserves only his wrath and punishment! Praise to his Name."

Hosea's lean dark face was naked in its joy, his large

brown eyes blazing with a new fire. He felt like a new man inside and his words had wings on them, catching the ears of his two listeners and lighting joy in their hearts. "I can't describe the song he gave me. The joy he filled my heart with came from his heart! When I saw him I fell at his feet, but he laid his hand on me and gave me water, and blessed me. And then he spoke to me, and his voice had power and sorrow and joy together— how can I explain it?"

"I understand," Amoz answered softly. "God has sorrow because of us, and joy because of his love for us. Who can fathom it?"

Hosea looked at him, perplexed. "That's just what my father used to say, that the anger of God and the sorrow of God are one and the same, and all springs from his love. I don't know how long the Man spoke to me, but it must have been days and days. I do remember getting lost after he was gone, and nearly passing out completely before I reached the trees by the Jordan."

"And there I found him, Abba, looking like death under the trees!" cried Isaiah, who felt he had been silent long enough. His laugh frightened away the birds nesting in the branches above them, but he stopped when he saw the hope in his father's eyes. "No, Abba, don't look at me like that. Think you not that I, too, had those hopes after Hosea told me what happened to him? I didn't see the Man; I heard no voices in the wilderness. But Hosea has renewed my hope, and I *know,* in here"— he struck his massive chest—"that God will speak to me. I know it, but I may well wait several years until the right time comes. Now my task is to attend King Uzziah, and I have already been away two weeks. Hosea, will you come home with us for a few days?"

Hosea stood up and Isaiah rose with him, dwarfing the Israelite. "I can't, my friend. You may not mind my origins, but the people in your city hate me for being an Israelite, one of the tribes who left their Temple. Even so, the voice of God still calls inside me, and I feel a new need to return to my people and tell them the glorious news, that he still loves them and cares for them, despite their wickedness."

Amoz nodded as he pulled his cloak around his shoulders. "See that you always remember that, young man, for I doubt you'll hear him often in the years ahead. Remember, the life of a messenger of God may read well in the ancient scrolls, but the way is terrible and lonely, and only others of your calling will be able to understand you and what it is you do. Even believers will revile you for the stand you take against the false gods and the wickedness they revel in every day. Do not let yourself grow bitter because of the path down which God leads you!"

Hosea's eyes were still shining. How could the old man speak so? "Have no fears for me, Amoz. Haven't I seen my Creator? What can life do to me to make me forget his love?"

Amoz remembered the anger that had been inside Hosea when they met, and sighed to himself. *The young are always so sure,* he thought. "I go now to let you make your farewells. No—not to me, I hate them. God guide you always, my son." He raised his hand in a blessing, and then turned away toward the city.

The two young men, left alone, found themselves at a loss for words momentarily. Then Isaiah cleared his throat and began. "Hosea, it may well be that we will never see each other in this life again." He pulled at his short curly beard, wondering how to go on. A bluff, hearty friend, he hated leavetakings as much as his father did. "But you've heartened me this past week. I will always remember that in Israel God has his prophet Hosea, and I will pray for him."

Hosea's eyes were misty, but he stood straight and his eyes were turned toward the hills to the north. "There is no loneliness for me now, my friend, for I know you'll be here in Jerusalem speaking for God as I will in Israel."

The stiffness and constraint grew, and neither knew what to say, for there were no words for their thoughts.

Finally Hosea reached out his arms, and Isaiah clasped them roughly. "May our God richly bless you," Hosea choked, realizing just how much this man meant to him, and agonizing over departure. But God led him away, and he must go.

Isaiah stood on the top of the hill and watched Hosea stride down the path, as his father had watched ten days before. The Israelite turned at the bottom and waved, and then was gone around the bend in the road.

T E N
Diblaim

Diblaim stood behind his counter, his shaking hands hidden from any customers behind a pile of goods. The noise of the shouters and buyers hurt his ears, and his eyes, rapidly growing dim with the years, saw only confusion in the multitude of color stretching to both ends of the market. *I'm getting old,* he thought. *I need a son to carry on my work here so that I can rest more at home. But I have no son, and Dan shows no inclination to come and join me.*

He gazed over the crowd, his back straight and his chin high, aware of glances cast furtively his way. For two years now the people of Samaria had watched him like that, and the children that used to come and play with Nathan now ran away if he so much as looked at them. He knew why, and the fact that they blamed him more than his daughter for her imprisonment hurt too much for him to dwell upon.

Diblaim's eyes were black with old sorrow, and he had

no one with whom to speak about it but God. Yet his constant tortured praying brought no comfort. His wife never mentioned their daughter on the roof, and his Rachel only gazed at him with her soft, puzzled eyes and said nothing. His heart cried out to them words he could never speak: *O my wife, O my Rachel, it tears me too, knowing she suffers up there!* Every time a night storm whipped around the city he would stand by the window in his large bedroom, listening, knowing her tiny tent was right above him and that the rain and hail were beating at the tanned hide walls in fury. *Are you safe?* he would cry out in his heart, but his mouth remained closed.

Every evening his wife would carry a bowl and a platter of bread and cheese up the stairs, leaving them at the top. She would wait until the dark form at the other end glanced up, and then she would leave. Diblaim knew that Shana never said a word to that small figure draped in sackcloth, for her sorrow was too great. But he also knew that Rachel, after supper, would slip outside and up the stairs herself, to watch her sister eat and whisper heartbroken prayers for her. To the younger girl this exile was inexplicable, but she had full faith in her father and never thought to reproach him. For this he was grateful. It helped ease his own painful questions.

Two years Gomer had lived on that roof, and in all that time he hadn't set eyes on her. He felt that she hated him, and that hurt even deeper than the Samaritans' scorn. *I did what was needed, and now God will see it through to whatever end he has written.* So he told himself, and so he prayed.

My daughter is a whore, he thought, standing amidst the gaiety of the market. The same thought had been there since the moment Zedediah had accosted him at the gates and thrown out his accusation. *My lovely daughter is a whore.* The twisted agony of his soul showed in the deep lines under his eyes, testifying to endless, sleepless nights spent in weeping prayers. *My Gomer is a whore! O my God, where did I go wrong? What didn't I teach her? What lack in her made her entice the heathen to her side? Maybe that wasn't the first time.* The thought of the faceless men Gomer had lain with flashed through his tortured mind. He moaned and slumped down on his stool, not caring who saw his pain.

His thoughts kept swirling on and on, and he found himself helpless to think of anything else. *She should have been stoned, she and my—my friend Senu-Amen, together outside the walls, killed in their blasphemy and sin.* But his heart recoiled from the thought even as his just mind realized the rightness of it—and the futility. The laws to govern the behavior and direction of his people had been given on Mount Sinai hundreds of years before, given to help Israel keep herself pure amid impure tribes who had already sold themselves to evil. The worship of the Old Ones had been almost stamped out in those days by the zealous Joshua and some of the jduges who followed him, but there had always been some who preferred the heady wines and gala feasts of Ba'al and Ashtaroth. Diblaim had spent long hours with his neighbor Beeri in their young and studious days, reading the history of Israel. So often their people had left the true worship of God, and so often they had been enslaved by other tribes before they thought to turn back to God—and always he had rescued them. Distress turns man to his God, Diblaim had learned, and that was why he was treating Gomer so. But who among his people could understand? Who would believe?

His people had again turned away from God, ever since the first Jeroboam rebelled against Solomon's son and led the ten northern tribes into idolatry. Who was left who kept the old feasts? Who followed the old ways of Moses? It was the Old Ones now, from farther back in time, who led Israel in their grip as once they had held Canaan.

My people are sick unto death, Diblaim thought, closing his tired eyes against the flurry of the crowd. *They show no desire to return to the Holy One now, and trouble breathes at our necks. Assyria presses in from the north, our brothers in Judea harass us to the south, and east and west are the vassals of Tiglath-pileser. Yet Israel goes on singing and dancing the nights away, reveling here in the square under the indulgent eyes of Levites who should be leading her back to her God in repentance.*

How long will you wait for her to return, O my God? How long will you hold back your wrath? Are you yet hoping to see her turn to you in repentance, as I hope for my Gomer? The knife twisted again inside the dark heart of the father.

"Diblaim?" A low, hesitant voice interrupted his prayers. Diblaim opened his eyes and stood up from the stool. At the side of his booth, one hand gently scratching behind Nathan's long ears, stood a slim youth, his dark brown eyes watching the merchant with lively interest. There was an elusive familiarity about the young man, but Diblaim doubted that he'd ever seen him before.

Diblaim

The merchant bowed. "I am Diblaim," he answered with quiet courtesy. "May I help you?"

The stranger's eyes lighted, and he smiled. His lean tired face lit up with an inner warmth, and Diblaim found himself instinctively liking the youth even as he scrutinized him carefully. Along his jaw was the beginning of what would soon be a thick, flowing black beard to match the hair waving in ragged locks to his shoulders. His robe was so faded that even the expert eyes of the merchant couldn't tell what color it had been. His skin was tanned so dark that it was possible he was an Ishmaelite from the desert, but what would he want in Samaria? The lad needed a wash and haircut, Diblaim decided, and a new robe. But he didn't look able to purchase any substantial amount of Diblaim's goods, although the cut of his dress showed he was a scholar. *Poor and dirty,* thought the merchant. Was he looking for a gift?

But the stranger had given Nathan a final scratch. He came around to the open back of the stall and clasped the startled Diblaim by his upper arms. His voice was choked, but the merchant felt strength in the youth's grip. "You don't remember me, Diblaim, but I remember well your kindness to my father, and in his name I have come to see you. His name was Beeri ben Obed."

"Hosea!" Diblaim pulled the younger man to him, and suddenly the dirt didn't matter any more. This was the son of his old friend—what was too good for him? He put his shaking hands on the broad shoulders and gazed into Hosea's sparkling eyes. "Hosea . . ." He searched the face as once he had searched the face of Shana. He saw strength and joy; yet he caught a glimpse of suffering. "Thanks be to God who has brought you back here after so long. Is it not twelve years? But where is my friend Beeri? Is he well?"

Hosea closed his eyes briefly, and then looked again at the merchant. "My father died defending Dan from some drunken Assyrians over a year ago, Diblaim."

Diblaim's shoulders slumped. "One more believer gone, and Israel is the poorer. My heart is sore for you, my friend. I remember the years of fellowship Beeri and I shared. But let us remember what King David said, that he would see his son again after this life. May it not be that God has another place besides dark Sheol, where the soul of a pure man like Beeri would be taken? It is in God's hands."

Diblaim sat again on his stool and motioned Hosea to take the other. For some reason, the memory that this was where Senu-Amen had sat made him angry for a brief second. But Hosea was an Israelite, and what was more, he had been brought up in the Laws and faith of their fathers. If it had been Hosea who had seen Gomer and desired her, the ending would have been so different. But now, what man who followed God would even want to look at his daughter? The old grief soured him again, and he let a few moments pass in silence as he struggled with his thoughts.

Hosea, meanwhile, was taking in the scene about him, and comparing it with twelve years before. There were many more foreigners now under Menahem than there had been under Jeroboam II. He saw men dressed in the fashions of the Egyptians, the Philistines, the Assyrians, traditional enemies of Israel who went openly before the Samaritans with their wares. Women dressed in bright colors and with coins around their mantles showed that Samaria had indeed grown more affluent and bold. The women's faces were painted, the men's beards oiled and curled, and most clothes were delicately decorated with embroidery.

Hosea wondered how his people could walk about so carelessly, chattering and laughing. Danger looked from every corner, where Assyrian soldiers stood or sat, all unsmiling, their eyes covering their contempt.

"Diblaim," he said slowly, and the merchant looked up. "I have walked through our land, and nowhere have I seen the wealth that is before me now. The caravans don't come into Dan because of the recent wars in Syria; and the people of Bethel and Shiloh are mostly poor. It's almost impossible that this is the same country."

Diblaim's interest had been caught. "You've been traveling, have you? Looking for work?"

Hosea smiled. It was so good to be able to talk to someone who would understand! Amoz had been right. He had been laughed out of most towns where he tried to speak to the people, and once or twice soldiers had escorted him to the gates, quite roughly. But the initial joy he had known in his desert encounter was still there, and he felt confident that soon a large number of people would listen to him and repent of their ways. How could they help it, when God cared so much for them? "It's a long story, Diblaim, and you're in the middle of a working day. Here's a customer now."

At that moment an old woman had wandered up to the stall and was fingering a bolt of blue wool. She was bent over with rheumatism and her gnarled hands clutched a cane, and she was dressed in torn gray linen. But the merchant jumped up to serve her, realizing that she was one of the richest women in town. She delighted in her disguise of old clothes, hoping that in that way she would reach a good bargain with traders, but they had caught on to her tricks long ago.

"Come home with me for supper, Hosea," Diblaim said over his shoulder, pulling out the wool for the woman to see it better. "My wife will be glad to see you again."

"And your daughters?" Hosea asked cheerfully, his mouth twitching into a grin. That was a dangerous thing to ask a fond father, he knew, for it would be instantly assumed that he was interested. Suddenly he found himself liking the idea of seeing Diblaim's girls again. Rachel had been a small, chubby baby who was still falling when she tried to walk, but her black eyes and laughing face had promised prettiness when she grew up. Easier to recall was the halo that the sun made around Gomer as she raced ahead of him through the meadow, her hair flying behind her like golden wings, her long legs taking her through the meadow grass as fast as himself. He remembered the day, just before he left for Dan, when he had suddenly realized that the sound of her soft laughter, floating back to him on the cool mountain air, was making him feel things he'd never felt before. He had looked at her, awed and a little frightened, and she had stood there laughing back at him, her childish mouth curved into a smile, a look of gleeful challenge in her brown eyes. And he had known himself her slave.

I had forgotten her, he was thinking now with surprise, *forgotten that bewitching seven-year-old who looked like a king's daughter!* He turned to Diblaim, laughing, to tell him what he had remembered. It was then he noticed the other's silence, and the pain on his face that whitened his mouth.

Hosea reached over quickly and caught the older man by the arm. "What ails you, my friend? Shouldn't you sit down again?"

"No, no, I'm all right, Hosea." Diblaim turned back to his customer, his mind whirling at Hosea's first question. His daughters . . . There would be the inevitable questions, the hesitant evasions, the silences he would have to hide behind. *God help me! What shall I do? Hosea, Hosea, why didn't you come back two years ago?*

Shana looked up from the fire when she heard the door open and blinked to clear her eyes, momentarily blinded by the flames. She had been stoking it so that the upper closed-in shelf would heat the bread inside. Diblaim liked it soft and hot.

In the doorway she could see two figures, but her constricted pupils could see no more. A sudden wild hope flared in her heart. Had her husband finally brought Gomer down?

Diblaim's voice roared through the kitchen and startled her. Why was he so happy? "Wife! We have a guest for supper! Come and see if you recognize him!" Then it wasn't Gomer. She put down her poker and slowly stood, fighting her resentment down. She would welcome the man if for no other reason than that he had brought back that lilt to her husband's voice. Smiling a trifle wistfully, she walked forward, thinking that it had been too many years since her husband had stormed in like that and swept her into his strong arms, his face laughing and his dark brown eyes glowing with love.

Hosea stood just inside the door as Diblaim closed it and slipped out of his sandals. He looked about the room, remembering how Shana and his mother had once worked here preparing Shabbat, gossiping happily about the goings-on in the city. Over there was a huge table that had held so many places during Passover. In one corner were the usual high mounds of bleached linen, smaller now than they had seemed to a boy just learning to climb. Almost he expected to see his mother come in from the workroom, smiling, scolding him for being out so late.

Shana stood in front of him and he bowed to her, dismayed. How gray and weary she looked, when once she had glowed with health. How rounded were her shoulders! Could twelve years have done this to her, giving her the deep lines of pain around her mouth and eyes—the same lines that Diblaim had?

Shana's large black eyes, still as warm and comforting as they had been the night his mother died, looked straight into his. She hesitated a brief moment, and then a smile banished the grief from her face. "It is Yona's son," she said softly and laid her hand on his. "You are welcome for your mother's sake, who was my beloved friend."

His mother's name brought a mist to Hosea's eyes, and he reached out his arms to Shana. She hugged him tightly, and he held her for a moment, both aware of the other's sorrow but not knowing its origin.

A footstep sounded from the workroom and Hosea released Shana, looking at the doorway expectantly. A girl came out of the darkness holding an oil lamp, and she was as he remembered the small mother beside him. It's Rachel, he told himself, aware of a certain disappointment. Her black eyes shone with peaceful laughter; her small mouth curved into easy smiles when she saw that they had company. She put down her handful of threads and waited for her father to introduce her, then caught herself admiring the way this young man held his head. He seemed excited and almost proud, she thought, not like humble Dan. Feeling a slight guilt, she scolded herself for making comparisons.

Diblaim reached out eagerly to his daughter and leaned over to kiss her smooth forehead. "You remember my Rachel, Hosea? Daughter, this is the young man who left many years ago with his father while you were still learning how to talk."

"I remember Gomer telling me about him." She smiled, and then clapped her hand to her mouth. She looked at her father fearfully. Had she done wrong? The words had come so naturally.

Diblaim's lips thinned, but he ignored what she had said. "She is promised to her cousin Dan, Hosea. You remember the boy of my farming brother? Yes, you used to play with him when—" He stopped and cursed himself for his foolishness in bringing up old times. Must all conversation lead to Gomer?

Hosea was completely bewildered by now. Rachel had scurried away to the fire as if pursued by guilt. What had she said that was so terrible? And Diblaim looked like a man with terrible pain. He opened his mouth to ask the whereabouts of the other daughter when he noticed a silent drama being acted out by the fire.

Rachel had picked up a tray and turned toward the door when her father reached her with swift steps and motioned her angrily to lay it down again. She did, her face puzzled and hurt. Hosea noticed bread and cheese on the tray, with a bowl of soup.

Shana was having none of this. She stood up quickly from the fire, where she had sat watching, and with a swift movement picked up the tray and went to the door, anger in every firm step. Hosea had never seen her like that, and his bewilderment grew. What was going on?

Diblaim lifted his hands with a sigh as his wife slammed the door behind her, and a moment later they heard her steps on the outside stairs. Was there a sick servant on the roof? wondered Hosea. If so, why this intense emotional byplay?

"The meat, Rachel," said Diblaim, and the girl, who had been standing before the fire twisting her hands and looking at Hosea with troubled eyes, came to life again. Shana returned in a moment and, without glancing at her husband, ladled out the soup. In a moment, the four of them sat down to eat.

Hosea took a few mouthfuls, and complimented his hostess on her cooking. She merely nodded. No one else spoke. Finally, Hosea could stand it no longer. He said, "You have not told me about my playmate, Diblaim. Have I missed Gomer's wedding? Is she away visiting relatives?"

Diblaim went pale and his lips stiffened. "She . . . is not with us, Hosea." That was all.

But Hosea noticed that Shana was watching him with a strange gleam in her usually gentle eyes. This made him slightly uneasy, and he would have been horrified to know that she was just beginning to realize that he might be the means of forcing her husband to end Gomer's exile. How, she couldn't fathom, but in between mouthfuls she started to pray fervently. *Let it be so, Adonai! Let this youth who remembers my daughter be the one to make her live again!*

After the meal the two men relaxed by the fire, and

Rachel took up the sewing as Shana pounded out the dough for tomorrow's bread. Both women kept their mouths closed and their ears open, eager to hear what passed between Diblaim and Hosea.

They heard of Hosea's travels after he left Dan, and wept at the cause of his leaving. Was it so true, then, that almost no one still believed in the ever-merciful God of Israel?

Hosea told of his search, how only one farmer in all those he met still held to the faith. He told of the wicked orgies he had seen in the village squares, unwilling to go into detail. "There is no sin they did not commit before my eyes," was all he would say, his face aching with the tears of mortification and shame he held back.

Diblaim understood. "I've seen it all here in Samaria," he answered, thinking of the girl upstairs wrapped in her coarse woolen cloak, the girl who would probably hate him for the rest of her life.

Now Hosea was hunched forward, his deep eyes glowing in the light of the oil lamp, and he told of his meeting with Amoz, of his days in the desert—and of the Man who met him there. "I have seen our Adonai face to face and have lived," he said intently, his whole face glowing with uncontainable joy.

He told of how he had been found half-dead by the huge son of Amoz, this man Isaiah who sought God as he had. "There are some, Diblaim. Take hope in that. Some men do seek him."

He told of the walk back to Israel, with God surely protecting him because none stopped or harassed him. Then he had walked into Bethel to see if the other golden calf, twin to the one in Dan, still existed. "They have a new temple there, and a man I met told me that a builder from the Greeklands built it for the god. It looks lovely from the outside, but is dark inside except for the sacrificial fire where—where children are offered to the god. But in front of the temple a man stood preaching the day I arrived, and I heard him gladly, for he spoke of God and warned our people to beware of the coming destruction if we went on in our evil ways. He was a Judean and the people pelted him with mud and stones, but day after day he came back. He was an older man, bent with suffering and pain, but how he must have loved our Adonai to preach his words to such people! He told me his name was Amos, and that he knew my friends Isaiah and Amoz. The last time I saw him he was being chased down the road by Assyrian soldiers who were threatening to cut off his . . . his manhood, should he return to Israel. May God give me such courage when my time should come!"

Diblaim sat up very straight, and for once the shaking of his hands was stilled. His voice was quivering with excitement as he asked, "Your time, Hosea—your time? Then—" He choked, unable to continue.

Hosea smiled at him and the women, who had crept slowly up to the fire and were watching him with parted lips. "Our Adonai spoke to me of Israel, and his voice was full of sorrow because of our evil ways. But then he told me how he still loved us, and he gave me hope that our people will respond to his love through my words. I stood on Mount Gerizim yesterday after giving sacrifice to God, for I needed cleansing for this work. I knew then that he was directing me to Samaria, and I exulted, for who can tell? Perhaps Menahem himself will come to the market and hear the words of God from my lips, and then the whole nation will turn back to God before disaster comes upon us!"

"Is it possible?" stammered Diblaim, eyes wide with hope.

Hosea stood up and held his hands, his lips trembling. "My friend, help me with this task. It is so large, and he has chosen *me* to do it! How is it possible?" Yet Rachel noticed that his nostrils flared with pride, and she felt a small fear for this man inside her heart. Did he yet understand this task to which God had directed him? Or did he envision himself as the converter of his people, as the man chosen to guide their king? Had he fully seen the sorrow of God, as her father had?

Diblaim, too, had risen, and he laid his hands upon Hosea's bowed shoulders. "God is doing a new thing in you, Hosea, and with your friend Isaiah, and with that Judean Amos. He gives you words that fill your hearts and which you must speak, as once he did for Abraham and Moses. Your ears hear him while ours are deaf. We have only the scrolls to know him by, but you have received the very Spirit of our God!"

A silence fell upon the house, and Diblaim and Hosea knelt down to pray. Rachel and Shana looked at each other, and both were thinking the same thing. Was Hosea still too young to really know the words he spoke? Was the joy blinding him to the sorrow?

The mother put her hand over the girl's and whispered, "We can only pray. It is the men who act." Rachel suddenly knew that Shana's chief prayer was still for Gomer.

ELEVEN
City of Darkness

The first golden rays of the sun lit the rooftops of Samaria the next morning, just as the first early risers were finding their way through the streets. Facing the east, the walls of the magnificent royal palace, built two hundred years before by Omri and added to by his son Ahab, were the first facades to welcome the dawn. Polished ivory facings reflected to the people below the sun they as yet couldn't see, and lightened somewhat the dark way they traveled.

Running past the palace was the broad avenue that led down to the market square, and already it was becoming crowded as servants, slaves, and merchants started their daily duties. Within the ornate walls that glistened above them lay, they knew, King Menahem and his nobles. But they felt no awe or shyness, fully aware that those of the court would still be sleeping off their drunken orgy of the night before. They, the common folk, might indulge in such pastimes if they so chose, but they still had to be up before the sun to get about their daily business. Only the wealthy could afford to sleep away the daytime.

Samaria was not a large city—so the Assyrian soldiers claimed who had to spend any time there. Built originally to give Omri central command of his ten tribes, it of necessity stayed within the double walls he had constructed for safety. Compared, of course, to the sprawling expanse of Nineveh to which these Assyrian soldiers were accustomed, containing as it did some five cities plus residential suburbs, Samaria was definitely just a provincial town, housing no more than 3,000 people, half of whom lived in the palace. But the Samaritans worked long and hard, so their city was quite wealthy. They felt no need to act humble before the sneering men of Tiglath-pileser.

The land Omri had purchased from Shemer and then, with characteristic generosity, named after him was now entirely lost under a maze of streets and buildings. The royal avenue and the market square were the only planned events within the walls. Every other house had been put wherever the builder wished, and in the resulting chaos such streets as one could find were similar to the first attempt of a child at drawing a straight line. The only rule of thumb followed by the owners was that the closer one built to the palace, the richer one had to be, so that his house would not disgrace the city nor offer offense should the royal eyes happen to glance out of a palace window.

At the opposite end of the city from the palace and farthest down the slope stood the east gate. Around it had once lived those who tried to follow the old ways of Israel and had no desire to join in, or see, the festivals held in the square. The area was considered respectable, and no group ever tried to invade those houses to hold an orgy. As a result, some of the families of the district were among Samaria's poorest, for no modern-day Israelite cared to buy from someone who was apt to start reproaching him about his life. Over the two centuries, however, even that small band of the faithful had dwindled, although the families kept up the tradition of being poor. Diblaim was one who had reached a certain level of prosperity in his partnership with Senu-Amen, but few of his neighbors had been so blessed.

Such, then, was the city to which Hosea returned.

Shana was up from her bed an hour before the sunrise, stepping quietly around the bedroom she shared with Diblaim. Without the aid of an oil lamp, she found her soft linen tunic where she had laid it the evening before on the one chair in the room. Pulling it hastily over her head, she smoothed the folds out and then tied her girdle about her waist, not noticing her plump rolls there anymore as once she had with regret. Reaching down for her overskirt, she tied that on with another girdle, broader and looser than the first. Running an ivory comb through her thinning hair, she caught herself remembering the time Diblaim had given it to her as her betrothal gift, the one item of beauty she had ever owned. She had tended it well over the years so that not one carved tooth had been broken. It was more than a lovely treasure, for it reminded her of the days when she had been pretty, and Diblaim had been thinking of other things than his trade when he complimented her weaving.

Putting her memories down along with her comb, she picked up the small pot beside her, used for night emergencies, and passed quietly through the curtained doorway. She had asked Diblaim years before to remove the wooden door once held there by iron hinges. It had been too thick for her to hear her children should they cry out in the night.

The stone steps of the stairway were cold on her feet as she descended swiftly, keeping her free hand against the wall to steady herself. Reaching the bottom, she looked over at the fireplace and smiled softly. Hosea was still stretched out before the dead embers fast asleep, completely exhausted from his long walk the day before from Mount Gerizim.

Laying the pot by the door, Shana walked over to her large flour vat and removed the lid. Her iron pot was there waiting to be filled, one of the few iron pots in the city. Diblaim had obtained it from a Greek merchant who had bargained shrewdly, and Shana still wondered wistfully if it was worth the two lengths of Persian silk her husband had finally given for it. But it had lasted twenty years, she reminded herself as she ladled flour into it, and no pot made of clay could boast such a lifetime.

The quiet rummaging behind him awoke Hosea, and he sat up quickly to look around. "Shana! I—I'm sorry, I must be in your way." He jumped hastily to his feet, and was suddenly conscious of his short tunic reaching barely halfway down his thighs and looking hopelessly rumpled. His outer tunic lay across the bench beside him and he reached for it hurriedly, the cloak he had used to cover him falling away from his arm. Blushing under Shana's amused gaze, he fumbled with the sleeves and finally managed to get into his robe and tie it around his slim waist.

"I did often see you tumbling around in the dirt outside with nothing on, you know," she reminded him with a twinkle, and he grinned back, his face still a deep red. Taking pity on him, Shana knelt down before the coals and started to build another fire. "Did you sleep well? Were you warm enough?" she asked.

"Very well and very warm. Your fire lasted until I fell asleep, and my cloak kept out any drafts. But I must look today for a place to live. I don't want to keep imposing on you this way."

Shana looked at him gravely, her busy hands still for a moment. "You have brought joy to a household that has been without joy for too long, Hosea." But she couldn't tell him to stay. Who knew what Diblaim would say to that? And what about her daughter up on the roof?

By the time Diblaim came downstairs, the sweet aroma of spiced lentils was steaming from the pot. Rachel was busy spreading wild honey on unleavened biscuits, and she greeted her father with a cheerful kiss. "Good morning, Abba! I thought I'd use the honey Dan brought us from his farm, since it's a special day today."

Hosea looked at her uncertainly. "Have I forgotten a feast day? What is special about today?"

"You're here, aren't you, my friend?" answered Diblaim, his heavy voice sounding young and hearty. The time he and Hosea had spent in prayer the night before had refreshed him so much that he wished the younger man was his own son, so that he might never have to leave them at all.

Less than an hour later, Hosea stood alone outside Diblaim's door. He had been invited to accompany the family to Dan's farm where Shabbat was being held that evening, but he declined, saying that he'd be there later for the evening celebration. "I wish to see the city," he told them, and noticed the frown on Diblaim's face. "Yes, I know there is evil here and you don't want me to see it, but I must. Our beloved Adonai has brought me here to speak his words, and I must know to what conditions I speak."

So the three had wished him Godspeed and gone to Dan's. None of them had yet breathed a word about Gomer, and Hosea was greatly perplexed about it. But he put it in the back of his mind, sure that sooner or later he would see Gomer again and find out how his childhood playmate had turned out as a woman.

There were two things about Samaria that had struck Hosea the afternoon before when he had entered the city, and he knew it would take many days before he could ignore them as well as the townsfolk did. These two things were the smell and the noise. The first was nauseous, the second deafening.

Hosea remembered that the smell of the town of Dan hadn't been this bad. Frequent mountain rains there had washed the streets every week or so, and garbage never accumulated to any great degree. But in Samaria, except in a heavy rainy season, refuse and filth overflowed from the alleyways between the houses onto each street, until those walking by found themselves wading ankle-deep through the muck. No one noticed or complained, though. The inhabitants thought it normal. Only the caravan workers wondered at city dwellers who hadn't the sense to carry their garbage outside the gates and burn it. The farmers preferred not to think about Samaria at all, even while they were in it. Standing now before the door, Hosea remembered the pots Shana had dumped in the alley before breakfast, and he felt his stomach churn. The rains were a month away, and already Samaria lay under four months of garbage and reeked in every corner. And as often as not if it did rain, houses would be flooded and the water would only spread the filth around the floors. Some would find its way through the streets and down into the valley, bringing fertilizer to the farms, and for this the farmers were grateful. Hosea found the whole process sickening after his months of wandering through the fresh countryside, and caught himself longing for a whiff of trees sending off their sweet after-rain smells.

The noise was quite another thing. The smell offended only the nose, but the clamor of the city rang through his head until he was sure it would burst open like an overripe pomegranate. The quiet of his journey had ill prepared him for a capital city in full cry, full of shoving townsfolk, greedy tradesmen hawking their wares, and bawling children. The animals, too, added their part to the din, as reluctant camels and stubborn donkeys milled around the gates and resisted their owners' attempts to control them. A camel bellowing is not a pleasant sound, even at a distance.

Occasionally a rider on horseback would canter through the double gates, pushing his tall, strong animal through the crowd. These men were so obviously either king's messengers or noblemen that the crowd resisted its natural impulse to shove back and made way without squabble.

Hosea stayed in front of Diblaim's house, watching the crowd in the gate square for quite a while. He felt suddenly very small and inadequate for the job presented to him, and wondered how he was meant to begin. Just go to the market and start talking? Wait until an orgy started and break it up with well-spoken warnings? What did a man of God really do?

Suddenly he felt something heavy and soft resting on his bare foot, and he looked down. Perched on his toes was a huge rat, its long whiskers twitching as it looked back up at him, in its paws the leftover bite of someone's lamb leg. He quickly kicked it away, shuddering. It obviously was used to such treatment, for it picked itself up unconcernedly and waddled back into the dark alley. He watched it go with disgust, wondering how long the rats of Samaria had been that bold. Approaching a man in broad daylight was incredible. He thought of the dozens of parties that went on all over the city during the week, and knew that there was probably more than enough left over to feed an army of rats, which it seemed Samaria possessed.

No, Samaria, he thought with despair, *your darkness is greater than your beauty.* He remembered his first glimpse of the city the day before as he came into the valley and looked up the slope at the other end. He had been impressed by the well-kept walls, the industrious reapers in the fields, the shining painted houses which from that distance made the gray stone white in the sun. Crowning the whole view, the palace itself dominated the city with its splendor and royalty.

But now he stood within the walls, amid the rats and filth. He listened to the jokes of the youths passing by. He heard the maligning gossip of the women on their way to the well near the gates. He saw the greed in the eyes that met his. And he knew his would be no easy task.

TWELVE
Restoration

At the insistence of his host, Hosea had spent a full week
at Diblaim's house, sleeping in front of the fireplace.
Enjoying as he was the food and company of his father's
old friend, Hosea was yet acutely conscious of an unexplained tension in the household. Even stranger was the
fact that whenever his footsteps wandered toward the
outside stairs, he was courteously but firmly steered
away.

But the night came when Hosea was unusually rest-
less, having spent seven nights indoors and seven days
wandering about the marketplace listening to the people. He felt a yearning to see the stars again, the stars he
had grown to know so well on his travels.

Supper was just over. Shana and Rachel sat before
the fire, their busy hands sewing some torn garments.
Diblaim sat on the bench, frowning over his accounts.
For the moment no one was watching him, so Hosea
stepped quietly to the door and opened it, passing out
into the twilight.

It was Rachel who first heard the footsteps on the outside stairs. She jumped to her feet. "Abba! Where's Hosea? I thought I heard—"

"No!" The word barely escaped Diblaim's tight lips. Then he noticed a faint smile on his wife's mouth as they listened to the footsteps reach the top. Suddenly he realized that she had been waiting for this, and the fear and anger so long bottled up inside was suddenly deflated.

He sat down hard, head in his hands. Was God showing him that the time had come?

Hosea took a deep breath when he reached the roof, letting the cool air fill his cramped lungs. The pungent scents of the city were blown away by a faint breeze from the north, and above his head hung the stars in white splendor, drawing his hungry soul out of the depression in which he had been living in the past few days. Pure and clear, they reminded him of the God who had created them, and he found once again the peace he had known in the Plains of Moab.

Sauntering slowly along the roof edge, Hosea ran his hand over the rough stones, humming a tune he had learned in his boyhood. Samaria felt a hundred miles away, Samaria and all the cares he must know for her.

He reached the wall overlooking the valley and leaned on it with a sigh of content, letting his eyes roam over the contours of the distant hills surrounding the city on all sides. Cool and dark, soft and hazy, Israel spread herself out before him, and he felt that he could hold the whole country in an outstretched palm.

A scuffling noise from behind startled him and he turned quickly, expecting to see Diblaim come to join him. But no one was on the roof with him, and he frowned thoughtfully. Were there rats up here as well as in the alley? If so, he should do his host a favor and rout them out before they chewed the flax left to dry by those vats in the corner.

Walking slowly toward the place from where the sound came, he glanced about, waiting for the rats to break cover at his approach. But none did, and then he noticed something that perplexed him. At the other side of the vats stood a tiny tent, made of goatskins, judging by the smell. Were the rats in there? Or maybe this was the sick servant whose food Shana brought up each day.

Kneeling down a few feet from the dark opening, he peered into the tent and heard again a faint scuffle. "Hello," he said tentatively. "God give you peace; I mean you no harm."

Silence answered him. Maybe it was rats after all, or else whoever was in there was very frightened. He came closer. Now he could see a small shape huddled against the wall at the end of the tent. "Are you well, my friend? Do you need help at all?"

A stifled sob answered him, and he saw a small hand clutching at the dark robe to pull it closer. Hosea's bewilderment grew. What was wrong?

Suddenly determined to get to the bottom of this mystery in Diblaim's house, Hosea reached inside the tent and touched that hand. *I am not just a man,* he thought. *I am a man of God and must reach out to his people. If this is a woman, she must be made to understand that; otherwise I am breaking Moses' injunctions about touching women.* But before he could speak, the hand pulled away from him and hid inside the folds of what he now saw was sackcloth. The apparent destitution of this person touched Hosea, and he spoke again. "Please don't think I come to harm you. I have been sent by God to Samaria to tell the people of God that he calls for their repentance and love. You seem so alone up here. I've never heard Diblaim speak of you. Cannot you let God relieve that loneliness with his presence, as he has relieved mine? But you don't know my name. I am Hosea ben Beeri, staying here—"

A painful gasp interrupted him, and the figure in the tent jerked away from him as far as the space allowed. He reached out again, amazed at this reaction to his name. "Please . . ." he began again, and then the words froze on his lips.

A lock of hair had fallen from the mantle covering the head of this mysterious person, and the moonlight streaming over Hosea's shoulder caught that lock in its silver radiance. That hair. . . It shone with its own glow in the moonlight, a ruddy golden shining that mocked the sun with its intertwining lights. He knew it hung dank and dirty to the floor, but he was seeing it as it had floated in a mountain breeze against his shoulder, framing a face that laughed with childish glee up at him.

Just then he heard heavy footsteps behind him, and he turned to see Diblaim at the top of the stairs. He stood up and walked over to meet his host, still feeling stunned by what he had just discovered. The two men stood and looked at each other for the space of a caught breath.

"Hosea, I didn't want you ever to come up here."

"I needed to see the stars tonight before I slept, Diblaim. You never asked me not to come here before." Hosea's voice sounded strange to himself, and he found it a struggle not to be angry at the mystery confronting him. "Tell me, my friend, who is in the tent behind us?"

He saw the hope spring up in Diblaim's eyes, and knew the other was thinking that he hadn't seen anything yet. "It's—it's my wife's servant, Hosea. She . . . is unclean, some rash on her body, and this is the only place to keep her until she is pure again."

Hosea felt his horror growing as he listened to words he knew were hasty lies. Diblaim faltered to a stop, aware somehow that his guest was angry. He saw a sternness in the younger man's eyes that bounced his own words back to him, and he heard how hollow they were.

Suddenly unable to bear the sight of his host a second longer, Hosea turned quickly around and strode back to the tent, his muscles screaming under the iron control that kept him from lashing out at this man he had respected from childhood. Why should he lie? What terrible secret could force this man to break Moses' Law?

The tent reared up before him and he lashed out at it, tearing the goatskin hide from the pegs. He felt a dark satisfaction in the sound that ripped across the roof.

Exposed to the sudden light of the moon, the person who had been hiding in the tent gave a low cry like a cornered rabbit, and huddled against the nearest dye vat. Diblaim gave a queer strangled groan at the sound, and stumbled back to the stairs. He didn't want to see what Hosea would do next. He didn't want to hear whatever words were said.

Hosea dropped the goatskin and looked at the crouching figure at his feet. The man of God stood before the harlot of Samaria, a confrontation known before the world was made.

Gomer clutched at the sackcloth around her, trem-

bling with fear and biting her hand to keep from screaming. Alone for two years and suddenly confronted by this
stranger from the past, she felt her hazy mind go blank,
and she didn't know what to do except stay as still as
possible. Through the heavy material covering her head
she could see the man who stood over her, his broad
shoulders looming dark against the starry sky.

Hosea . . . A gentle memory found its way through her
fear, a memory of adoring brown eyes and clumsy,
helpful hands lifting her to a rock that had defeated her
small scrambling feet. She had cried when he left home,
cried because he was the only one of the boys who
listened to her stories of the places she was going to visit
when she grew up, the only one who really talked to her
as if she were no longer a baby. Now here he stood. He
had defied her father; she had seen him turn away from
that old man who had once whipped her so heartlessly.
Now he stood before her, and she was afraid.

What if he should see her face? She could feel the
dryness that ate away at her once smooth skin, caused
by the hot searing sun. Her hands were rough now too,
swollen and red. Underneath her robe her bones showed
against her skin, so thin had she become on the food her
mother brought once a day. The memory of what she
had been scorched her eyes with tears, and she hung her
head in silent beseeching. *Go away, go away. I don't
want you here to see my shame.*

Hosea reached down his hand when he saw her head
fall, and she looked at it in wonder. No one had touched
her since her father had pushed her up to this roof a
lifetime ago. Yet, there was a hand before her eyes, the
fingers long and strong and supple on that hand

stretched out from a tattered sleeve. Did he really want to touch her, the unclean one?

Hesitant, too terrified to even think of what she was doing, Gomer opened one hand and let her mantle go. It fell from her face as she slowly raised her hand to his. She felt the fingers close over hers, and the forgotten feeling of companionship flooded through her. Someone really was here with her. After all those dreams she had seen in her fevered nights, someone was here.

Hosea pulled gently at her hand and slid his other arm under her bent shoulders. With a great effort she gathered her feet under her shaking legs and stood up.

Now the moon shone full on her face, and Hosea felt his horror flood hotly through his whole body. Her deep, expressive eyes were the same; only they stared at him with terror instead of laughter. But she seemed small and shrunken in on herself, although he realized that if she stood straight she would be almost as tall as he. Scales dug into his hand as he held her fingers tighter, and he found himself shuddering. What work had she been doing to have a hand like that?

He lifted her chin with his free hand and looked into her eyes. "Gomer . . ." She was so thin and weather-beaten, with her once generous mouth sullen and rigid. Suddenly he knew that he must stay with her, to bring back the lost joy to her heart, to make up to her whatever had happened, to give her the love and friendship she had obviously not had for too long.

"Ho . . . Hos . . ." She was trying to speak, but her unused voice cracked.

His pity made him tender. "Yes, Gomer. It's your Hosea. I've come home to you, Gomer." He smiled into her startled eyes. In the moment of silence that followed, as she tried to understand why he should say such a mad thing, Hosea thanked God for bringing him to Samaria. *I shall love her as you do Israel, my Adonai,* he promised. *I shall cherish her and banish the fear inside, and she shall grow in love and joy as I have done. Only let her blossom as your daughter should, only let her grow in her beauty and your joy, and all Israel shall see what you do for those who turn to you! Whatever brought her here shall be forgotten.*

He noticed that her eyes had closed in weakness, and she was sagging against his arm. So he picked her up and held her close against his chest, and felt her relax against him. *She trusts me,* he thought, and exulted in his new determination to win her as his wife. Gomer . . . The dream of a nine-year-old boy might yet come true.

Down the stairs and into the front door strode Hosea, still carrying Gomer, a new manliness in his walk. Shana and Rachel stood together in the middle of the floor, their eyes obviously long glued to the door through which he had just come. Diblaim sat before the fire on his bench, his forgotten accounting books under his drumming fingers. He glanced quickly up when Hosea came in, and a strange expression of relief lit his heavy features when he saw Gomer. So the time really had come.

No one moved at first. Hosea stood inside the door, legs spread apart for balance, face grim as his arms tightened around the slight figure, wrapped in sackcloth, that leaned on his chest. Shana noticed that he held her as tenderly as he would a newborn babe, and she knew she had been right about this man. She said quietly, "Rachel, get the food."

Rachel ran over to the fire and picked up the tray she

had prepared to carry up to the roof. She was confused and happy, and ready to do whatever her mother said with no questions asked.

Gomer slowly opened her heavy eyelids and saw Shana's face before her. "Imma?"

That one little word broke through Shana's years of reticence and acceptance. "My daughter!" she sobbed, clasping the two swollen hands to her breast. It had been too long since she saw those eyes fixed on her in child-like trust, too long since she had heard that word from Gomer's lips. Too long since the men in the marketplace had told Gomer their northern stories, since her play-mates had taught her boyish freedom and slang, since Zedediah had spread his tales and created unease in her mother's heart. "Oh, my daughter," she said softly, her tears falling on the sackcloth over Gomer's arms, "my Gomer, thank God he's given you back to me. Thank God."

Gomer closed her eyes again, wondering why her mother thanked God instead of Hosea. But then, her family had always been rather peculiar. She was too tired to think it through, and the fire was bringing a pleasant warmth to her chilled bones.

Hosea carried Gomer into her old room and laid her gently on the pallet there. Shana and Rachel instantly shooed him out, their eyes shining with gratitude. He left them, letting the wooden door swing shut behind him.

Diblaim looked up again as Hosea drew slowly closer to the fire, and the pain in his eyes made the younger man quail. What right had Hosea to intrude with his questions and his anger? The father's grief was too deep. Yet if Hosea wanted Gomer, he had to speak.

"Diblaim, I must ask your forgiveness for what I did."

"No." The merchant rasped out his words with agonizing clarity. "God has sent you here, and whatever you do I accept from him."

Hosea was staggered by that, and for a moment fearful. "I—I must beg you not to do that. I am but a man."

"So am I, Hosea. So am I." Diblaim rubbed his forehead wearily. "I'm also a father, though, and I must act as I feel God would have me."

"Diblaim, can you tell me . . . why?"

The room was silent except for the crackling fire. Then Diblaim sighed and straightened, so that he looked Hosea in the eye. "My daughter is a whore."

THIRTEEN
On Trial

Hosea pulled himself up onto the large rock overhanging the source of Samaria's river, and sat down amid the damp green moss on top. Bare feet dangling over into the spray, he let his eyes roam over the peaceful scene before him, only a ten-minute walk up the hill from the east gate. *I can think here,* he told himself, *here where God's trees and birds surround me. At least, I hope I can think.*

But the story he had heard from Diblaim the night before was too terrible even to think about the clear morning after. Both men had wept before they slept, their heartbroken sobs drowned by the torrent of rain outside. Gratitude that Gomer was safe from any more storms helped to calm Hosea's pain and unexplainable hurt, but he still couldn't credit her actions. Had she really—but she couldn't have, not Gomer!

"My daughter is a whore." He had shrunk from the word, hitting out at it in fear and horror. No wonder

Diblaim had aged so; no wonder Shana had been pathetically glad of the joy and good news Hosea had brought with him. He was sure Rachel was totally unaware of the reason for her sister's punishment, but he knew her enthusiasm over Gomer's restoration was unassumed and deep. *Rachel,* he thought, *so pure and untouched. I'm sure Dan has never even held her hand as they planned their future.* But Gomer—she is supposed to have enticed a man, a pagan at that, going in the teeth of all her father's teaching! No, it was impossible. Two sisters could not be so unlike, and the Gomer he had left behind had been well grounded in Moses' teachings and the fear of their Adonai. She had been a little wild, yes, but of what account was that? She was a woman now, far past the age most girls married.

Hosea jumped down from his perch and started pacing the small grassy bank, his mind in a turmoil. There were only two things of which he was sure: one, that God had brought him to Samaria and led him to Gomer; the other, that she was *not* a whore. Remembering Zedediah from his boyhood, he recalled the skinny man's delight in Gomer, his constant reaching out to her as she flitted past like a butterfly. He hadn't been surprised, when he returned a week ago, to find the man had moved into his father's house. Beeri had never trusted Zedediah, reminding his son that there were many who partook of Shabbat with them at Diblaim's house, yet yearned after evil in their hearts.

He stopped pacing and stared ahead unseeing. Was this the cause? Diblaim had the facts from Zedediah. What if the source were false? Could it be possible somehow to show this lie, to wipe Gomer's name clean and enable her father to accept her again?

Closing his eyes and raising his hands, Hosea breathed a fervent prayer to the skies. *Adonai, Adonai, hear me, my beloved Adonai! Hear my cry and aid me in this time of need! I need your guidance, O my God.*

He opened his eyes, and suddenly the lost memory came of his father's patient teaching of the Law to a young and bewildered boy. It had been a sultry night during harvest their first year in Dan, and he had eagerly questioned his father about the reason for punishments which seemed so severe. Beeri had told him case after case of women and men who had sinned, the precautions built into the Law to prevent miscarriage of justice, the end result of guilt and/or innocence.

His father's quiet words were coming back clearly, and Hosea laughed aloud with joy. *"Thank you, my Adonai. Blessed be your name forever!"* he shouted, for he saw his way straight before him now.

A jeweled bird flitted among the tamaracks as he bolted down the path back to the city. It was free and wild, and shied away as he dashed by, but followed at a shy distance wondering at his joyful song.

Gomer woke up to the feeling of a soft hand on her brow, and she fearfully opened her eyes. Brilliant sunshine flooded the room and lit up Rachel's eyes as she bent over her sister with a glad smile. *Am I dreaming again?* she thought feverishly. *Is this another time when I think I'm a child again?*

But the smell of lentil soup convinced her this was no dream, and she struggled to sit up. Rachel supported her until she could lean against the wall, talking cheerfully all the while. "Wasn't it so good of Hosea to bring you down again, Gomer? And Abba—I've never seen him so quiet as this morning! Imma says it's because he's wondering now what to do about you, but I'm sure I don't understand the problem. No one ever told me what you'd done, and I knew it couldn't possibly have been breaking one of the commandments because you wouldn't *do* anything like that!" She chattered on, her naturally shy manner for once forgotten in this momentous event. She was like the little sister who once had run to Gomer with every problem, pain, or joy, and Gomer watched her with tired affection as her sister prepared breakfast by the bed.

An hour later Shana felt eyes upon her, and she laid down her shuttle to turn around. Framed in the doorway of the workroom were Gomer and Rachel, the older leaning heavily on the younger's sturdy arm. Gomer was transformed, and Shana could only stare at her a moment, sure this couldn't be the forlorn creature Hosea had carried in the night before.

Rachel had washed Gomer's hair and brushed it till it shone, and now it hung in its old glory below her waist in thick glowing waves. Her large eyes still seemed bewildered and shy, but her unhappy mouth now had a tiny smile in the corners as she met her mother's eyes. One of her dyed dresses had been dug out of an old chest by Rachel, and now clung in green splendor to her slender form. It was almost as if the ghost of Gomer's former happy self had been dug up too—from the years before she ever saw that Egyptian.

Shana felt her mouth trembling as she struggled to hold back her tears. She had wept enough the night before. She stood up slowly and came over to the two girls, her arms stretched out in love. "My own daughters," she said with a sob, and pulled them to her.

Gomer stood before the six men who sat in the kitchen before the fire. Her mouth was dry with fear as her eyes flicked over them one by one, knowing why they had come. Hosea stood to one side watching her. She could feel the intensity of his gaze, and it troubled her for some reason.

On the two benches drawn up to the fire were the only men left in Samaria who still called upon the Name of God. Her cousin Dan's rough tunic looked poor beside Zedediah's gaudy blue cloak, but at least *he* was looking at her with pity. The old man had hunched his shoulders over his thin chest and coughed continually, but never took his beady eyes off her face.

Also from the valley, with Dan, had come Jephthah and Elnathan, cousins to each other but unrelated to Diblaim. Their faces, ruddy from the sun, were calm, and their eyes serious under straight brows. Gomer felt her soul naked before them, and was afraid.

Her father sat at the end. She knew he was worried because his fingers were drumming an obscure rhythm on the wood. Rachel and Shana stood outside of the oil lamp's circle of light, their hands joined for comfort.

After a quiet day spent with her mother and sister, Gomer had been totally unprepared for this confrontation, thinking that everything must be all settled now. But when Hosea had led these men in, she had run into her room and clutched at the windowsill for support. Only when her mother came and gently brought her back into the kitchen had she calmed down enough to face them. After all, this had had to come sometime. This was her trial.

Hosea stepped forward and began with a deep bow to her. This confused her. Was he not her judge, kind and strong though he had been last night? Why then this courtesy? She was sure that these men were here to condemn her, and that the stoning she had escaped two years before waited with the dawn.

"My host, and friends from Samaria, it has been many years since my father and I were among you, but you are all remembered." Here Hosea's eyes looked straight at Zedediah, but the old man's attention was too fixed on Gomer to notice. "My father, Beeri ben Obed, was descended from the princes of Dan through his mother, but we have long been scribes in our family. We have held faithfully to the writings of Moses, and from genera-tion to generation have passed down the accumulated scrolls we have copied containing the Laws and the histories of Israel. I shall be bringing them to Samaria soon for all to read who are able.

"In training for this age-old skill, I learned all the Laws by memory and learned how to copy them exactly, so that not one letter of the sayings of Moses should be lost. For, my brothers, it was to keep Israel pure and peaceful that God gave these Laws to Moses, and no other tribes can claim a better system than ours. So it is that I am well-qualified as a judge in Israel to decide the guilt or innocence of any person within our boundaries."

From the benches came murmurs of assent. Zede-diah's nod was absentmindedly given, however. His ea-ger eyes had seen Gomer's fear, and he could see himself next morning crushing that beautiful face with a well-aimed rock, sweet revenge for all the ignoring she had done!

Hosea went on, his low steady voice growing stronger with an intensity and passion that told Shana more than words could have done that he was already deeply in love with her daughter, and cared more than any impartial judge should about the outcome of this case. "We have before us, brothers, a woman accused of harlotry, a crime punishable in Israel by death from . . . stoning." He cleared his throat. "She has instead been imprisoned on her father's roof by that same father, and lived in a tent with barely enough food to survive, while she worked from dawn to dusk without stopping. Her father felt that by doing this—well, I'll let him say it in his own words now."

Diblaim sighed, and slowly rose to his feet. He glanced quickly at his wife, who nodded encouragement. He couldn't look at Gomer, afraid of the hate he was sure was in her eyes. He bowed to Hosea, and Zedediah frowned. Who was this son of Beeri to merit such respect? "From the mouth of the messenger of God has come the command to speak, and I shall bare my soul before this company."

Zedediah sat up straight and for the first time really looked at Hosea, whom he had always considered a pretentious brat. For the first time, also, he found himself wondering if the trial would go as he anticipated. Then he scoffed at his fears. She *had* to die, according to the Law, because of what he would say. He leaned back on the wall, smugly content, and waited for the words he knew were coming from his distraught neighbor.

"All my life, brothers, I have lived in the fear of the God of our fathers, and have sought to teach my children to do the same. Great was my sorrow to hear, then, that often my eldest daughter spent much time during her growing years in the market listening to the stories of the pagans, and playing with their children. When the time came for her childhood to end, I forbade her the market except when she shopped with her mother. Later I stopped even that, for I heard she was sporting with the young men at the well and before our door. I feared for her safety, for men were wont to watch her and I knew the hearts of Samaritans that were wicked."

For the first time her father's anguish penetrated Gomer's heart, and she finally understood what her innocent play had meant to him who traded with the men of Samaria and heard their talk. Older now and wiser in the ways of men since Senu-Amen had shattered her innocent dreams, she realized that her father *had* been right, and that his seeming cruelty had only been for her protection. *Why didn't I see it before,* she thought with regret, *but it's too late now, far too late, and I shall die labeled a whore. If only I had thought to tell him that the Egyptian had promised marriage. Then he might have realized that I meant no harm to him.*

Diblaim, not realizing that his daughter's heart was beginning to soften toward him, continued his painful story. "One day Zedediah came to me and said that— that Gomer had enticed a man, with whom I traded, into my house, a heathen from Egypt. I was filled with fear for her virtue, but from what my neighbor said it was far too late. Indeed, he hinted that she had lost it long before." Diblaim's voice, raw with emotion, faltered. He was ashamed before these men. Gomer was trembling with anger now, knowing the years Zedediah had filled her father's ears with lies, knowing that if given the chance she would blast those lies with her truth—if they let her speak.

"My neighbor told me the heathen was gone, and when I entered my house I found Gomer here, in the kitchen lying on the material I had planned to sell the next week. Needless to say, I burned it all the next day. I knew Gomer could not be stoned as the Law demanded, even though she had been caught this time in her harlotry. So I—I whipped her, and led her up to the roof. I know the heart of God, that he wishes his people to repent and not to perish, and I prayed night and day that my daughter would confess her evil and sacrifice for atonement on Mount Gerizim. I was ready at any time to take her if she had but asked. Once a week I instructed my wife to ask Gomer if she wished to do this, but no answer was ever given."

Hosea's heart ached for Gomer, but outwardly he looked calm. *Of course she didn't repent,* he thought. *She had done nothing!* To live such an existence for two years and never complain—he wondered at her courage, and loved her the more. "Zedediah, we will hear you now," Hosea said.

The old man jumped up, smirking, his eyes leisurely studying the woman before him. She stared right through him as she had always done. *Not tomorrow you won't, harlot, not tomorrow!* "I will tell you what these two eyes of mine saw! Yes, listen well, my brothers. I will speak the truth as Moses spoke it on Mount

Sinai, and none can deny it, not even you, harlot!"

"Enough!" barked Hosea. "No verdict has yet been given."

Zedediah growled something none could understand, and then spoke. "I was standing at my door early that awful morning, and I saw Diblaim"—he bowed to his neighbor—"head for the gate, and I remembered that he had a gift for the caravan leader outside the gates." *How had he known that?* wondered Diblaim angrily. Then he remembered that Zedediah was the town gossip and knew everything almost before it happened. "Then his good wife Shana and their lovely daughter Rachel also went out the door, heading for market as they were accustomed to doing before Shabbat. Gomer at that time each day went to the roof to work, but that day she didn't."

Diblaim was frowning. He hadn't realized that this old man watched his family so closely each day. There was something wrong here. Had the donkey trader nothing better to do?

"I then saw a tall man in desert dress come inside the gate just as Gomer came out the door and headed for the well with her pitcher. She ran to meet him and they—they . . . Well, much went on which as a son of Jacob I am ashamed to mention. I heard Gomer say she was alone, and the two went inside. Now often I have seen her do this thing and wondered if I should warn her father, but he had ignored my hints, and the men were always long gone. But I thought this time would be different. Diblaim might come back through the gate at any moment, and there was the man to substantiate my story. But it was an hour before he arrived, and the man left just before that. Brothers, what could I do? This woman was ruining the good name of her father. Could I as a son of Jacob, brought up in the Law of Moses, keep silent any longer? So when Diblaim came through the gate I told him what I had seen, as I have told you." He bowed, trying not to smile with triumph, but the grin came anyway. He sat beside Elnathan, not noticing the imperceptible drawing away of the farmer.

"I will now speak." Hosea stepped forward, his face grim. Zedediah's story had sickened him, sure as he was that it was fabricated by an evil heart. All sat up straight, knowing the end was coming. "We have heard the evidence, my brothers, and I have only two things to say.

"First: a woman who lies with one man is *not* a harlot, and only one man has been identified, the Egyptian. The rest are nameless shadows, and no facts are before us to show that they ever existed. If a man lies with an unbetrothed virgin he must pay the bride-price and wed her, if the father agrees to the marriage. If the father objects to the man, such as in this case with an Egyptian, the man is still commanded to pay the bride-price for having deflowered a daughter of Israel. If the Egyptian lay with Gomer, he should have paid that money, but he was gone before Diblaim was told what had happened.

"Second, and most importantly: all the evidence against Gomer has been presented by one man, Zedediah. The Law states that for a case to hold, there must be two witnesses to a crime. One is not enough. I say, therefore, that Gomer should not have been found guilty on the word of this one man. Furthermore, since only he has ever said that she behaved like a harlot, and no other man has come forward to agree, we will never more call Gomer a harlot. Before the Law she is a true and obedient daughter of Israel."

Tears were coursing down Diblaim's leathery cheeks,

released after all those years of torment by this sentence of mercy. A joyful hosanna came from shy Shana. But Gomer stood as still as stone in the middle of the room.

Zedediah sat on the bench with his mouth open wide for a moment, and then let out a shrill scream. "She did! She did! She did!"

Hosea walked quickly over to him and pulled the old man roughly to his feet. "Old man, you've done enough harm here," he said, his voice dangerously quiet. "Get out!" None too gently, he shoved Zedediah toward the door and shut it behind him.

"Now what shall we do, Hosea?" Diblaim asked, his shaking hands stretched toward the younger man. Hosea swiftly came to him and guided him back to the bench, where Dan put his huge arm gently around the trembling shoulders of the merchant.

"We shall begin again for Gomer, my friend," Hosea smiled. "We know now what happened and can accept her as once we did, as a true daughter of—"

"May I not speak?" Her level voice cut him off, and he turned to stare at her. She was watching him with her eyes wide. He couldn't read her thoughts in them, but the sensation in his midriff caused by her gaze told him that she saw him as her savior.

"There is no need for you to say anything," he said gently. Walking slowly to her, he held her eyes with his own intensity. "Zedediah lied. He couldn't have seen you with a man by the well, for it was on the other side of your father's house, and no man can see through thick walls. And he couldn't have heard anything said on that street unless it was screamed aloud, for the stones absorb any sound unless it is very clamorous. I know, because I have tried it just this morning. Gomer, you spent two years on that roof for nothing, because of a lie."

Gomer was staring at him, her mouth partway open to say the words that scorched her tongue, unable to believe what she was hearing. *Hosea, what are you thinking? Do you all believe now that no one came to me that morning? Hosea, Hosea, must you make me as clean as you want? Can't you accept me as I am, a woman who did give herself to a man?*

Hosea was still smiling, thinking her silence was relief. "We know you, Gomer. You're incapable of doing such a thing as bringing a heathen to your side, whether his intentions were honorable or not. After all, how can a girl brought up as you and Rachel have been even entertain such thoughts, let alone go through with the actions?"

Diblaim was standing beside him now, his black eyes beseeching his daughter for forgiveness. "Gomer..." His voice trailed off, for she didn't move, too stunned by Hosea's words to respond. *No, no, you're wrong, you're all wrong,* her mind screamed at them. *How can you be so blind?*

In her despair she jerked away from Hosea and her father, and saw Shana at her side. The mother saw her face, and instantly put her arms around her daughter's frail waist. "Gomer, it's all right, it's all over now. Can you not see that?" Her soothing voice had no effect, so she tightened her hold.

Hosea reached out a hand to Diblaim, joy lighting his lean face. "My friend, now I may speak the words that have burned in my heart since I saw your daughter once more. May I pay the bride-price for her, an unsullied daughter of Israel, and claim her for my wife?"

Diblaim heard these words in a daze, remembering his

wish that it had been Hosea who came two years ago.
Now there never had been another man, and Hosea had
made his offer in purity and honor. . . . *Adonai, Adonai,
can any man be happier than I?*

He opened his mouth to answer, but Shana's sharp
cry interrupted him. "Help me, Diblaim, Hosea! Gomer—she's fainted!"

F O U R T E E N
Shana

A week had passed. Hosea had been gone from Samaria five days, having taken Nathan to fetch his father's scrolls in Dan. He was expected back by the next Shabbat.

Shana had woven her daughter a wedding gown, and now the two were adding the finishing touches of embroidery around the neck and sleeves. Rachel had spent the days on the roof practicing the songs Gomer had requested, so glad in her spirit that each melody was warbled with tearful praise.

Diblaim had been at home all that week, making a wall to divide his bedroom in half. He had decreed that Gomer and Hosea would live in one half, saying, "I have never had a son, and I do not wish to lose my daughter a second time." Hosea had readily agreed. The two resulting rooms were spacious and airy, both having a window overlooking the valley. And the new son was even going to join Diblaim in his business, "for there are not many who wish for a scribe to copy the old Laws, and that is the only writing I will do. Even a prophet must work!"

Everyone was happy and excited about the approaching wedding—except Gomer. She was still weak from her long ordeal, but her form had started to fill out, and her face had lost its gaunt look. Yet, her eyes were still haunted with a trace of fear, and Rachel was puzzled about her lack of gaiety. Why did she never laugh? Why did she never speak of her future husband? The younger girl knew that if *her* wedding day were coming so quickly, *she* wouldn't be able to sit down a moment.

Shana watched Gomer closely, but said nothing until the day Hosea was expected back. Two years was a long pause after which to pick up the threads of motherhood again, and she really didn't know how to instruct Gomer concerning her duties as a wife.

Gomer, hunched over the sleeve she was embroidering, felt as taut inside as a strung bow. She had dreamed about the Egyptian the night before for the first time since he had left her, and the dream had left her considerably shaken. The Egyptian had been laughing, his sharp face looming before her, and he had mocked Hosea and his gullibility. But hadn't he just been speaking her own thoughts aloud? Now this man who loved the girl she had once been was returning today for her. She had avoided him since his proposal, and her retiring actions had made Diblaim sense how wrong he had been about her. How could he ever have thought of this shy woman, who left the room when Hosea entered, as a harlot?

Shana, more aware of the workings of a woman's mind, saw Gomer's reticence, and her heart ached. She knew that Hosea would make the best of all possible husbands for her daughter. Where was another God-fearing man so willing to marry her, so tender, so awed by her? He would cherish her, the mother knew, and love her till the day death parted them. But Gomer . . . something was different about her, something that couldn't be accounted for by her exile.

Shana laid down her embroidery and rubbed her aching eyes. Gomer glanced up, then took another stitch. "Gomer, I should speak with you about—about what is coming to you."

Gomer's head came up slowly, and then she looked her mother in the eyes. The words on Shana's lips died away, and the two stared at each other. *O my God, we were wrong. O my Adonai!*

"Don't be afraid," the mother said suddenly, and then bit her lip. Why should she say that? Would not Hosea's gentleness banish all fear?

Gomer took another stitch, her mouth grim. "Afraid, Imma? Of what should I be afraid? The girl Hosea loves has nothing to fear."

Shana groaned. "Gomer, what can I say except that I will be praying for you."

Gomer jerked up her head and glared at Shana, her nostrils flaring. Her mother gasped at Gomer's fury, and frantically asked herself what had happened. *What is wrong with my daughter?*

"To what god shall you pray, Imma?" Gomer asked in insulting tones, laying down her work and standing up. The other woman felt small and weak now, as if accused of wrong. "To what god, Imma? Father's god, who condemned me to death? I escaped him, didn't I? Canaan's Ba'al? Egypt's Osiris? What god will answer prayers for you, Imma?"

Gomer passed sedately from the room, a new arrogance tilting her head high. Shana watched her leave, numbed and bruised by her daughter's words. *Indeed I will pray,* she thought fervently and with unshattered faith. *I shall pray for a man of God who follows his guidance—and for his wife who does not.*

"Gomer."

She looked at him in the fading light of the sunset, and her eyes softened. How strong he looked standing there, how commanding, with his large brown eyes fixed on her in adoration. The anger within her faded with the sun as she wondered if she could ever return the love she saw in his face. Could he melt the dead weight that was her heart and plant a scented flower there instead?

Hosea felt his heart lurch as she looked at him, so nearly his own height. *How lovely she is,* he thought wistfully. *Will she really be mine tomorrow? Shall I truly stand with her and say, "She is my wife and I am her husband, from this day, forever"?* Then they would be one in the sight of God and man. This breathtaking woman, who stood so silently by his side, would never leave him until the day they died.

The last shreds of color were fading from the western sky behind them as they stood within the shadow of the gate arch. The song of a distant shepherd's pipe floated lightly through the gathering mist, and the silent music of the evening folded around the distant hills. Gomer ached to let the beauty of it carry her senses, to let go of this darkness within and admit the light of Hosea's love.

As if he heard her thoughts, Hosea reached out and gripped her cold hand. "I love you," he said tenderly. His words entered her heart and nestled there like newborn babes.

She gazed up at him, hoping, almost praying. Maybe someday . . . maybe someday she could say the same thing to him.

FIFTEEN
Rachel

The day was soft and green, the sky gentle above the two as they walked through the valley toward the small town of Karnaim. They had crossed the deep blue Sea of Galilee the day before, rowed across by some kind fishermen. Gomer had leaned over the edge of the boat, enchanted by the subtle play of light and shade upon the surface of the water. It was the first time she had ever seen a lake.

The fishermen, between their heaving grunts, told the couple stories of the many sudden storms that had often capsized experienced rowers, and so descriptive were their tales that Hosea caught himself watching the horizon for clouds. But the day had remained fair, and when they reached shore the two climbed the nearest hill to look back at the beach they had left that morning. The tiny sea had shimmered like a giant blue sapphire below them, each wave reflecting the sun. Hosea had grabbed his wife's hand and laughed like a boy, free and happy again as in their childhood.

Now they walked slowly through this quiet valley, listening to the birds welcoming the springtime. Hosea held her hand, because no one was around to notice this lack of decorum. Sometimes she squeezed his in return, glad to see him so joyful. The months since they had been married had been busy ones, filled with the making of their furniture and with the learning of the merchant trade for Hosea. Gomer had become content in those months, for Hosea paid her every attention and always treated her with care. Her lithesome figure had blossomed once more, and the golden sheen of her skin was ruddy with health. Shana, watching her closely for signs of contempt toward her husband, saw none, and put away her fears.

Hosea was talking now about his travels through this part of Israel, how sometimes the occupying Assyrian soldiers, stronger here in the north, had joined the mockers and butted him with their spears whenever he asked his questions of the village elders. Once, indeed, he had spent a night in a dried-out cistern because a man complained that he had been bothering him with impious questions. Remembering that, Hosea could laugh now at the irony of it. Gomer smiled stiffly.

Suddenly Hosea paused in midstride, looking down at the ground. Gomer, puzzled, looked down too and saw several odd-shaped stones lying around. They were squared off at each end, and many had carvings on one side. Here and there she caught a glimpse of broken-off pillars stuck into the ground at strange angles. Everything was covered with light green moss, and a strange dead silence hung over the area. Even the birds flew silently overhead.

Hosea stepped over to a stone which he saw held an

inscription and said excitedly, "This is old Canaanite, Gomer! Maybe this is a ruin of one of the cities Joshua destroyed. This is the area through which they entered the Promised Land."

He knelt to decipher the script, and so intent was he on his task that he missed Gomer's angry look. She turned away to pace through the ruins, thinking furious thoughts. Men had died here protecting their homes, died because of a battle ordered by Joshua's god, and their wives and children had been slain without mercy. Because their religion was called evil? Who was Joshua to decide what was evil?

She saw something sticking out of the debris near a broken pillar, and knelt to pull it out. It was the statue of a woman, her breasts bulging down over her rotund stomach, her plump arms outstretched. The paint had long since been stripped by the elements, but her jeweled eyes still looked out at Gomer with a mysterious smirk. *What would she say if she could speak?* wondered Gomer. She stood up with the statuette in her hand.

Hosea had the gist of the inscription now, and he called out for her to come over. He watched her come, enjoying her unhurried dignified way of walking. The breeze played with her long hair and her billowing skirt, forming both like another skin around her body. Hosea sighed. Even after all these months, he could scarcely believe that she was really his.

She knelt down beside him, her glowing hair falling over his shoulder. He gathered up the locks in one hand and kissed them, and the slight perfume of the herbs she used to clean herself wafted to his nostrils. His throat thickened, and he breathed a song of worship to the God who had formed her for him. *O Adonai, Adonai, thank you for my Gomer.*

"What does it say?"

He broke his concentration away from her to answer. "Let's see . . . it starts here: 'Dedicated to the honor and goodness of our Lady, the queen of our land forever, Ashtaroth; this is a temple for her habitation built by her son and servant, Og the King. May she long bless us.'

"Gomer! This must be the city of Ashtaroth where Joshua defeated King Og and claimed the land for God. So it is written in the histories. Just think, my beloved! Right where we're standing the great Joshua led our fathers to victory! But what's that in your hand?"

Gomer clung to the statuette, hot anger bubbling again just below her surface. Always, always the people of Israel were in the right, if they obeyed their god! Always their god must win! But what if this Lady she held had won? What would have happened to the wandering tribes then? And what would have happened to their all-powerful god?

"It is a statue." She had managed to speak calmly. Hosea took it from her hand and examined it curiously. Then she saw him go white.

"Ashtaroth," he murmured. He was remembering the dream he had had that had forced his departure from Dan. *She* had tried to entice him, her shining black body promising the delights he had found honorably with his wife. But it almost seemed like her mocking eyes called to him again out of that heavy darkness.

He shook his head to clear it, but it seemed like those eyes were still staring at him. No, it was his wife, but why did she have that strange, almost contemptuous expression in her lovely eyes? If he hadn't known her so well he'd have thought she hated him, she looked so fierce . . . as Ashtaroth had looked.

"Gomer?" He dropped the statue and kicked it away, loathing what it represented, and reached for her hand. But she had followed the fall of the figure with eyes wide with fury and didn't see his gesture. *So he kicked her, did he, this arrogant man of God?*

"Leave her alone." Her voice hissed with suppressed emotion.

Hosea stared at her, not believing his ears. "Leave her alone? Leave who alone?"

"The Lady." She stared back at him, and he suddenly realized that he hadn't been wrong about the hate. There were depths in her eyes he had never seen before.

"Gomer, how can you talk so?" Was this the woman he had been led by God to wed? "That is no lady; it is a mere stone carving. How can you speak as if there really is an Ashtaroth? She is a lie, my beloved, made up by wicked men to replace the one true God."

Gomer turned away. "Just because your god won this land in battle gives you no right to speak so of the Old Ones!"

Hosea felt himself foundering in surging, unknown waters. Was she saying what he thought she was saying? *"My god?* Gomer, what do you mean, *my* god? He is *our* God, Adonai of all Israel. He has guarded us and cared for us since this world was created! There are no other gods for him to defeat, only deluded and wicked people who worship nothing! Gomer, they are lies!"

But she was walking away from him down the valley, and he had to hurry to catch up to her. They walked side by side the rest of the way to Karnaim, not speaking. Both seethed inside, one with rage and the other with bewilderment. Gomer was remembering the tales she had been told in the market about the Lady: her goodness, her bounty, her way with men that the young and innocent daughter of Diblaim hadn't understood.

Hosea was experiencing a new and hitherto unknown fear: What if his wife didn't understand his calling? Worse, what if she didn't believe in it at all? He had told her often the story of his meeting with the Man in the Plains of Moab, and she had always listened intently. But as he now recalled, she had never said a word. When Shabbat came, she sat silently through the psalms and hosannas. And—he groaned inwardly, wondering why he hadn't thought more of it before—whenever they came to a town, she always waited for him outside the gates as he spoke to the people about their God who awaited their repentance. He had thought her shy about being among people after her ordeal. *What if—O Adonai, let it not be! Is she as pagan as the rest of them?*

"Gomer," he said, hesitant to break the long silence. "Will you come into Karnaim with me today? I have a cousin there with whom we can spend the night instead of in the meadows."

"No."

His heart failed him, and he bowed his head in despair. All the joy he had found in the day fled, and left him empty and grief-stricken. *Adonai, Adonai, what is wrong? Did you not lead me to her? Adonai, answer me. What is wrong?*

Rachel was sweeping the accumulated dust from her sister's floor, and sneezing from the cloud her broom had raised. They had been gone over four months on

Hosea's mission, but she had dreamed that morning that they were walking through the city gate, and Rachel had implicit faith in her dreams. Singing cheerfully, her heart full of gladness, she caught up the bagful of dirt and tossed it out the window.

Turning back inside, she brushed her dusty hands on her housedress. But a sudden faintness made her clutch at the windowsill, and she laughed at herself. What was this, being tired long before the noon meal was ready! She rubbed her hand over her forehead, frowning slightly at the ache in her head. Oh well, she was probably far too excited these days.

Dan had finally asked her father if they could wed next month, for he had his flock built up and he had raised a new home for them further down the valley. She started to sing again, remembering the way her father had laughed and cried at the same time. He would miss her, she knew. She must make sure that she and Dan spent Shabbat with him as often as possible.

O Dan! Dan! she hummed, swishing her cloth over the chairs and table where Hosea's scrolls lay piled high. *Soon we'll be together at last, at last!*

"Rachel . . ." She whirled around on the balls of her feet to see who called from the door, then laughed happily. Gomer stood there smiling at her, hair and dress dusty from the final walk to Samaria.

"Gomer!" She ran forward and threw her chubby arms about her sister. "You're home! I knew it, I knew it! I had a dream last night that you would return!"

Gomer returned the hug, trying not to be envious of Rachel's simple joy. *Dear Rachel, so happy and open and pure! So full of life and song! If only Hosea had asked for you.* She remembered the strain that had been between them since that morning near Karnaim, and wanted to weep onto the round shoulder below her face. But no, how could Rachel ever understand?

"Gomer, it's true, isn't it . . . I mean—" Rachel's twinkling eyes saw Gomer's blush. "I had a dream a month or so ago of a new arrival in our home."

"Are you spying on us, Rachel?" Gomer laughed, and for a moment her face lit up. "Yes, it's true. I just told Hosea this morning, and he still hasn't come down from the clouds." Maybe a baby would be the answer for them. Maybe in rearing a child she could find the release for her buried love.

She had tried hard, so hard to love Hosea as he deserved to be loved, but every time a growth of tenderness started to sprout, something would happen to squash it. Like that time by Karnaim, or the day outside Shiloh before that when he had been brutally whipped by the people and had barely managed to crawl to the cave where she had set up house. For a week she had ministered to him, cooling his fever with water. She had begged him to give up this trip and return home to Samaria and the cloth trade. But he just prayed for those people, that they would still repent!

I'll never understand him, she thought now as she watched Rachel shaking out the covers on their bed. *Never, because God fills his whole life . . . and I hate his god.*

She noticed suddenly that Rachel had dropped the covers in a heap on the bed and was just standing there. "What's wrong, Rachel?" she asked, wondering if her sister was daydreaming.

Rachel turned slowly and faced her, trying to smile, but her forehead was puckered with pain. "I—I'm all—

all right." Her face was going white. Suddenly her arms were trembling and her legs had started to buckle beneath her. "Gomer!" she called in a tiny voice. "Gomer, where are you? I—I can't see." She reached out to clutch at the air, gasping for breath.

Gomer ran forward. "Rachel!" She grabbed the girl's shoulders just as the floor rose to meet her fainting body. "Rachel . . . Rachel . . . RACHEL!"

Diblaim stumbled over a stone, then stared down at it uncomprehendingly. Shana looked over at him, sighed, and took his arm. They continued their slow walk, both feeling too old, their shoulders stooped and small under the heavy weight of ripped sackcloth. They trudged forward in rhythm, unaware of themselves, their eyes swollen and sore.

Hosea helped Gomer along behind them, and she leaned on his shoulder. Sorrow hung heavy like the child within her, and it was all she could do to move her feet forward one at a time.

Rachel rode before them, lying still under the soft white linen, her hands folded calmly, her face a mirror of peace. Dan watched her from his back corner of the bier, and his eyes were wide and staring. She looked like an untouched heavenly seraph.

The bier was covered with her favorite yellow flowers, and they tumbled about with every jolt of the bearers. Jephthah and Elnathan held the two front poles, and Shana's nephew Benath was opposite Dan.

The high sharp wails of the hired mourners behind them assailed the ears of the family. Gomer walked on with her eyes closed, loathing the sound. How much sweeter had Rachel sung at her wedding, her lovely voice soaring over all of them as she sang with all her heart, "The heavens declare the glory of our God; all the heavens show forth his workmanship."

A tear slid out from under Gomer's eyelid, but her mouth was closed. The truly bereaved walked on in numbed silence, their cries so piercing only God could hear them—if he heard at all—their grief so deep only their hearts knew the bottom.

Sweet Rachel! thought Gomer, *singing now with the seraphs who surround your god! My sister, I learned too late to love you for yourself, too late. My anger at Father's preferring you blinded me to your goodness, your loveliness. O my Rachel of the loving eyes and gentle voice, why are you gone from me?*

Diblaim shuffled on up the valley, following the bier. He remembered the day he had buried his brother Dan. The cave had remained shut ever since, and now it would be opened . . . for Rachel. Only that morning she had opened her eyes and smiled at him, had whispered that she loved her dear Abba. Then she had reached out for her husband-to-be, just before the end. *Rachel! How can I live without you, my little dove, my heart's joy!*

Underneath a small withered cedar was the family tomb, the covered mouth hidden among the profuse green growth in that moist valley where the life mocked their grief. Dan and Benath rolled away the stone after laying the bier gently on the grass, and then the four bearers tenderly lifted that small form and carried it into that deep eternal darkness.

Dan seemed not to realize what he was doing until he emerged again into the bright sunlight. He blinked and looked about him. Shana reached out her hand to him with compassion, but he stared at her like a blind man. A huge sob ripped out of his throat. He turned and ran from them into the trees, and they let him go.

Gomer was glad he was gone. Maybe among the trees he could find comfort as he wept into the grass, calling her name who would never again answer him.

She turned and walked back, unable to wait. She had no word to say to anyone. She felt as dead as the rounded body that lay behind that rock, and the darkening silence she walked in was just another tomb.

SIXTEEN
Trapped

Gomer stood close to the wall in her room, listening to her father and her husband going over the day's accounts in the next room. They had apparently made some very good sales, for they sounded jubilant.

She sighed, rubbing her side. She still ached from her latest childbirth, and had often caught herself hoping that there would be no more. True, the tearing, drowning pain that had engulfed her when Jezreel was born hadn't been repeated, but she was too narrow for the large children she always seemed to conceive. Now the three were playing on the floor behind her, absorbed in a game with blocks that her father had carved for them, and Jezreel was teaching the younger two how to count with them.

The rain outside came steadily down, unwilling to stop for the night. Supper was over, and soon it would be time to put the two boys down in Rachel's old room. *Rachel . . .* The old grief touched her softly for a moment, and she rested her head against the cold stones of the wall. It had been five years since her sister had gone, yet she still missed her sorely. It was as if the brighter side of her own self had been buried in that hillside cave, for since that day laughter had been a stranger to her.

Ruhamah was tugging at her skirt, and Gomer bent down to the tiny girl with a smile. In fussing over a small cut finger she found the only pleasure she had. The children had indeed filled a void for her as she had hoped, for since that morning near Karnaim Hosea had steadily drawn himself further and further away from her. Or had it been herself who had discouraged any hesitant efforts on his part to recover the contentment they had known in the beginning? She didn't know, and she didn't really care enough to find out.

Jezreel started scolding little Ammi, who was pouting about a letter he had written upside down. Gomer intervened with a small pat on both heads and the admonition, "He's only two, Jezreel!" Then suddenly she was surrounded by all three, hugging and laughing as they pulled her to the ground. Yes, they loved her, because she was always there, because she seldom scolded or lost her temper, but it was Hosea they adored. He was so intensely proud of all three that if she had loved him, she might have been jealous. They filled an emptiness in him too, she knew, and didn't begrudge him any of the children's affections. Already he was teaching the boys how to write and was boasting of their successes. When Diblaim asked doubtfully if Ammi was not too young for such brainwork, Hosea would grin and say that at his age he could read the whole Torah! No one believed him, of course, but it spurred the boys on to greater efforts.

Hosea strode into the room just then, and all three

pounced on him with squeals and shouts. Gomer walked over to the window and watched them from there, smiling quizzically, for the four made a happy picture. At that moment, she felt at peace with herself and her world. The puzzling, hurting battles she had quietly fought with Hosea were long past, and even if she couldn't understand or accept his passionate love for his beloved Adonai, she never spoke against him. Her hardest moments had come when he so arbitrarily named the children. Jezreel was to remind the Israelites of the battle fought on that plain between General Jehu and King Ahab. The victor, Jehu, instead of giving glory to God, had proceeded to grab more power for himself. Ruhamah had been named Lo-ruhamah, a cry of Hosea's to Israel that if she persisted in her sins, God could regard her as "his beloved no longer." And little, laughing Ammi had been called Lo-ammi, a desperate plea by his father for Israel to realize that if she continued to follow after false gods she "could no longer be called his people." Hosea even claimed that God had told him what to name the children and why. Hosea's talk was sometimes like a foreign language to Gomer.

Gomer had stormed at Hosea for days after the naming of baby Jezreel, sure in her heart that it would do her son no good to be a constant reminder to Israel of her past sins. Hosea had set his jaw and stood firm, and Diblaim had backed him the whole way. "He is the messenger of God, my daughter"—and that was that. She had then expected the other two to be named without being consulted, and she had been right.

She watched her family play on the floor, Hosea forgetting his dignity in a rough tumble with the boys. Once, when they were first married, she had thought that Hosea had come to release her from the bondage of life with her father into a new life of contented love. But all too soon she had realized that Hosea's love was just another form of bondage, for he feared for her safety in the streets of the city more than Diblaim had ever done. Once again she was forbidden to leave the house, even to hear him speak to the people on the rare occasion when he was asked to do so. Four walls hemmed her in, and she had learned to live with her frustrations—so she thought.

Gomer sat down on her chair, picking up the shirt for Ammi she was putting together. The baby had grown too fast lately, and she wondered where the years had fled. Hosea glanced over at her from his perch on the floor and wondered what she thought as she sat there, a lovely picture framed by the halo of the oil lamp. She hadn't grown older than the day he had wed her, so it seemed. Heavy work hadn't bent her shoulders, child-bearing hadn't bulged her slim figure. But he knew now that if he had realized her lack of faith he would never have bound himself to her, no matter how deep his passion might have run. He still loved her with a silent, hidden ache she didn't know was in him, for he couldn't bear to show it in the face of her affectionate indifference.

She was his wife, and he still knew that God had meant that to be. Someday she would come to love and worship his God as he did—how, he couldn't say, but he had the assurance that it would happen, and each morning he prayed that this day would see the breakthrough.

Jezreel and Ammi were begging for a story, so Hosea pulled them onto his lap while Ruhamah hung over his shoulder. Before he started, he glanced again at his wife.

She was watching him and smiling gently. He smiled back, the never-ending hope in his heart that maybe, this night, she would return to his bed from the pallet she had set up near the door. But her smile held no such promise, so he sighed and turned back to the children.

Not many days later, a knock came heavily at the front door. Hosea and Diblaim glanced at each other over the dinner table and nodded. "That would be Dan," Hosea said and stood up to let him in.

Shana frowned. "But it is the end of Shabbat. How could he come now? Should he not be at his prayers?"

"He will eat this meal with us," her husband said impatiently, his eyes fixed on the door. Dan strode inside, his round face wearing a troubled frown, and he nodded at the company without a word. Gomer fetched him a bowl, while the children jumped up and down with glee at seeing their favorite uncle. But instead of picking up all three at once, as was his wont, he merely hugged them with a distant smile, all the while watching Diblaim.

The meal passed in silence, the men preoccupied with some common problem. The women were puzzled and the children subdued by the air of gloom in the room. Finally Diblaim pushed back his chair and said, "It's time to go." Dan and Hosea hastily dropped their bread and got to their feet.

Shana stood up also. "Is it too presumptuous of me to ask why you break the Shabbat like this? What is this all about?"

Diblaim glared at her, shaking his head to indicate that he had no wish to explain, but Hosea interposed, "We had best tell them, I think, in case anything goes wrong."

Gomer caught her breath and stared at him. What was going on that could hurt him? She might not love him, but he was her comfort and security, and she couldn't imagine living without him any more than without her parents.

"It's the new king in Samaria, Pekahiah. He has called a celebration for this afternoon for his god, whom he proposes to make our nation's protector. We intend to go and remind our people that Shabbat is just over, the day sacred to the God of our fathers, and that no other god is fit to stand in his place." Hosea's face was calm, but Gomer noticed that his fist was opening and shutting from the tension within, the urge to disrupt this outrageous ceremony in the Name of his God controlling his emotion.

Something pushed up inside of Gomer, a half-remembered habit of rebellion. "Let me go with you!" she pleaded, rising from the bench to face her husband.

He stared at her, appalled. "My beloved, what are you saying? All the evil men of our city will be in the market today—and you want to go among them?"

"Daughter, what's wrong with you?" demanded Diblaim, his eyes black with his old suspicions. "It's a pagan festival we go to break up, not a decent gathering. It's no place for our women to wander!"

Gomer lowered her head in submission, but the rebellion was growing stronger inside. The forgotten heat of anger burned her throat, and she glared at the door as it shut behind the three men, keeping her in and all the world out. Suddenly she knew she could stand it no longer.

She remembered what Hosea had said and asked Shana, "My husband said it was the *new* king who has

called this—this festival. What has happened to Menahem?"

Her mother was busy clearing off the table. "He died
last month," she said briefly, "and his son has come back
from Assyria to take the throne. Thanks be to God there
was no bloodshed this time."

Gomer tightened her mouth. Hosea not only kept her
hidden in her own home, but evidently he had decided
to keep her ignorant of outside events as well.

Shana was calling the children into the workroom, for
she intended to teach them a "game": how to crush the
flowers needed for dyeing. Gomer waited until they were
all grouped at the other end of the workroom and
couldn't see into the kitchen. She heard shouts of laughter and her mother's gentle voice, and she knew the
noise they made would cover any sound she might
create.

Carefully, she slipped upstairs to her room and got her
gray cloak. Then, tightly wrapped from prying eyes, she
crept back down the stairs as stealthily as before. Paus-
ing a moment, she heard Ruhamah's high-pitched voice
giggling at the story her grandmother wove into the
game. Then she headed for the door. Pulling it open, she
held her breath, hoping it wouldn't creak on its old
hinges. There was no sound. She slipped through and
pulled it closed behind her.

She was outside.

S E V E N T E E N
In the Marketplace

The most beautiful feeling of freedom swept over her as she stood there, and like a half-remembered song from the sunny years of childhood it filled her heart so that she lifted her face to the sun and laughed softly with the joy it held. She was alone and free, with nothing to do but what she wished, nowhere to go but where she willed.

Her mantle had fallen from her head in her swift exuberant laugh, and she smiled as she rearranged it over her hair and part of her face. Hosea must not see her, nor her father, because if they did Dan would be forced to accompany her home, and she was determined to see what was going on. Running quickly through the twisted streets, she soon heard the low rumble of the crowd gathered in the marketplace.

Hurrying around the last turn, she stopped, appalled by the solid mass of backs that met her gaze. She realized instantly that she couldn't stay here. For one thing, she'd see nothing of the show; and for another, she caught a swift glimpse of Hosea's head a few rows deep in the throng. Standing still a moment, she pursed her lips in thought. Wasn't her father's friend the carpenter always out to these pagan festivals? And his house was halfway around the square with its back door opening out to the spot in the market where he kept his booth.

Her mind made up, she turned and ran for that front door she remembered from her childhood. Peeking in cautiously through the window, she decided the house was empty and smiled with satisfaction. All was clear.

Pushing open the door, she slipped through the house and without hesitation pulled open the back door. She found herself in a small open space, long and narrow, and was puzzled. Then she saw that a new platform had been erected that came almost over to the wall of the next house, and abutted onto the back wall of the carpenter's. No one had noticed the small space, a cubit's span from the wall beside her. She closed the door behind her and stepped carefully forward until she was sure no one in the crowd could see her, hidden as she was in the shadow of the tall platform. Suddenly she realized that she would be able to see everything that went on much better than her menfolk, and she chuckled. How high their anger would rise could they see her now!

The crowd was talking and laughing in a holiday mood. She didn't recognize any of the faces nearby, but she pulled her mantle tighter anyway. Just then the rumble of chariot wheels came from the royal avenue, and everyone turned toward the sound. All chatter stopped, and in the sudden hush Gomer could hear her heart pounding with excitement. Since she was taller than any of the women and many of the men, she had a clear view of the opening opposite the platform at the other end of the square. *Any moment I shall see the king,* she thought.

Then he came, sweeping up the dust of the road with his wheels, his golden chariot drawn by a matched pair of white Arabians who tossed their long manes and stretched their long legs through the crowd. Scattering before the chariot, the people started to cheer wildly, and soon the air was resounding with the deafening clamor. Three more chariots followed the first, the last bearing a covered litter, but no one paid them any attention. They had come to see the king for the first time.

He drew rein before the wooden platform, his swirling blue cloak falling in rich folds from his broad shoulders and flying out behind him like wings. His tunic, falling to his knees, was a bright yellow and was bound at the waist with a blue sash. His wide chest was covered with a thin silver-worked breastplate.

The people cheered him without pause, and he laughed, a full deep laugh that came from the earth, yet held the gaiety of the sun. He dropped his reins and turned to jump onto the platform. Then he saw Gomer.

She had forgotten to hold her mantle, and it had slid to her shoulders. Her face was upturned to his where she stood in the shadow of the platform. She had watched him coming and had forgotten everything else in the world but him. An instant flew up from the stream of time to hang suspended above them. He stopped moving; she stopped breathing.

Her heart was exploding. O the splendor of this man! He stood above her tall and firm, like a god, like a flashing seraph, and she loved him. His eyes threw fire into hers, a fire that she sensed would never die this side of death. She saw his curling black hair, his firm proud mouth, his lean strong jaw that bespoke a commanding spirit. His eyes held hers. Both felt a surge of knowing that stripped away all need of words and pretenses and lifted them into a high and lofty glory that neither had known existed.

Then a nobleman called to him from the chariot behind. The world reclaimed them both and swept them apart.

The crowd was still cheering, and no one had noticed the king's momentary hesitation. He smiled at them and raised his hand in triumphant acknowledgment of their praise, and the noise died away. The arrogant tilt of his head made the woman by the platform feel faint, and she clutched at the raw edge to steady herself, not noticing the splinters that bit into her palm.

"My people!" called Pekahiah. "Friends! It's been too long since I was here among you, and it's sad that the death of my father was the signal for my return." The cheering erupted again and he smiled, his eyes sparkling. "Yes . . . Thank you . . . And *this* is my home, no matter how many years I spent serving the Great King, our adonai Tiglath-pileser, truly the lord of the world!" Not enough cheered this phrase, and the Assyrian soldiers on the edge of the crowd growled into their square beards. Someday . . .

"Will the priests come forward?" Pekahiah called. Four from the third chariot climbed the platform, dressed simply in long white robes, their bowed heads shaved clean. On their shoulders they carried the covered litter from the fourth chariot, its purple drapery swaying mysteriously. They laid their burden before the king and stepped back. "Today, my people, will be the new feast day for the god who has led me victoriously in battle—the great Tammuz whom you call Adonis, the husband of our Lady Ashtaroth, who descends yearly to the underworld and returns to bring spring to our lands. Praise be to Tammuz and his Lady!"

The people cheered sporadically through this speech, and then grew silent as the king approached the litter and called softly. Two girls stepped out then into the sunlight, and the men broke into a roar of approval. The women were silent, recognizing with narrowed eyes the lovely priestesses of Ashtaroth from Shiloh. The two slim girls swayed their bodies gently under the gauzy Egyptian drapery that flowed over their young limbs. Their faces were hidden under masks of white and gold paint; their breasts rose with difficulty under heavy amulets carved in the likeness of their Lady.

But they were meant only as decoration. Both started a rhythmic dance around the litter and slowly pulled the purple curtain back. There was Tammuz, standing tall and slim before the crowd. An unknown artist had worked long and lovingly on the four-cubit statue, a masterpiece of cunning and skill. He seemed alive as the sunlight played upon the curving planes of his ebony body, and his jeweled eyes, sunk deep above his smiling mouth, seemed to see all. The people were yelling madly, hysterically. Pekahiah stood behind his god, smiling.

Just then a commotion started at the platform base as someone tried to push up the steps. Gomer glanced over quickly and gasped. It was Hosea! Hastily she wrapped herself again in her cloak and shrank back into the deep shadow of the wall.

Before anyone could stop him, Hosea had leaped onto the platform and was striding toward the two priestesses, still swaying before the statue. He pulled off his large brown cloak and with his jaw set in the firm way that Gomer recognized, he threw the cloak over the two sets of bare shoulders before him. Before the stunned girls could break away he had them pinned together, their bodies completely covered for the moment. But he couldn't cover their mouths, and he was blushing uncontrollably because of the vile words they were pouring into his defenseless ears.

Gomer understood none of the girls' scathing phrases, but the king obviously knew their meaning, for he was laughing hard even as he signaled his guards to close in.

Hosea was caught in two hard grips as the soldiers turned him away from the priestesses. They pushed him forward until he faced the king. The two looked closely at each other as if they had all the time in the world, this haughty young prince and the angry man of God. Both pairs of eyes flashed with suppressed emotion, but both men were well under control.

Pekahiah spoke first. "Who are you, and why have you desecrated Tammuz's feast day?"

Hosea tossed the ragged locks of hair from his eyes and gazed steadily into the king's black eyes. "The people know me, O King. I have stood here in the marketplace for six years telling them what I now shall tell you."

"Are you a seer or diviner, or one who watches the stars?" Such men were highly respected in every king's court, and nothing was decided without their advice. Yet the king's tone was amused, as if he said he had no use for such charlatans.

"No, O King." Hosea's voice was quiet, and Gomer found herself biting her lips from tension. *Hosea, Hosea, don't make him angry!* "I am Hosea ben Beeri, sent by the God of the Israelites, who has no Name we can speak, to remind his people of their covenant with him, made on Mount Sinai hundreds of years ago. They swore to honor and worship him, but they have forgotten how." His voice was getting louder, and the passion in his face startled Pekahiah, who stepped backward in momentary awe. "Hear, O Israel! The God Adonai is ours; he is one! Do you remember the days when you worshiped that One, the true God? Have you forgotten the love he held for you when he led you out of Egypt under Moses, when he led you to conquer this Canaan under Joshua? These gods you worship today were defeated then. They are false gods with no power in them! This Tammuz—is he not just a mere statue made with human hands, and no god at all?"

The king's eyes were growing blacker, but Hosea had twisted around in the soldiers' grip and was aiming his words at the silent mob. His face was shining, his eyes full of something that frightened the people for the moment. "Listen to me, O Israel! Our God has warned me that the day comes quickly when you must account to him for your turning away. And though you mock or kill me, his messenger, my children remain to remind you of my words: Lo-Ruhamah! Lo-Ammi! Can't you hear the words of our Adonai? O my people! O my beloved! Repent—repent of your wicked ways and put away your false gods, or the day will come when they will fall powerless from their high places as the enemy arrives at your walls!"

The king signaled to the soldiers, and they pushed

the shouting Hosea to his knees. The prophet stopped abruptly as the hard floor hit his legs, then looked up into the stern face of Pekahiah. But before either could say a word, a high shrill cry came from the crowd and was taken up with fervor. "Stone the blasphemer! Stone him! Kill him! He dares say wicked things against Tammuz and our Lady! Stone him! Stone him!"

A stone whistled through the air and the king ducked. It just missed his head. The soldiers, seeing their leader's danger, grabbed Hosea by the shoulders and shoved him off the platform, and the people shouted with delight. Hosea felt hands pulling at him, until a stone struck his temple and everything went black.

Gomer was beside herself with fear. Where was he? What was happening to him? She ran out of her hiding place and tried to push her way to him through the crowd, but to no avail. In her terror she even tried to claw her way over a man's back, but he shook her off with ease.

Looking up, she saw the king standing beside his statue as he watched the seething mass at his feet. She flung herself against the platform and called up to him, "Please, please, O King! Hear me!"

Pekahiah turned his head and looked around, seeking the source of that desperate cry. Then he saw her, clinging to the edge of the platform while the maddened people shoved past her to get to the prophet. In two steps he was standing over her, and he knelt so that their faces were close together. He saw her fear, and reached out a hand to touch her hair.

"O King, please stop them!" Her voice, low and tense, came to him between her painful gasps. "Please! Don't let them kill him! He's my husband. Please!"

His hand jerked back as if it had been stung by her words. They stared into each other's eyes for another breathless second. Then he sprang up and ran over to the dense mob still fighting by the steps. "Cease!" he roared, and the ones closest looked up in surprise. When they saw the king, they backed away hurriedly from the limp figure on the ground.

Pekahiah looked down and saw blood dribbling from a blow on Hosea's temple. His clothes were ripped to shreds. That was as far as the crowd had gotten, because so eager were they to kill him that they had been in each other's way.

The people gradually quieted, and the king still stood there gazing at the prone figure on the ground. *Strange that such a man should still exist,* he thought, *eager to speak for his god, aching for his people to return to the old ways.* His father had written him once about this man, warning that he was a possible troublemaker or center for revolt. Now Pekahiah knew this to be false. Here was no soldier after the throne, but a peaceful scholar somehow fired with the passion of the times he studied.

Two men had come up to Hosea and knelt beside him. The king jumped off the platform and watched as they tenderly drew Hosea's cloak over him and prepared to carry him away. The older of the two, tears running into his long gray beard, paused for a moment to gaze at the young prince. "He is a good man," he said, choking. "If he dies for this day's folly, our God will have payment in full."

The king frowned, but said nothing. The god of Israel had certainly once been powerful and feared, and Pekahiah was not one to incur the wrath of any man's deity.

Watching the two carry Hosea through the crowd that parted to let them pass, he caught himself hoping that the prophet wouldn't die. There had been that about the prophet that had been attractive—a courage, a recklessness in the face of certain danger that was strange in a scholar. He would do anything for his god. Indeed a strange man, mused Pekahiah. He turned to the platform to continue the festivities.

It was then that he remembered the woman who had pleaded with him to intervene, and he glanced around to see if she had seen his success.

She was gone.

Hosea lay in his bed, head well-wrapped with fresh linen, and thanked God that he was still alive. It had been very close at first, but the faithful nursing of his wife had pulled him through. She had sat up night and day beside him, pale and silent, and had constantly bathed his bruised body with oils to soothe the pain. "Thanks be to God," he whispered again, watching the flies dancing through the window. He was so glad just to be able to see the sand gnats that he forgot how irritating he had always found them.

Gomer came into the room carrying a bowl of hot pottage, and his nostrils quivered at the smell. He was very hungry, having been unable to eat until three days after his mauling.

She lowered the plate to him and watched him eat. She remembered when Diblaim and Dan had brought him in the door, and she had been there to receive them. Her mother hadn't even noticed that she had gone out, assuming that she had retired to her bedroom to rest. So no questions had been directed at her, only at Diblaim.

But Hosea lived after that day, and for that she was glad.

Still, the memory of the king tormented her in the midst of that gladness as she nursed her husband. She kept seeing those dark quizzical eyes so close to hers, with a question in them only for her. *Pekahiah,* she thought—*he looked at me, and for a moment we were just man and woman caught outside space and time.*

Hosea started coughing, and she hastily bent down to lift him into a sitting position. When he was finished eating, she lowered him again, taking away the bowl.

He took her hand and gazed up at her with his eyes full of weak tears. "Gomer," he whispered, "my beloved, you are so good to me. And yet, I still wonder if it wouldn't have been best had I died."

She went pale, afraid. "You mustn't talk so, Hosea! Please! You are alive, and they will never do such a thing to you again."

He frowned, puzzled. "What do you mean?"

She busied herself with the wrappings she kept in a pile by the bed, not looking at him. "Now can you not see that—that it's useless to go on talking like this to the people? They have laughed at you for years, and now they've almost killed you. Please—can't you give it up and just work with Father?"

Hosea closed his eyes. She still didn't understand. All the closeness and care he had felt from her this past week evaporated with her words, and he groaned. "Gomer, Gomer, can't you see that I *can't* stop? God has given me a task to do and I must do it. The success or failure of this task is up to him, not me. But I must not stop. Yes, you're right that they won't listen to me, and that's why I say maybe I should have died. Then maybe they might realize I mean every word I say. O my beloved! If only you could see it the way I do, Gomer. I hate telling them they're wicked! It gives me no joy to threaten them! Sometimes I want to reach out and wipe them off the face of the earth for their insults to God, but I cannot. Why must it be me, Gomer?" He gazed up at her, and suddenly he was like a bewildered child.

She gave a smothered sob and knelt beside him, pressing his face to her breast. "Hosea, that's what I can't understand, and why I wish you'd give this up. They don't care about you. Can't you see that?" She held his face between her hands and made him look into her eyes. "My husband, we haven't spoken of these things since we were first married, and I have kept my silence. But I must tell you now. I can take no more of this life! I want a husband who will live to old age with me, talk with me, share himself with me—and let me share my true self with him. But you don't want to know me, you don't care about my feelings about the Old Ones, and you turn away anything I might have to say about our people. You go out and spend months away from me and the children spreading a message no one wants to hear. Hosea, I know them, I know why they turn from you, I know why they want to kill you! And I say this god of yours isn't worth dying for! What has he given you but sorrow and pain and the hatred of your own people? Hosea? Are you listening to me?"

He had shut his eyes so that she couldn't read the deep anguish of his soul. Every word she had said ripped him to shreds worse than any mob could have done. *My beloved, my wife, why are you so far from me?*

Finally he opened his eyes again to see that she had left him and was staring out the window. "Gomer," he said. She turned around, and her face was filled with unhappiness. *I put that sorrow there,* he thought, and hated what he had to say. "You ask what God has given me. Can you question the mission he bestowed upon me? Have you forgotten my long search that finally ended at his feet? O my wife, God has given me joy."

EIGHTEEN

Flight

The slam of the door behind her still vibrated in her ears as she stood in the hall, her breasts heaving. *I hate you,* she thought passionately. *I hate you, hate you, hate you! You give him joy, he claims! And where does this terrible joy lead him to but death? I spit upon your joy!*

She turned and ran down the stairs, hardly seeing the children playing in the middle of the floor. Shana knelt before the fire and stood up at her approach, appalled by the fire in her daughter's eyes. "Gomer, what—"

Gomer looked right through her, and Shana recognized the insane fury she had seen only twice before—when they had quarreled on the roof so long ago, and when Gomer had spat out that she would never pray to God.

Jezreel's sudden wail from the corner made Shana turn to him instantly. When she picked him up and turned back again, Gomer was gone.

Pekahiah paced up and down his sumptuously furnished bedroom, moodily biting his lip. In the past two weeks he had successfully taken over his father's kingdom without the usual bloodshed, and all his nobles except one seemed satisfied with their new ruler. The one mutterer, Pekah, he had banished to his lands north of Hazor, because Pekah, general of the horses, had tried to entice the army into open revolt. Pekahiah had decided not to kill the man but to set a policy of mercy for his new reign, but now he wondered if he had made a mistake. Only the future could answer him.

Just as important as winning the favor of the nobles, he had also taken intact his father's harem. One or two of the generals had asked for a woman, but he had turned them down curtly. To have the concubine of a deceased king was tantamount to a claim on the throne, and Pekahiah wanted no pretenders.

He had not as yet visited the harem, being still faithful to the memory of the tiny Ethiopian mistress who had died a year before. There was only one woman he had ever seen who might be the one to suit his various moods and needs, and she walked the streets of Samaria—so he thought—the wife of that prophet of Israel's god.

The thought of the man of God continually pestered him, and he had sent to see if the man still lived, curiously relieved when the answer came back that Hosea had survived. Yet the memory of the man's wife kept swimming through his mind, and whenever it did he caught his breath in wonder. A woman in a thousand, he had thought when he first saw her, and the scanty light where she stood had made her hair a radiant cloud about her face.

He was no man to go hunting a woman, and he tried to forget her. But today, for some reason, she wouldn't leave his mind.

Irritated with himself, he finally strode out of his room and called for his man Gor. "I wish to ride to the market and see Tammuz," he said, and the hunchback saluted and ran for the stables. Wrapping his long blue cloak about him for the breezy ride, Pekahiah followed, still deep in troubled thought.

Gomer took a deep breath and stopped pushing her way through the mob. She had fled without mantle or cloak, but was unaware of the curious stares her beauty caused. It had been too many years since she had run free as a child for the townsfolk to recall her lovely light coloring. They had no idea who she was.

She looked up at Tammuz, standing regally on his cedar base, then closed her eyes. She had done it, she told him, she had finally run away from the stifling atmosphere of her home. She had left them all behind and ended up here before him, before the statue her husband called an abomination.

"Lady . . ." she murmured, knowing that wherever Tammuz stood, his wife must be close by. "Help me, Ashtaroth, help me! I have left those who still worship the god of Moses. I don't know where to go now, Lady. Help me."

A horse stepped lightly behind her, and she heard the thud of feet hitting the cobblestones as a rider dismounted. Silence seemed to penetrate the fire in her aching heart, and she turned around. It was the king.

He stood there looking deep into her eyes, gripping the reins of his horse tightly in his large hands. He had no words for her, but somehow he knew he needed none, knew that she had been remembering him as he had remembered her.

She gazed up at him, caught his eyes, and he didn't seem a stranger at all. The breeze played joyfully with his cloak and her long mantle of hair, and it seemed to be twining them about the two still figures in that busy square.

They knew each other again, seeing in each other's eyes a heart that yearned after the same bright dreams, a soul with the same hungers that came in the lonely hours.

He turned away from her and vaulted into his gilt saddle, then looked down at her where she stood so still, her hands clasped to her breast as she wondered what he would do or say.

He reached down his hand to her and touched her flushed cheek. Pent with emotion, his voice reached her ears with a command: "Come."

She reached up her hands to him.

PART II
PEKAHIAH

NINETEEN
In the Harem

The soft swish of the peacock-feathered fan was the only sound within the harem. It was the hour after midday, and the wives and concubines had settled down for their afternoon nap. Draped over any convenient couch that had offered itself, they sighed and murmured in their drug-like sleep, the fan keeping the flies and gnats from settling upon their emotionless, upturned faces.

The dry season had come once more, and all the open windows were covered with thick layers of Persian silks to keep out the relentless sun and its accompanying heat. But some breezes straight from the eastern desert over the Jordan still managed to waft in around the curtains and, unfortunately for the women, there was only the one fan to lighten their misery. However, being basically of the phlegmatic nature of eastern women, they endured the heat as they endured their luxurious prison.

The slave who flourished the cumbersome fan was a short, solemn man with a round, moonlike face, his head utterly devoid of hair. He seldom spoke, for he had acquired a stammer on that day forty years before when as a boy he had been captured on his farm east of the Tigris River by marauding Assyrian soldiers, had lost his manhood, and had been carried west to be sold as a slave. But his small black eyes shone with suppressed intelligence, for he watched all and was usually on top of any potentially troublesome plot before it got anywhere. He well knew that many kings had been deposed because of the doings in the harem, and he was determined that his master should have no such worries.

Pacing up and down between the couches, he watched the indolent women as they slept, fully aware that they were as much slaves as he was. They did nothing all day, however, but chatter in the harem tongue that was a combination of every language under the sun; or they slept, their oiled, brown bodies rolled on top of cushions as plump as themselves. If perchance the king asked for a woman at night, the slave might have to choose among these screaming, jealous women ready to tear his eyes out with their long nails. He was very grateful to the lady in the Great Chamber that such nights came fairly infrequently. But now they were still, these terrible noisy women, and he could laugh inside at them as he pleased.

One couch was empty, he knew, although he couldn't see it. Closest to the door of this huge room that covered the whole second floor of the west wing of the palace was a chamber that was curtained off from the rest. Since the days of Omri, who had built these splendid

royal quarters, that room had been the chamber of the
Great Lady of the court, usually the mother of the king if
she still lived, or else the chief wife. The room was high
and spacious, the curtains that contained it made of a
shimmering gold material from the far east, and it had
large windows that overlooked the bustling courtyard
below. The couch was set along one wall and was covered with dark blue silks and red pillows. The few pieces
of furniture—some chairs and a low table for perfumes
and paint pots—were of delicately carved cedar inlaid
with ivory. It was, in fact, the feminine counterpart of the
king's room that stood across the hall and up a short
flight of stairs from the harem door.

It was indeed a queen's room, thought the eunuch,
Nuri, as he wielded the heavy fan with his muscular
arms. But no matter who the woman was who occupied
that room, be she old or young, ugly or fair, she was
deeply hated by the rest of the harem because of the
favoritism shown her by the king. She was mistress of
them all by tradition.

The present king's mother had died five years before
he had returned from Nineveh to take his throne, and he
had as yet chosen no chief wife from the surrounding
nations. The women in the harem at the time were either
remnants from the previous king's bevy of beauties, or
else had been presents from allies at the time of ascen-
sion. Thus, by rights, the Great Chamber should have
had no occupant. But all remembered the day, two years
before, when Pekahiah the king had led a strange woman to the door and instructed Nuri that she was to be
treated as the chief wife from now on. No, they had not
been married, for she was already some other man's

woman, but they had contracted between themselves before Ashtaroth in the palace temple that afternoon, he said, to be lovers forever. Any children born of the union, he declared, would be his heirs. The other women bit their tongues to prevent screams of rage from pouring forth.

The Samaritan woman had not understood at first the great honor her lover had bestowed upon her, and soon she came to Nuri with her puzzled questions. He had taken great delight in telling her of the former occupants of that room, and she had listened intently. From that time to this, he had been her devoted slave in mind as well as fact, because she didn't treat him as a thing the way the others did, but like a friend. She was always courteous, asking him for things in a low, soft voice quite different from the raucous yell of the other women. She never screamed or threw things, or asked him to perform certain distasteful tasks.

The other concubines hated the stranger with a deep and fierce fire. She seemed to be Pekahiah's companion all the time, except when she was in recluse for her monthly impurity. Even in this respect Nuri found her much better, for the other women cared not a whit for cleanliness and lived like animals, and jeered when he carried hot water in for the Samaritan woman's daily wash. He preferred that task to the monumental one he undertook twice a year that consisted in turning all the women out onto the balcony and having other slaves brought into the harem to wash everything down, shovel out the dirt, and sprinkle the floor and curtains with sweet nard. Jasmine and roses were always kept in pots to mask the odors, but the freshness in the Great Chamber always seemed like a garden to Nuri.

But the Chamber was empty now. Gomer did not stay there, and Nuri smiled to himself at this evidence of the Samaritan woman's superiority. O gods, was she not indeed a worthy one for his beloved master?

TWENTY

For Love

Gomer sat on a cushion in the sunlit corner of the palace library, her lips moving softly as she made out the wedge-like characters on the tablet she held in her hand. She still found it difficult, even after a year, to read this ancient script, and after a time laid it down with a sigh. The scribes on the stools along the corridor, bent in concentration over their papyrus rolls, heard her and smiled gently, their nearsighted eyes blinking with approval. She was coming along, their lovely student, and soon would be equal to them.

Gomer laid her head against the stone window ledge behind her and closed her eyes, enjoying the warmth of the sun's rays on her hair. It had been a day like this, she remembered, when she first entered this room. Bored with the afternoon hours that plodded along, too energetic to indulge in a daily afternoon nap, she had pestered Nuri for something to do. "The kitchen?" he had suggested in his high voice, but she had wrinkled her nose with the distaste of long association with such things. She would not be welcome in the stables, he had rambled on, and he wasn't sure if the library would be to her liking. . . .

Her interest had been caught. A library? Hosea had once told her that his father had worked there, doing the king's business. Brushing him out of her mind, she asked for explicit directions, for the palace was like a mindless maze even to those who knew it. Soon she was gliding silently through the dim corridors, a soft green cloak about her, and without much difficulty she reached her objective.

The scribes, imprisoned all day long in their musty room, were delighted with her appearance. A month later, she informed the impressed Nuri that she was learning to read. However, when he asked if she would write too, her face clouded and she shook her head as memories of Hosea bent over his scrolls flooded through her mind. That night, the only night it happened, she had stood at the window after her lover went to sleep and wondered how it was with those she had left below in the streets of Samaria.

Gomer, after learning to read Hebrew from Pekahiah's Israelite scribe, was engrossed for months in the histories of her land that were kept in the large vases stored under the tables. Later, exhausting this material, she learned the language of old Canaan, for there were several tablets there filled with the tales of ancient heroes and gods, and she found her longing for adventures and high fantasies well satisfied with these stories. The Egyptian scribe agreed with her that they were certainly far more interesting than those told about the austere, pleasure-hating god of Moses.

The Assyrian scribe who had accompanied Pekahiah and his soldiers to Samaria two years before had given in to her pleas and taught her his native tongue. Now she conversed with him like his sister, and the old men sat about her and listened with pleasure to her soft twisting of words that were new to her. She was daughter to all of them, and brought a glow to their dusty lives that enriched them all. Her low voice, her gay laugh, her well-bred ways made their afternoons a rare pleasure, and they all prayed that Pekahiah would never tire of her and send her away.

Gomer found diversion in the library and great delight in stretching the muscles of her mind as she never had before. But her life, the real time for her, was spent behind the closed door of Pekahiah's room. There, surrounded by the accumulated wealth of centuries, with a small oil lamp burning to the end of its wick near the window, she found the deep contentment, the fulfillment she had always dreamed of and never found until she came to the palace with Pekahiah.

The people in the palace, she knew, wondered what magic she had worked, what god she had captured to so enslave their king, and many made the sign against the evil eye when she passed. Her lover had laughed, his deep rich voice filling her ear as he said, "You are my Ashtaroth," and he would hold her bright hair to his lips in adoration. Then the happiness that welled up inside made her want to cry.

Surrounded daily by eastern opulence and richness beyond her wildest youthful dreams, Gomer soon felt as if she had always lived in the palace and had always been loved by Pekahiah. *This is truly my life, this is why I was born,* she would tell herself as she looked into her mirror, the only one in the palace, which Pekahiah had ordered placed in her room. Perfumes, silks, dancing lessons, pastries, wines from Hebron and the north . . . all and everything was hers, as she wished, he told her. She would stand in the center of his room and gaze at him, her eyes glowing, and say, "But I want only you, my life." Then he would come to her and hold her tightly by the shoulders, his large black eyes searching hers, and he would wonder if it was really true, that this lovely goddess was really his, that her eyes were really filled with liquid love for him.

He would tell her the stories of Greece that he had learned from the northern merchants in the court of the Great King at Nineveh. His voice captivated her imagination, making her see pictures of willful goddesses and playful gods who enjoyed pretending to be mortal. "You are my Aphrodite," he would say with a smile, his strong fingers intertwined in the locks of her hair, and she would laugh back at him. "Then you are my warlike Ares." They would reach for each other, not noticing the breeze that blew out the lamp.

They were like careless lovers those long evenings, and no hint of the careworn soldier-king came into that room, even if he had spent the day ordering the suppression of pocket rebellions, or tried to dredge up more money to pay the Assyrian tribute. None of the cares of his kingship could prevent him from coming to her side, and she in her turn made a haven of rest out of the room that had once seemed so empty to him. She would listen to him, talk with him, make him laugh and relax in her arms, and as the months had gone by he found that he couldn't live through a day without the thought of seeing her at the end of it.

She, in her turn, had left behind her former life, for her days and nights were full of either Pekahiah's commanding presence or else the memory of him, and any thought in her mind was usually connected with loving him, with bringing him joy.

Once he lifted her hair idly in his hand and watched the play of the moonlight on her tresses as they slid through his fingers. "Why is it, my love, that your hair holds the lights of the sun and the moon, and your skin has a lighter shade than any other Israelite woman I have ever seen? Can it be that your mother was not always true?"

Gomer had stiffened at his words, and her eyes smoldered as she said, "Do not speak so of those of my family who know what honor is, even if I have left it behind."

He sensed immediately that he had hurt her, and cursed himself for being so tactless. He should have realized that she would see a hidden reproach in his words. "My love, you mistake me. I spoke in jest. You are faithful, so your mother must have been as well. I have seen my soldiers watching you—and I am proud of you that you stay close to me."

She leaned over and brushed his curls from his damp forehead, for the night was sultry and the air lay heavy about them. "Could I do otherwise, my king? Yes, I am true—to you."

He sighed and wished he hadn't spoken, for the memory of Hosea stood between them, the memory of a man who still lived and walked and spoke less than a mile from where they lay. "I just wondered—why you are so fair of face and hair."

Gomer looked up at the sky, and the stars reflected in her eyes. *How lovely she is,* he thought, *and she grows more so each day. So slim and strong, so tall and graceful, a true queen among women—and I cannot place her beside me because of that man who claimed her first, and I cannot order him killed because of what it would do to her.* He knew that he couldn't do it even if she hadn't cared at all, for the memory of the bravery which that man had shown in their brief meeting called for respect from king to prophet. A god certainly held the man, even if it was a god his wife had hated and run from—into the king's arms. He sighed again, and found her looking at him with a slight smile.

"You asked me a question I can't answer, my king," she said and leaned her head on his shoulder. He caught a whiff of myrrh and buried his nose in her hair. His breath caught in his throat, but he forced himself to listen. "My—my mother never told me why I look so different, although I used to ask her often. My father always looked angry when I asked, so I soon stopped. 'When you are older,' Mother said, but I suppose I never was old enough."

He wrapped her slight form in his arms and held her tightly. "Maybe there is northern blood in you and your father is ashamed of it. Who knows? Not all your people are adverse to marrying outside of your tribes."

"They are your people too, my adonai," she murmured, and heard him chuckle deep in his chest.

"Only partly, little one, only through my father. My

mother was from Tyre, and taught me early not to belittle her people as most Israelites do."

She was growing sleepy and yawned. "I don't really care," she said softly, and he chuckled again. Lifting her easily in his arms, he carried her in from the terrace, into the private darkness of his chamber.

T W E N T Y - O N E
Nuri

When Gomer came out of her chamber the next morning after the servant girl had taken away her breakfast
tray, she found Nuri at the harem door, his full lips
forming a frown and his small eyes darting about in a
frantic fashion. When he saw his Great Lady, he bowed
low, his hands pressed together before his huge belly.
"Mistress," he murmured in his own tongue, and she
smiled.

"Speak, O servant," she answered back in the same
language, and his eyes brightened.

"The Great Lady is indeed gracious, to speak such a
sweet language to one who rarely hears it." His hands
pressed against his heart, and his pathetic gratitude hurt
her.

"It is a great tongue, Nuri, for does not the Great King
speak it in his halls? But come, tell me why you're
looking so worried." She motioned to him to follow, and
she walked over to the balcony door. He waddled after

her, sighing deeply as he watched her flowing walk and her queenly bearing. *Such women were meant for kings,* he thought, *and it is my sorrow to not even be a man.*

Gomer stepped out into the sunshine and winced as the bright daylight hit her eyes. The terrace stretched before her for quite a distance, being the roof of the first floor kitchens, kept specially for the women's sunning and play. A small statue of Ashtaroth stood beneath a marble inset against the outer wall, so that the women didn't need to go to the temple at the back of the palace for their prayers. Often Gomer had knelt before the Lady in the early morning after leaving Pekahiah, and watched the sun rise over the eastern hills as she softly whispered her heartfelt thanksgiving. She thought of those times now as she led Nuri toward the statue, and she smiled slightly. So often the amused, friendly face of Ashtaroth had watched her cry her happy tears, and the plump breasts had seemed to swell with sympathetic ardor. *Yes, Ashtaroth is indeed my Lady,* thought Gomer, *a great and powerful Lady who rules my life and has placed me within the love of my adonai king. Blessed be Ashtaroth! And cursed be any who deny the joy she has brought my way.*

Gomer sat down on her little stool that she had left outside the week before. Now that the rainy season was long gone, there seemed no danger in leaving it exposed to the weather. Nuri sat at her feet, his baggy green trousers billowing out all about him and disturbing the sandy rooftop. The flies, long awake and looking for someone to pester, started to swarm about the two as they talked, but the conversants soon were so absorbed that they didn't even slap at the little biters.

Nuri began immediately, a sure sign that he was greatly worried, for he usually waited for her to speak. "Mistress, there is something going on in the harem, and I
can't seem to dig it out at all."

Gomer frowned thoughtfully. It never occurred to her
to question Nuri's judgment, for he was always right.
"How has this come to your notice then, my friend?"

Nuri was rubbing his sweating palms together, and his
stutter was in full force. "It—it is the women, m-mis-
tress. They have been unusually qui-quiet this morning,
and this is not the first morning th-this has happened.
The king's man, Gor, was at the door this morning while
I—I was at the other, giving sick Sarai her breakfast.
He—he just stood there watching me, until one of the
women went over and handed something to him, and
I—I thought it looked like a scroll. I ran over, of course,
to chastise her, but she just laughed at me and walked
away! Mistress, it is unthinkable that she should do such
a thing! Am I not master in the harem? Do I not carry a
whip?" He jumped up and paced back and forth in front
of her, his dark brown skin shiny with sweat and the
nostrils of his tiny nose quivering.

Gomer had shivered with disgust at the name of Gor.
She had never been able to overcome a queasy feeling
when the king's hunchbacked slave was around, and she
couldn't understand it. The man was inoffensive
enough, bowing to her whenever she entered the chamber, walking about on silent feet doing whatever Pekahiah told him to do. Maybe it was the guarded look in his
eyes; maybe it was the half-leer she had caught on his
face the first time her lover had led her into his chamber.

Whatever it was, she was quite willing to believe that if Gor was involved in something secret, it was not for her own good.

"Nuri," she said slowly, "Gor shouldn't have been at the harem door, but he may merely have been taking a message from the woman to the king. After all, she is his—his woman." It hurt unbearably to say such a thing. If it weren't for the fact that possession of the harem was a large part of Pekahiah's kingship, Gomer wouldn't have been able to bear its presence. The woman may have been complaining of the lack of the king's attention and threatening to make trouble with his allies. It had happened once before, and Gomer had cried many nights away in her lovely golden chamber while Pekahiah had gone through every single one of the women, in order to appease their furies. As far as she knew, no complaint had been made after that to any neighboring country. Whether complaining would do any good for the woman, Gomer didn't know, for kings have a tendency to ignore a woman, especially if she is complaining about something. But Pekahiah had wanted to be sure no ill winds would blow about his throne, for too many kings had been killed in Israel for any to feel at all secure.

Nuri was shaking his head, standing still and facing the smug little statue of Ashtaroth. "If only she would speak," he muttered, "and tell us the secrets she has heard on this terrace."

Gomer stood up and walked restlessly about, kicking a pebble with her gold-worked sandal. The thoughts going through her head in the past few moments were kindling a smoldering fire against the women in the harem. "Go on, Nuri. That can't be all. That alone wouldn't upset you. What else have you seen?"

He hesitated, his fleshy brow furrowed. "It—it's only a feeling, mistress, but it's a strong one. The women have often been huddled together in groups about one couch, and—and when I approach, they fall silent. Yes, that happens all the time, b-but now they are smiling, and their smiles are evil when they l-look my way. The two who can write, the concubine from Tyre and the concubine from the Ephraimites, have been very busy lately a-as well, and many scrolls have disappeared from the pile kept for their use. Why all this writing, Lady? To my eyes, there is a plot b-being hatched under my very nose, but it's being so well done that I have no way of stopping it, because I don't know who is doing it or if they are all in it. And h-how can I accuse Gor? He is over me i-in the palace, if not in the harem." The small man from the Tigris was nearly jumping up and down in his panic, and Gomer reached out her hand in a calming gesture as she sat down again.

"Nuri, Nuri, calm yourself, my friend, or else we are lost already. Now, if there *is* a plot—and we don't know that for sure—then something will come to light that you can tell the king. After all, a plan to depose a king needs aid. The harem can't do it alone."

Nuri nodded his bald head, relieved. "You are r-right, Great Lady, and I am a fool. It may be just letters to their homes for gifts, it may be a surprise they plan for the king! It-it's just their looks that disturb me, the—the gloating in their eyes when you leave for the king's bed in the evening. They used to glare; now they smile."

Gomer was pale, but she held her trembling lips

steady. "Nuri, I will speak to the king tonight about this, but in the meantime say nothing to anyone else, unless you see the king's captain, Renin. He is loyal, for he served with Pekahiah in every battle our master fought and saved his life more than once. Would a man come all the way from Nineveh to Samaria unless he was loyal to the man he followed? Yes, tell Renin and he will keep his eyes open. A rebellion needs soldiers, don't forget, and Renin will notice any restlessness among the men."

Nuri was smiling now, relieved. "Yes, yes, my L-Lady, I will go right now and find him. And—and thank you for listening to my foolishness." He bowed to her and waited for dismissal.

Gomer stood up and brushed the sand from her lap that had settled there, brought by the slight breeze from the east. "You are not foolish, my friend, and I'm glad you told me about your worries. It is the king we serve, is it not, and his life we will save if there is a plot? Go then."

She watched him waddle off and disappear through the door into the darkness of the harem. She frowned. The woman from Tyre had been standing back in the shadows, but Gomer was sure even her sharp ears wouldn't have been able to catch the words that had been said.

The fear in her heart, planted by Nuri's words, was growing, and she closed her eyes against the sun. "Gods, O gods Tammuz, Ashtaroth, Ba'al, watch over my love, keep your hands extended over my adonai." The pulse in her throat beat violently as she struggled to keep back the tears, for the women must not suspect that she knew anything. But the thought of her lover dead . . . killed. . . . A picture flashed into her mind of his dead face staring blankly into hers, and she groaned softly and pushed it away. "No, No."

The woman from Tyre stood in the doorway and watched as the Samaritan turned toward Ashtaroth and knelt, her bright hair falling to the rooftop in a chaotic golden wave. She smiled to herself, sure that she knew what the two of them, the sorceress and her familiar, had been speaking about, for surely their dark powers were able to discover that something was going on. But the spells of Dagon, long known to her family, had been spoken over every whispered meeting with the others and over every scroll that she had written. No magic of Ashtaroth's would be able to ferret out their plans, and soon—*please Dagon, soon!*—the proud witch of Samaria would die as she deserved.

Renin listened to Nuri's stammering speech, his handsome young face misshapen by a furious frown. He didn't know that his fierce look was making Nuri even more nervous, and wouldn't have cared if he had known. He had nothing but contempt for eunuchs, and only the obvious intelligence of this harem master had obtained him the ear of the captain of the king's bodyguards.

"You suspect Gor?" He glowered down upon the little man, just over half his height, for the soldier's feet were encased in boots of iron meant to frighten everyone he stomped past. It was a whimsical invention of the former king Menahem, and his soldiers had hated it. Renin, however, found the boots useful in dealing with drunken servants and various other troublemakers, not to mention the nobles of Israel who were continually annoying his master. One flourish of the left foot and they would hobble away, learning the value of silence.

But Gor was another matter. Being the king's personal slave, he was accountable only to Pekahiah. "So the king's concubine sends a message to someone via the king's slave. That is certainly an unusual occurrence, yes?"

Nuri nodded, hating himself for his fear of this man. But ever since the soldiers of Nineveh had taken him away from his father's land, the sight of their curled beards and shining helmets had always filled him with despair. He had to admit, though, that the king's captain had never treated him with anything worse than disdain, and he was used to that from the highborn. "Master, th-there is more, but as I told the Great Lady I have no proof, only s-suspicions."

Renin looked away and saw through the window at the end of the hall that the sun was nearing midday. Gomer . . . the king's woman, the Great Lady. He remembered the day Pekahiah had brought her here, how he had felt sure that a goddess was approaching him. Pekahiah had stopped at the palace gate, where Renin had been standing on guard, and introduced him. "My dear and loyal friend and captain," he had been called. Renin remembered how he had flushed with embarrassment, a thing that he, a hardened soldier and a ladies' man, had never done before. She had smiled at him then, and ever since he had listened for her footsteps and gay laugh. He gladly performed guard duty for her when she wished to go to the temple behind the palace, and had personally supervised the arrival of the gifts Pekahiah had ordered for her from Nineveh. Gomer must not come to harm. Her beautiful face must never know the tears of grief she would shed should anything happen to their king. The two beings Renin worshiped in this world, Pekahiah and Gomer, must not be brought down by the plotting of mindless, chattering females who had too much time on their hands.

"I will watch," he said finally, and didn't see Nuri's relieved smile or hear his murmur of appreciation. He didn't even hear the eunuch running back down the hall. All he could hear in his mind's ear was the soft laugh of the king's woman.

TWENTY-TWO
"Here Am I; Send Me"

The people of the tiny village south of Shiloh were just as adept at ignoring him as the sophisticated people of Samaria, Hosea was discovering. He had stood in their market square now for three days, calling to them to listen to one sent from God, and they had hurried past him, their faces hidden, their ears closed to his hoarse pleas. Each night he had gone out of the gates discouraged, but each morning he had returned with new hope. So far not even one person had shown any interest in what he had to say.

Munching on his bread and cheese which he had bought at a market stall, Hosea pulled from his pocket the scroll that had been tapping against his thigh with every step. He knew it by heart, but he felt renewed courage each time he read it. Sitting under the doubtful shade of an ancient cedar tree which had lost most of its branches to time and weather, he unrolled the scroll and started to read it again.

"Isaiah ben Amoz, late the servant of Uzziah and now the servant of Elohim, writes to his friend Hosea." Hosea smiled at the opening, realizing now the excitement that had held Isaiah in its grip as he wrote that line. It had been almost ten years since the two had parted outside Jerusalem, and once Hosea had been able to send a letter with a caravan that was planning to stop at that city. No answer had come, and he had wondered whether Isaiah had finally gone abroad to seek his calling. Finally this letter had come, and Hosea had found his face wet with happy tears by the time he had finished reading it.

"It has been long since I received your letter, my friend, but I purposefully waited to answer until I had something to write about comparable to your own experience. Your wife has, I trust, since presented you with more children after your firstborn son." Always, at that point, Hosea had to close his eyes with pain, as the image of Gomer came to life in his mind and he saw her again as she had been the day she went away, angry, bitter, frustrated, yet so beautiful. But she had broken faith with him; she had trodden her marriage contract in the dust by becoming a lover of the king.

He remembered his first bewildered agony when Diblaim had come home from the market, weeping, to tell what had been passed on to him by the other merchants who had seen it happen. She had actually been worshiping the idol Tammuz, with her hair uncovered in a brazen invitation to any man who looked—and the king had looked. At first Hosea's hidden love had soured within him, and he had fled the city to journey alone through Israel. His messages then had been furious, angry ones, blasting his listeners who had broken faith with their God as Gomer had with him. How clearly he saw the parallel, and how bitterly did he grasp the enormity of what Israel had been doing to her God for hundreds of years. Mocking him, worshiping other gods when their fathers had sworn to only follow God, Israel was, to him, another Gomer. God's pain became his; God's frustration with a disobedient people became his; God's wrath became his.

Yet there was still something missing in his messages. Some vital ingredient that had once been a part of him had gone with Gomer, and his listeners could tell the difference. The children of Samaria were afraid of him now, and even his own three children didn't run to greet him as they once had. As each month had passed, Hosea had grown more and more morose and lonely, and even Shana's determined cheerfulness grated on his high-strung nerves. The gentleness in him was gone, but he sensed somehow that his lack was due to more than that.

Hosea opened his eyes and glanced up at the sun shining through the green lacework of leaves above his head. The joy he had known in each day, since his meeting with the Man in the desert of Moab, was also gone. All he cared about was being able to get to the next town. The first bitter reaction was long gone now as well, and he could usually think calmly about the past, accepting it as past and not hoping that Gomer would return. *She has shown herself for the woman she was,* he thought, *and I was a fool not to realize it before. I had enough warning, but I wanted to believe her a pure woman like her mother, like Rachel. I was a fool to love her and marry her, and I have paid indeed for my folly. I am a mockery to the people in*

Samaria, for while I call to them in the marketplace, my wife plays the whore with the king in the palace that looks down on me.

As if he saw Israel totally identified with Gomer, Hosea had stopped beseeching her to return to God. He now saw the full extent of her betrayal, and realized the utter impossibility of any reconciliation between God and Israel. The covenant between them had been broken centuries before, and all that remained now for Israel was her deserved punishment, spelled out by Moses so long ago. *Israel has broken the rules; she now must pay the price,* thought Hosea.

But always he had to stop there in his words and his mind, for always the question came: What if Gomer loses the protection of the king? What if she comes to the place where she, too, must pay the price for her adultery?

When that point in his thoughts came, Hosea always shied away hastily before the picture of Gomer's punishment could come: her lovely, graceful body stretched out against the rocks by the gate, blood pouring over her lifeless limbs, her golden eyes open and staring at the sun, while the stones that had brought her death lay heaped around her. Never, not even in his most bitter agony, had he been able to wish her that.

Hosea managed to turn away from his thoughts and started to read the letter again. "I have every assurance that the road along which you have been called will show you again and again the power and might of the God whom we both adore. And now I wish to tell you how, at last, I have heard his voice.

"My king died in wretchedness and poverty when the spring rains had passed their height, and I alone of all the court was there when he was buried. Even Jotham did not come, but I wasn't surprised. The son of the good Uzziah has already shown, in his neglect of his father, the contempt in which he holds our customs and our worship.

"With no desire to return to the palace and take up my duties there, after the burial I went to the Temple to pray, for my father was very ill at the time and I did not wish to go into the desert. I washed myself, I sacrificed a lamb to God, but the priest who performed for me made me angry in his indifference. So I left him and went to the Hekal, the Holy Place, to pray. But you haven't been there, my friend. You know from your knowledge of Moses' writings on the Tabernacle that the Hekal is where only true Israelites are allowed, where we can look upon the veil that separates us from the Debir, the Holy of Holies, where our God is present. The veil is beautifully woven, Hosea, like the silks from the east you sent me, but more precious is the thought that behind that veil, where the High Priest sets foot once a year, is the place for our God.

"There were no priests in the Hekal when I entered, it being the hour for the meal, and I was alone with the table of showbread and the lit candles. It was very quiet, for the noise from the streets cannot penetrate Solomon's thick walls. I knelt to pray, and know not how long I stayed that way. I was unhappy, for nothing had happened in the years since we met except that my people now hardly ever sacrifice to our God and never observe Shabbat. The feasts are a time for drunkenness and adultery, as you told me it is in Samaria. All this I prayed about, Hosea, and I was in deep anguish of soul. I saw the filth of our people, and I knew I was no better, for have I not often yearned after the prostitutes in the streets of David's city?

"I lifted my hands in prayer after these thoughts, to beg for cleansing, and I saw him. Hosea, I saw him! You say he was as a man, but I say he was to me as God, Elohim, the One above all others.

"He was seated on a throne that shone as the sun, but his own face was brighter. All about me were his seraphim. They crowded the Hekal to the walls, and they were singing a song that has not yet left my ears, so loud and ringing was their cry: *Qathosh, Qathosh Yewah— Qathosh Yewah!* I have written what I dare not speak: the Name of the One I saw. I have written the words of the song I dare not sing, for my life would flee from me.

"I fell full length on the Temple floor, and I felt as a woman's bloody rag before him. I cried, 'Woe is me, woe! For here is a man unclean in his mouth, living with people who have unclean mouths, and I have seen the King! I have seen my Adonai!' I thought I should die then, my friend, for what man can look upon our God and still live? But in his mercy he did not wipe me away from the face of the earth. His mighty hand that rested on his thigh instead beckoned to one of his fiery servants, who surely are a wonder in themselves! The servant came to me and placed a lump of burning flame inside my mouth and the pain seared through my whole body, yet I still lived. Did I dream, you ask, my friend? No, for the scars are still there. And the fiery one said to me, 'Behold! You have been touched by this, and your filth is as if it never was, for your sin is forgiven.'

"I was overcome, and near to fainting. But then I heard *his* voice, the one you say filled your whole being with joy. I know now what you meant, my friend! He said, 'Who will go for us?' And I cried as loud as I could with my burning lips, 'Here! Here am I! Send me!'

"He said more to me, the same as he said to you in the desert, how we were to speak in his Name the words of the covenant, and remind our people of the peril in which they stand unless they repent of their rebellion and return to him. But he said more, Hosea, which you have told me in your letter: that our people will not listen, that they will turn away even more from our God. And the end is near.

"Farewell, Hosea. I go to the court now, and will send this to Samaria with Jotham's messenger who has something for your king, Pekahiah. Keep well, my friend, and may God in his goodness bring us together in his own time.

"This scroll was written by the hand of Isaiah ben Amoz in the first year of Jotham king of Judea and the third year of Pekahiah king of Israel."

Hosea stood up and stretched himself, and once again the peace that always followed his reading of that letter came over him. His own life, since Gomer had left, had meant nothing to him, and even his eldest son was almost a stranger these days, for Shana and Diblaim had taken over the care of the children. But the knowledge that somewhere to the south there was another man like himself facing death and abuse in the Name of God gave him courage to go on. The joy might have died, the sense of a calling was often faint, but with Isaiah on the same road, he felt less alone.

Shaking the crumbs off his robe, and stuffing the scroll back into the pocket of his inner tunic, Hosea headed back to the village square.

TWENTY-THREE
Pekah's Rebellion

It wasn't until Hosea's second morning in Kedesh, near his own city of Dan, that he realized something was wrong. He had spent the last two months wandering north, and hadn't heard any news from Samaria for much longer than that. Therefore, it was with a shock that he realized that the soldiers in the barracks were preparing for war.

The marketplace was full of them, in their shining breastplates and high helmets, and they were all Gileadites from across the Jordan. He had asked one of the townsfolk what was going on, but had received a glare and an order to keep silent. However, being afraid for his family, he went to the captain, who was reviewing troops outside the walls, and asked him if there was going to be war.

"War, yes, and a just war it is, man," answered the captain, frowning. His face seemed familiar to Hosea, but it was so creased with wrinkles and so dark from the sun that it was impossible to tell either his age or his origin.

"Have you been in Samaria, captain?" asked Hosea, for a sudden alarm from deep within reached his thoughts, and he knew he must find out what was happening as soon as possible.

The captain grinned and spat to one side. His men, at ease for the moment and eating their rations, glanced over once in a while at their leader and the daring stranger who was questioning him. "Samaria!" growled the captain, his grin fading. "Yes, I've been in that flea-ridden village you call a city in these parts. The palace is a pig's sty, and yet—it's still a palace." He grinned, and his second-in-command choked back a laugh.

The warning signal inside Hosea was growing stronger, but as yet he had no idea what it meant. It made him more anxious than ever to make the captain divulge his intentions concerning this small army sprawled over the plain. A few tents were standing, but most had already been packed. Clearly, whatever action was being planned was about to be put into force.

"Please, captain, can you tell me—has the king ordered you to be in readiness for an attack from the north? Is the overlord in Assyria on his way to Israel?" Hosea tried to keep his voice calm, but the tightness in his neck muscles betrayed his tenseness. His back, too, was sweating, for the sun was hot and high above their heads, with no breeze to lessen its impact.

The captain took his time answering, gazing over his troops with a casual yet practiced eye. Hosea knew that here was no soft nobleman who had reached his rank by virtue of birth or wealth; he had probably come up through the ranks, fighting all the way. He had a greedy look to his face, and his teeth kept chomping on something in his mouth. Unwashed for several days, he yet kept his armor bright and his sword clean. Only the fact that Hosea had come right up to him while he was finishing his morning review of the men had gained him a hearing. Obviously, the captain was very busy with his plans, and had no time for scholars or anyone not directly involved with the army.

"I said it was a just war, man," he said finally, turning his back on Hosea. "War with Assyria would be a waste of time right now. That will have to come later; I'm not ready now. My war will be fought in Samaria where I, Pekah, was dishonorably put aside by that illegitimate son of Tyre! He shouldn't be on that throne any more than his impotent god should stand in the marketplace! I follow Ba'al, who has lived long in this land and demands the right of worship! So I go to dethrone that Tammuz and that Pekahiah, and you, scholar, you should go with me to shout to the people that my war is holy, my war is just!"

Pekah had turned back to Hosea, and had thrust his face too close for comfort, for he had recently been dining on onions. But Hosea was too disturbed to notice such things. The words that Pekah had said burned into his brain. A rebellion against Pekahiah! The thought flashed through his mind that now, if Pekah succeeded, Gomer would receive her just punishment, but he thrust it aside. This thing was much bigger than his own personal hurts.

Pekah grabbed his arm and squeezed it painfully, his huge paw hard as rock. "Are you with me, scholar? When I saw you coming and you asked me what I did, I knew that here was the man I needed to help me. You have the robes of a scribe. You know the history of our people and how we followed Ba'al for so long. Tell it to our people! Go before me now through the villages to Samaria, calling on all the faithful to help me rid the land of this false king and his false god!"

Hosea hadn't the strength to pull his arm away, but standing straight before the paunchy captain he said in a clear, ringing voice that caught the ears of all the men, "The god of Pekahiah is false, as you say. But the god you follow also is false, and will aid you no more than Pekahiah's god aids him. I come to you in the name of Israel's covenant God, who led us out of Egypt and into this land where he promised us abundance and peace! In return for his goodness we promised to worship *him,* but we turned to Ba'al! Remember, Pekah, remember that before Ba'al there was our own God! Let *him* be your guide now. Let him be the one to bring true worship back to your tribe of Manasseh and mine of Dan, and all the other tribes of Israel! Then I will gladly go before you through the land and proclaim your coming!"

Pekah's jaw had dropped so that his rotting teeth could be seen. An ugly and imposing sight at his best, right now he looked like an enraged bull unsure of his ground. He shook his huge head back and forth during the last part of Hosea's speech, but didn't move to stop him. Deeply religious himself, he was afraid of any man who spoke in the name of any god, although his loud confidence in front of his men had convinced them that he feared nothing. Now, losing face before the troops while this man ranted on, Pekah decided he had heard enough.

"You speak of another god, scholar," he growled. Hosea turned to face him, calm, with the old joy surging through him and giving him renewed strength.

"Yes, I speak of another god—the only God! And—"

"Enough!" roared the irate captain, his face going purple. "You have prattled enough of an enemy deity, and I wish to hear no more! My men are devoted to Ba'al, as am I myself, and you are a cancer in our sight! Be gone before I break the law that protects the seers and prophets and have you killed!"

Realizing that he could go no farther, Hosea turned and walked away. Soon the curve of the wall hid him from sight. Pekah watched until he was gone, and then turned to his lieutenant. "He has poisoned the air with his foul words, and Ba'al must be appeased before we start. Order two bulls to be burnt right away, so that our way may see success." The man nodded and left.

Alone now below the wall, his men finishing their last-minute preparations, Pekah brooded over his plans. He had waited two long years for this day, ever since the haughty and handsome king had threatened to have him, the general of the horses, beheaded for trying to incite rebellion among the royal troops. Hiding in the northern hills, recruiting men who hated the yoke of Assyria and only wanted to call themselves free Israel-ites again, he had trained and disciplined his men until they were, he felt, good enough to stand against Tiglath-pileser himself.

And now this scholar, at first harmless-looking, had brought into his camp an overlooked evil: the Name of that One who had conversed with Moses so long ago. The power of that god had long since died away, for Israel had been worshiping at other altars for hundreds of years since Solomon died, and nothing had yet happened to indicate that Israel would have to pay for breaking that covenant. No, Ba'al was the god who counted, and no prophet of any other god deserved even to live.

Pekah lifted his hand and beckoned to two of his best men who were loitering below beside his tent. Eager to serve, they bounded up the slight hill and bowed before him. "Yes, O King?" As far as his men were concerned, Pekah was as good as on the throne.

Pekah glanced up at the sun, squinting, his face thoughtful. "That man that was here——" he said softly, and they strained forward to hear him.

"We saw him and marked him well, adonai," muttered one, whose handsome face had been disfigured in a sword fight so that a white welt stood out starkly on his dusky cheek.

Pekah turned his back on his two men and closed his eyes, while his thin lips broadened out in an evil smile. "He has spoken against our god, has he not?"

The two men looked quickly at each other, their hearts beating fast. Here, at last, was a chance to serve Ba'al in a way few men would have: to kill the prophet of an enemy deity! Bowing to the impassive back, they ran swiftly over to the corral for their horses.

Hosea's heart was still beating furiously as he toiled up the last curve of the slope. To the west, the Great Sea glinted under the late afternoon sun, and to the east the roofs of Dan huddled back into the shade of evening. His headlong flight south after his encounter with Pekah had left him with no supplies and no hope of getting any for quite a while.

It seemed that the whole northern part of Israel was about to boil over into revolt, and he knew that no one in these parts would appreciate what he was doing, for he had made up his mind to warn Pekahiah.

Unable to see that God was behind either of these men, Hosea realized that the best thing for his family—and Gomer—was to keep Pekahiah on the throne. If Pekah won, then Israel would immediately cut off relations with Assyria, and it would not be long before the end came. Hosea had long dreaded the approaching judgment he knew would come if Israel didn't repent, and now it was almost breathing down his neck as he panted down the southbound trail. He had longed for Israel's retribution and yet, somehow, he flinched from the actual happening.

From his empty heart came the message that his old love was not dead, for suddenly grief surged up and he nearly cried aloud as he topped the rise. If Pekah won, what would happen to Gomer? He knew too well the fate meted out to the harem of a deposed king, and even if she *had* sinned against him he couldn't wish her that. No, he had to reach Samaria.

He caught a glimpse of a hut in the gloom ahead and sighed with relief. Surely, so far away from Kedesh and Dan, these people wouldn't have heard of the planned uprising! He staggered on, his stomach growling with every step, but just as the thought of a meal was becoming solid he heard horses galloping swiftly up the hill behind him. Instantly wary, he turned and sought a place to hide, but the nearest clump of trees was a good 150 paces away.

The riders were now nearly to him, and he heard a quick yell tear from the throat of one of the riders. "There he is!"

Hosea caught a flash of burnished iron as a spear flew

straight at him, and he ducked sideways. He felt the cold metal tear through his side, and a wash of hot pain flooded his body. He fell to the ground and darkness closed in.

TWENTY-FOUR
Death in the Night

The bedroom was in darkness, but Gomer could see faintly the profile of her lover as he lay next to her. For some reason, he was unable to sleep tonight, and she was being as still as she could so that she wouldn't disturb him. It had been a wonderful evening, and there had been a desperation in his hands that had excited and bewildered her at the same time. And now, when he should have gone right off to sleep, he was lying on his back gazing into the sultry darkness, his fingers restlessly pulling at the cover.

Suddenly, with a sigh, Pekahiah rolled over to face her. "Gomer?" he whispered, and she smiled. She reached out her arms and drew him near, and he laid his curly head upon her shoulder.

"Pekahiah, Pekahiah," she murmured, stroking his hair soothingly, "what keeps you awake, my beloved?"

"I—don't know. There's something in the air, and I can't figure out what it is." His strong arm was around her, holding her tightly against him, as if he needed the reassurance of her closeness.

"Has your council been making demands again?"

"No. In fact, half of my council wasn't here today, and that's partly what's been worrying me. Where have they gone? And Renin—he came and told me that a great number of my troops suddenly broke camp last night, and have left no trace of where they went."

Gomer felt hot fear flush through her heart, but she tried to speak calmly for his sake. "Maybe they just wanted to go home to their families, beloved," she answered, running her fingers across his face in a soft caress.

Pekahiah said nothing for a moment, then suddenly sat up and looked down at her. Her hair shone even in the darkness as it spread out on her pillow, and her dark eyes were intriguing pools in her pale face. The worry in his mind left before a rush of love for her, and the deep feeling shook him. He had to look away, so that she wouldn't catch the glint of tears in his eyes. "Gomer," he said brokenly, when he could trust his voice again, "if—if something should happen to me, would—would your husband take you back? Would he take care of you?"

Gomer was shocked, and clutched the cover to her face. "Why—why do you talk like that, Pekahiah?" she cried.

He looked at her again, and she saw the drawn lines around his mouth, as if he was in pain. "I—I must. We both know what a rebellious people Israel has always been, and that kings must expect and be prepared for civil wars. You aren't part of my harem, really, because I have kept you apart, but—if I should be killed, the usurper wouldn't realize your position. And I was just hoping that perhaps if you escaped the palace and went back home—"

Gomer raised herself up onto her elbow, tears coursing down her cheeks. "Please, please, my love, you mustn't talk like this! I will never leave you, not even if death faced me for staying. And—and I couldn't leave, for death faces me if I return to my family. To them I'm a whore. My father called me that many years ago, and I couldn't bear to hear it again."

"I know," he said gently, laying his hand against her wet cheek. "The penalty is stoning—a terrible death. How could supposedly civilized people do such a thing?"

She thought for a moment and then answered, "My adonai, if Renin, your sworn servant, broke his vows to you and rebelled, what would his penalty be if you defeated him?"

"Why, he'd be beheaded, of course, and the parts of his body sent to every corner of my kingdom as a warning."

"All right. Well, I've learned in my reading this past year that Israel made a covenant with the God of Moses hundreds of years ago, and part of that covenant was a promise to wipe out evil in the camp. Whores were a part of that evil, my beloved. And for love of you, I am a whore; I have broken that covenant with God." She was smiling, but her eyes were worried.

"Pah! A powerless god!" Pekahiah snorted in feigned disgust, but his mind was filled with fear—for her, and for Israel. Was this god, indeed once so powerful, as dead as he had seemed these past years? "Ba'al held this land before that god came, and Ashtaroth holds it now. She sees you not as a whore, but as a loving daughter. Did not Tammuz bring us together?"

Gomer lay back on her pillow. She believed him; she wanted so much for him to be right! But his questions had brought Hosea's face before her again, he whom she had managed so long to forget. Wasn't that Hosea's message—the breaking of the old covenant, and the punishments that must surely follow? They were written in the last book of Moses—terrible, powerful curses. What if Hosea should be right?

Pekahiah had lain back onto the pillows, his eyes closed, and even as Gomer glanced down at him she heard a soft snore. He had fallen into the quick sleep of the soldier, and all his fears and worries were forgotten. *Men,* she thought with a gentle smile, as she pulled the cover over him so that he wouldn't get chilled. *They talk out their troubles and then go to sleep, leaving us awake and worrying!* She snuggled down beside him and closed her eyes, and soon was asleep herself.

Gomer's eyes were open and she was staring into the darkness, trying to remember what noise it was that had awakened her. Had it been the quiet closing of their door?

Then she saw it—a dark shape coming closer to Pekahiah's side of the bed, a shape that was hump-backed and terrifying in its stealth. For a second she lay there, stunned, sure that she was dreaming, but then she saw the glint of metal as a knife appeared in the dark hand.

She flung herself across Pekahiah's still form with a sharp scream, and the figure stopped, startled. Then with a snarl, it sprang forward, knife uplifted and ready to strike.

Pekahiah woke up when Gomer's cry reached into

his dreams, and with an oath he grabbed her and rolled to the other side of the bed. Her hair over her face, Gomer twisted her neck to look back and saw the knife stuck in a pillow, and the assassin frantically trying to free it. But by then Pekahiah had his sword, and he slashed out into the darkness.

Gomer was on her feet and running around the bed when she heard the thump of a falling body. She froze, fear like a cold shroud around her body. Who had it been? Was her lover lying dead on the floor?

"Gomer, light the lamp." Relief flooded through her and she almost laughed in her nervous hysteria, but she calmed herself and went for the lamp. She lit it with a flint that lay beside it and carried it back to Pekahiah.

The king stood over a body, his sword dripping blood onto the Persian carpet, his naked body covered with a fine sheen of sweat. Trembling, she handed him the lamp, and he held it down to the floor. "Gor," he said shortly, his voice expressionless. The hunchback lay twisted grotesquely on the carpet, his eyes still wide open in dead fear.

Gomer slowly walked over to the chair that held her silken robe. She slipped into it and looked back. Pekahiah was cleaning his sword with a length of linen that had been left in the room, meant to be a new mantle for her. His face was stern and old, his eyes bleak. He glanced over at her. "He would not do this alone."

Gomer gulped and answered faintly, "No."

They both heard screams then from the harem across the hall, the harsh masculine shouts, and someone's high-pitched death cry. Stunned into motionless statues for a second, they merely looked at each other. Then the scramble of heavy feet outside the door shocked Pekahiah into action, and he grabbed for his shield. "Stay behind me!" he snapped. She ran over to him.

Just as she reached Pekahiah's back, the door to the chamber was flung open. A huge soldier stood there, his arm and sword covered with blood, malicious triumph on his face. Pekahiah stood very straight, his eyes blazing with scorn as he sneered, "Pekah the troublemaker returns!"

Pekah stepped up the stairs into the room. Gomer could see over her lover's shoulder that the hall was crowded with women and soldiers, and the women were singing! She recognized, in her fear, the face of the wife from Tyre, and the hatred in that woman's eyes made her blood run cold.

But she had no more time to look, for Pekahiah had stepped forward to engage the rebel in battle. Their long swords arched through the air, and the clanging of the metal was a terrible sound. Suddenly a great cheer went up in the hall, where the soldiers and harem women were watching, for Pekahiah had staggered and slipped in Gor's blood. In an instant, Pekah's sword sliced downward, and Gomer's lover lay gasping his life away at her feet.

"Gods, O gods, no, NO!" The harsh unreal scream tore at her throat, and she threw herself down upon her king as Pekah's sword went up again to cut off the king's head. She clung to Pekahiah's body, his blood pouring over her arms, and looked into his eyes. They were glazing over, but he recognized her, and out of his agony and fear, he whispered to her. "Beloved . . ."

His head fell back onto her arm, and he went limp.

Rough hands were pulling her away, and she didn't have the strength to cling to him any longer. He was dead, her beloved was dead. Why hadn't she died too?

A hard hand grabbed her neck, and she found herself looking into a pair of hard, cruel eyes. "So this is the queen of the harem, and we know who gets the queen, don't we, men?" Loud cheers erupted from the hall, where each soldier had already picked his woman. The women who had plotted and planned for this night found themselves finally in the arms of men who noticed their charms and were delighted with them. They could see Gomer's face as Pekah's hands took liberties, and they screamed with laughter as their captors bore them off into the darkened rooms.

Gomer fought him off, and he was surprised at her strength. *Nuri,* she thought desperately, *where is Nuri? He'll help me. What have they done with Nuri?* Tearing her robe in her quick dash for the door, she ran down the steps and into the harem across the hall. She heard heavy footsteps behind her and loud curses, and knew Pekah was following. But fear lent wings to her swift feet, and she ran through the harem to the terrace. *I'll jump off,* she thought. *I'll jump into the hay mound near the stables, but where's Nuri?*

Then she saw him—what was left of him. He was staring at her from across the terrace, his head stuck on top of a spear that had been shoved into the ground beside Ashtaroth's statue. She saw, and she screamed. The women must have torn him to pieces in their blood lust and fury, and the evidence of their hate was strewn all over.

There was no escape from the terrace, as she saw now, for soldiers were climbing up ladders and coming toward her. This must have been their entrance point, she realized now, for they knew that the harem would welcome them. *A good plan,* she thought dully.

Then Pekah caught up to her, and the fury on his face was the ultimate horror of this night of horrors. She clutched her torn robe to her in an absurd gesture of defiance, and her bloodsoaked hair streamed around her as she tried to stare him down.

"Whore," he breathed, desire and fury struggling for mastery of his mind, and he grabbed at her shoulder. She pulled away, but he caught her again and threw her down to the floor. She felt his heavy boots kick at her legs and then, mercifully, she fainted.

TWENTY-FIVE
Exile

Pekah sprawled on the throne, his fat legs spread apart, his face greasy from the meat he had been chomping as he waited for the prisoners to arrive. Three days ago he had invaded Samaria, and he had been welcomed with open arms. The Israelites saw in him a man who would free them from the Assyrian yoke, a man who jeered at the awesome Tiglath-pileser and spat at his ambassadors. All the Assyrian soldiers had fled back to their own lands, except for those palace guards whom Pekah had managed to capture. Unwilling to kill them outright, Pekah had spent the three days devising a means of humiliation that would make them the laughingstock of the countryside. He had finally thought of an idea this morning, and had sent for them.

They came toward him slowly, their legs sore after three days of being cramped into a small storage room. There were six soldiers and one woman, and they were dressed in sackcloth that hung in tatters to their knees.

The woman's hair was dirty and tangled, her face covered with filth except where the tears had made white channels through the grime. They all stood straight, however, and looked at the man on the throne with scorn. He sensed it, and clenched his teeth in rage. *Still haughty, were they? Still thinking of the difference between himself and their handsome king? Let them think it—they'll regret it soon enough!* He smiled to himself, thinking of the fury of the Assyrian overlord when he heard of the insult done to his finest soldiers.

"Closer," he growled, and his soldiers prodded the prisoners with the butt end of their spears until they were only a few feet away from the throne.

"Kneel," he ordered gruffly, and they knelt stiffly, unwillingly, their faces angry. He grinned at them, picking his teeth with his knife.

"Pekahiah is dead," he said brutally, and watched with delight as the woman's face paled and she moaned. The captain of the soldiers, Renin, merely glared. He was a tough one, this Assyrian, and certainly needed humbling.

The woman caught his eye again, for she had closed her eyes against her tears. She had been a failure that night, he thought, and wondered what Pekahiah had seen in her. She was much too thin for his taste; he preferred the plump, short ones. And she had fainted on him, so that his men had missed the pleasure of her screaming as he violated her. Oh well, the rest of the women certainly made up for her!

Pekah stood up and sauntered forward, twirling his knife. "I have decided what I'm going to do with you," he began, and enjoyed the suspense in their attitudes. "No, I won't kill you. I'm sending you back to Assyria where you belong." He saw the blaze of hope and relief in Renin's eyes, and laughed aloud. "That is, if you can get there. You'll go dressed just as you are now, no shoes, no horses, no food, no guide. And *if* you reach Nineveh, you can give your king my compliments, and tell him that I'll be glad to put his face in the dust any day he pleases."

His men were laughing, the townspeople were cheering, but the prisoners looked at each other in despair. It was a journey of hundreds of miles to Nineveh, through mountains infested with bandits and through desert crawling with scorpions and caravan robbers. Renin wasn't even sure he could remember the way there, for it had been almost three years since he followed his master into Israel. Now Pekahiah was dead! His eyes met Gomer's and he whispered, "Courage." It was a wonder, but she managed to smile back at him. He didn't care that she was filthy and covered with the crusted blood of her lover. She was his goddess, and for her he'd find the way back home.

The narrow streets of Samaria were lined with jeering crowds as the prisoners made their way to the eastern gate. Gomer, her back straight and her eyes fixed on Renin's head before her, scarcely heard the mockery or felt the spit that landed on her face. She knew the people recognized her and were delighted with her disgrace, and she was ashamed, for she knew her father and her husband would bear the brunt of the laughter. Were they here now, watching her? She doubted it, and she was right. Diblaim had shut himself up in his room, and Hosea—no one seemed to know where Hosea was.

Finally they reached the eastern gate, and Gomer risked a look at her old home. Someone was huddled on the roof, and suddenly the years she had spent there rushed back and she nearly cried out in her agony. The punishment she had borne then was as nothing to the exile into which she was now being sent, for her lover was dead, and there was no pain in the world equal to her pain.

The figure on the roof suddenly leaned over and waved to her. It was Shana, her gray hair cut short in mourning, her gray face covered with grief. Yet she waved as she saw her daughter's face raised to her, and she saw her daughter try to lift her bound hands in reply. They hadn't seen each other for two years and they had parted in anger, yet the mother's love in Shana forgot all that Gomer had done, and she reached down her hands as if to lift Gomer to herself.

Gomer saw the gesture, and her eyes were blinded with tears. *Imma,* she whispered to herself, *Imma.*

Then they were outside the gate, and Pekah's men were untying their bonds. Laughing, the conquerors pushed the conquered away from the wall and went inside as the gates swung shut. The small group huddled together under the shelter of the walls for a moment, unsure and afraid. Then Renin took command, his young and handsome face quite stern as he barked, "Into file!"

Instinctively his men obeyed him, but Gomer looked confused. He stood over her, wishing he could banish that agony from her beautiful eyes that once had laughed as the sun. "Great Lady," he said, as she waited for him to tell her what to do, "our master asked me barely a week ago to watch over you, if—if anything should happen to him. I will keep that promise. Lady, we will make it to Nineveh, and you must not be afraid."

He sounded so stiff and official that Gomer was amused even in her grief. She managed a smile at him, and he felt his heart glow. "Thank you, Renin," she said softly, and he bowed to her and went to the head of the small column.

"Forward!" he barked, and they moved off down the slope. The lone watcher on the roof raised her trembling hand in a blessing, and her soft lips moved in a beseeching prayer for their safety. *"And let her return, Adonai. Let her return."*

They were weary, but they didn't dare stop near a town. So Renin made camp the second night on top of a hill and went off to hunt for meat. Gomer huddled close to the fire, unaware that barely fifty yards away a tiny hut nestled among the trees. The old couple inside had seen them and had doused their lamp, praying that they would not notice the hut. The man who lay on the mat by the fire, the man they had found bleeding and nearly dead, slept soundly, unaware of his hosts' fears. He was still too feverish to understand what was happening around him, anyway.

The next morning the exiles left, fresh meat on their backs, and the old couple breathed easier again. They watched the men and woman shuffle down the hill, wondered briefly who they were, and then forgot them, for the man on the pallet was tossing again in his pain.

Gomer was unaware of where she was. All she knew was that each step was taking her farther away from her lover, and the pain in her breast knew only one cry as she walked, a cry that held all her sorrow and agony and that dinned through her mind ceaselessly. *Pekahiah,* she moaned, *Pekahiah, oh, my beloved, will you never again reach out your hand to me?*

PART III
TIGLATH-PILESER

TWENTY-SIX
Nineveh

The dog raised his huge, hairy head and watched his master as he paced back and forth on the balcony. Lying there in the corner, panting in the dry heat of the day, he obviously thought that his human master was worse than foolish for wanting to move in such pressing weather. But the man paid no attention to the question in the animal's large brown eyes as his feet took him back and forth across the stones.

He was a huge man, as his dog was a huge dog and as his favorite horse topped the rest of his stables by two hands. Taller than the soldiers he commanded, broad through the shoulders and covered with thick muscles, he was an imposing sight, and fear came to the heart of the most foolhardy of his subjects when he was seen on the streets of his cities. His face was square, a powerful face that radiated power and competence. The square beard, trademark of all Assyrian soldiers, jutted out from his massive chin and put a scowl on a face that was otherwise expressionless. No woman would have called him handsome, but she might have been attracted by the virility of his manner and the supple spring of his walk, for though he was nearing fifty he could ride farther and faster than any youngster in the ranks. He was Tukulti-apil-esharra, the favored of the son of Esharra, Ninib of the strong hands. He was the third overlord of Assyria to take the title, putting aside forever his family name of Pul. He would be known on statues and pillars in every land he had conquered as Tiglath-pileser.

He had clawed his way up through the ranks until he had reached the top administrative post of the empire, and then he had brought the army to Nineveh and deposed the old king who was frittering away his lands with bargains and promises. From being an unknown of one of the old royal families, he had become king, taking the throne for himself and thrusting the Sargonids into exile. He had made the name of Assyria feared once more from the shores of the Great Sea to the mountains of far-east India, and those who were not directly under his rule paid tribute to be left alone. They were his greatest worry, those small countries who gave him money and then schemed to destroy him, for they could undo the work of his whole life with one well-aimed knife——if their man got past his guards.

This palace he had built for himself ten years before was meant to be unscalable, and none could enter it save past the towers to the west, where twenty top soldiers stood night and day at full alert. Kalakh was his dream in stone, a huge architectural altar to Ninib, as his whole empire was an altar for that god. The double colonnade that ran the whole front length of the palace within the protecting walls drew attention to the many statues around the pillars, held up by blood-stained stones. These were the gods of Assyria, the pantheon that had ruled Nineveh since time began, and they had blessed this man who called upon their ancient and powerful names. Had they not been neglected in the previous reigns, when a foreign god from the west had demanded recognition through his prophet? This king slaughtered bulls for them under the colonnade, and sprinkled incense in his gardens to please their nostrils. And they had indeed rewarded him.

But new problems always arise to plague rulers just as they think that finally their work is done, and a problem had been brought to Tiglath-pileser that morning. He had left the small countries to the southeast alone now for years, for his friend and companion-in-arms, Pekahiah, was in charge in Samaria. They had once been inseparable, since the day Menahem had sent his son to the court of Nineveh as a sign of trust and goodwill between the two countries. Pekahiah, handsome, eager to please, astute and full of common sense, had found a place beside the king-general right away—first as his cupbearer, that he might learn the arts of state affairs, and then as his shield-bearer, that he might learn the arts of war. But what good had all that training done him when treachery struck? Far from being grief-stricken at the news of Pekahiah's death, great anger and rage filled the king, and he vowed to bring down Pekah when next he took his army south.

Now, this morning, he had heard things that made him wonder if Pekah was not eager for a confrontation. He had treated the Assyrian troops at the border of Syria badly enough, attacking without provocation six months ago and sending them packing off to Nineveh without their armor. That his men should be treated so was galling enough for the proud king, but to do as he had done with Pekahiah's picked bodyguard was even worse. It was four months since Pekah had exiled them from Samaria, and they and that woman of Pekahiah's had spent all that time trekking to Nineveh. They had then been sent down the River Tigris on one of the king's royal barges to reach him here at Kalakh, but a rider had raced ahead by land to inform the king of what had happened. The news had made Tiglath-pileser pace his balcony, much to the consternation of his favorite hound.

Stopping a moment to rub the erect ears, the king grinned down into his dog's adoring eyes. "Ah, no questions from you, old man! You love and you obey, and I never have a problem with you. No! But these others!"

The dog jumped up and whined, unsure, for the harsh note in his master's voice sounded accusing. But the king walked away, frowning deeply, his hands clasped behind his back. He wore only a brown shift, clasped by a gold belt sent to him by the Pharoah of Egypt. These two kings held the world between them, and maintained an uneasy balance of power along the shores of the Great Sea. Tiglath-pileser wondered for a moment if the Pharoah was backing Pekah, and then dismissed it. His agents had seen no Egyptian gold in the marketplace of Samaria. It was more likely that Pekah was a braggart and a power-mad rebel, impulsive and reactive, intent on righting what he considered to be old wrongs. If so, then he could be easily dealt with at some future date. But for now, he had to take care of the people who had been so cruelly handled by the usurper.

A discreet knock came at the door, and the king growled, "Enter." A short dark servant, his large black eyes round with fear, pushed open the door and bowed to his master.

"O King, those who were sent from Nineveh are here."

"Bring them in. No, wait. Take them fresh clothes and let them bathe. i hear one is a woman. Let her not be more shamed than she has already been."

"I hear and obey, O King." The door closed quickly behind the retreating form of the trembling Sumerian slave, and the king grinned to himself and shook his head. They were so afraid of him! And it was so strange, because he only executed for disobedience. As long as they obeyed . . .

A sudden great loneliness fell over the king, and he strode back out onto the balcony and stared at the sun. They were all afraid of him, even the priests and priestesses, since he had ordered one killed for refusing to return to the old ways. Only his dog and his horse welcomed him with any show of affection since Pekahiah had gone away to rule his country. And now this one friend, the only one who had ever heard the secrets of his soul, had been sent to dwell in the shades.

I am too old to ever have another friend, he thought, *nor would I choose to be close to any of my weak-kneed counselors. Even the women fear me, and the nights I spend in Ishtar's temple have no joy. I am a great man, a king, and yet the toiler in my fields is happier than I, for he can trust his family and those about him. I can trust no one since Pekahiah is now gone.*

Another knock on the door roused him from his gloom, and he called out, "Enter!"

The door opened, and the Sumerian was in the room again, bobbing his shaved head several times as he said, "Here they are, O King, as you commanded." Six soldiers marched into the room in single file. He knew they were soldiers although they wore no armor, for they marched the way his men marched, and their faces wore the same proud, fierce look his men wore. They lined up before him and saluted, eyes straight ahead, fists on chests.

Tiglath-pileser returned their salute, his face grim with pride. These men had walked hundreds of miles to reach him. They had starved and fought bandits and desert dogs. Yet they still stood tall and straight as true sons of Ashur should.

He walked to the captain, and put his hands on the young man's shoulders. "Renin, welcome home. You have done well."

His face flushed, Renin smiled at his general. "I would I had done better, adonai. Then our friend would still be alive today."

"Do not question the gods, Renin. But have no fear. Pekah will pay for his crime, and you will be there."

"I ask nothing more, O King," the captain answered through clenched teeth, his handsome face growing dark with suppressed anger.

"Good," approved the general. He looked at the door, just as his chief wife came through it leading a woman. "Ishanath, you have Pekahiah's woman with you?"

"Yes, adonai," Ishanath answered, her black face sullen with jealousy. She was lovely when she was happy, and her long dark tresses and lithe body had made the king very glad—twenty years ago. But now every time a new woman entered the harem or the temple, Ishanath went into seclusion for a week and cried.

She led Gomer to Tiglath-pileser and stepped back, angered at the gleam in his eyes. She had dressed the Samaritan woman in a soft Persian blue silk dress that clung to her form and swept the floor at her feet. Gomer's long bright hair had been freshly washed and combed, and it hung below her waist in rippling waves.

Renin stood there, unable to move, taking in her loveliness, his eyes worshiping her as his heart longed for her. But then he, too, saw the king's glance, and knew a quick, deep sorrow. He was only a captain, and such a goddess was only for the gods.

"So you are the woman my friend wrote to me about, his sun, moon, and stars." Tiglath-pileser's voice had grown soft, and he meant to woo her with it, but she merely looked at him.

Gomer was still like a lifeless doll that can be led, but that cannot feel. The long trip had made her too thin and had left her deeply tanned and weary. The hot, soothing bath, the skilled fingers of the masseuse, the careful attentions of the dressmaker and the hairdresser—none of this had managed to dispel the resignation and sorrow of her manner.

She heard what the king said, but could not smile. Instead, a large tear rolled down her cheek as she said clearly, "Pekahiah is dead." It was the only thought her mind had known since that awful day.

The king set his jaw. "Yes, my friend has been most foully murdered. But the man will pay—have no fear. And now"—he turned to the soldiers—"for your valor, you will join my personal guard, and you, Renin, will wear the red stripe that denotes bravery, and you will be my captain of the chamber guards." Waving aside their stammered gratitude, he went on, "Go to the citadel now, and receive your armor. My servant will show you the way. Undoubtedly he is trembling outside," he added dryly.

The soldiers saluted and marched out, their faces red with pleasure.

Tiglath-pileser then nodded to his chief wife to go, but Ishanath stood her ground with the stubbornness born of desperation. "Adonai, do you not wish this woman to be put in the kitchens? After all, she is but a peasant from—"

"Enough," growled the king. She took one more look at his outthrust jaw and fled, closing the door behind her.

Gomer stood alone in the middle of the room, the sun's rays turning her long hair into a shimmering halo about her too-slender figure. The king looked long at her, and felt the flush of youth in his veins for the first time in many a year. He walked over and stood before her, and met her empty gaze. "Now, I want you to tell me what happened—that night." When she flinched and looked away, he added, "You must. You were the only eyewitness, I hear. Remember, Pekahiah was my friend, my companion-in-arms, and what has killed him has also wounded me. But first, tell me how you came to know him."

She told him the whole story in a low toneless voice, her hands hanging loosely by her side. When she had finished her tale, the king nodded several times. "You remember well."

"Every detail of that night is burned into my heart forever," she answered. He noticed she didn't address him as either "adonai" or "king," and he understood. For her, Pekahiah would always be the only king.

"You loved him well and brought him happiness, and for that you have my eternal gratitude," he said. He pursed his lips in thought, and then continued, "But now, Gomer, you must still live, and I have it in mind that you should enter my harem. There you shall have peace and companionship, no labor at all, and someday, when I send for you, you can know the joys of the body again."

She turned her head away from his gaze, and shame colored her face. "Was not my lover your friend? Must you treat me like the spoils of war?"

He grinned, glad to see that her spirit was still unbroken in spite of the shocked state in which she moved about. "But didn't you come to Pekahiah from another man? Surely you don't expect me to believe that you're anything else than what you seem, a woman devoted to the pleasures of men!"

Anger made her empty eyes flash. For the first time since Pekahiah's death, emotion flooded her heart. "You speak like a whoremaster," she spat at him.

He frowned. "Watch how you speak to me," he warned. "I am the king."

She lifted her chin, not caring what happened to her now. "Does that give you the right to insult your friend's beloved?"

He turned to the balcony, his hands lifted in surrender. "All right—I am sorry. You have no wish to be one of my women, although many women are eager to have that privilege. You tell me that you and Pekahiah dedicated your love to Ashtaroth, whom we call here Ishtar. By the way, how came you to speak our tongue?"

"A scribe taught me in Pekahiah's palace," she answered. Her large, lovely eyes had dulled again, the momentary anger past. *What a woman she must have been when she was happy,* thought the king, and found himself envying his dead friend.

"You speak it well," he answered, but his thoughts were busy with another solution. "How is this, then, beloved of my friend? You have been dedicated to Ishtar in love. Will you enter her temple as a priestess?"

She shrugged. "Why not? I have nothing to live for, so it would be good to give my days to the goddess who brought me love once."

He was looking at her very intently now, but she seemed not to notice. "So you will serve Ishtar! Yes, you have the look of one who belongs to a goddess, or a god. Ishtar will be pleased!" He smiled into his beard.

It would have been better for Gomer if she had remembered what Pekahiah had told her, that unlike Israel and Judea, Assyria and Sumer regarded their kings as the sons of the gods.

TWENTY-SEVEN
Ishtar

Dominating the quiet park which surrounded it, the temple of Ishtar rose to the skies like a huge, squat, round arm, its roofs reaching up like fingers to the clouds. Designed by an imaginative Greek who hated pillars and friezes, the temple was like nothing else the world had ever seen, or would see again. Built with white limestone imported over the desert from Egypt at great cost, it had been molded with love and care into the marvel it was in Tiglath-pileser's reign. He had rewarded the Greek handsomely, sure that now the Lady Ishtar would be pleased, as she evidently had been. The priestess' lands were flourishing, as year after year bumper crops were gathered into the granaries. Fortunate omens were consistently forthcoming from the priestess' mouth during her trances when the goddess visited her. All in all, Tiglath-pileser felt he had done well by the Lady, and she had returned in kind.

Gomer, having read the creation accounts of Assyria

in her afternoons with Pekahiah's scribes, knew all about the Lady, and when she first walked under the lofty green cypresses that were sacred, she felt that she had come at last to a harbor and refuge. Here would be peace and contentment; so the whispering breeze promised her as it played with the leaves overhead. Here her heart would find ease and, maybe, joy again. Surely the Lady had been good to her in Samaria when she brought her to her lover, and now she seemed to promise everlasting comfort in her holy place.

Gomer wore a simple white shift, for she was to be trained as a novitiate for the next few months. The priestess, when at first confronted with the king's order to admit this foreign woman to her group of sacred women, balked in anger. Was not this one defiled already? Had she not lain with a man, nay, maybe several men? She was unfit for divine servitude.

The king stood tall and commanding before her in her presence chamber, and the priestess found her objections fading into a whisper. She was old and ugly, her nose disfigured with warts; and Gomer, standing beside the huge king, looking wistful and forlorn, roused the jealousy that lay just below the priestess' polite surface. But the look in the king's eye warned her to silence, in spite of her obviously excellent reasons.

"You shall admit her."

There was a scornful pause. "Aye, adonai, but—"

"She was dedicated to Ishtar in her own country by my friend. Is it not fitting that she continue in the same service here?"

The priestess was not stupid. She sensed immediately what Tiglath-pileser meant, although she could see

Gomer's bewilderment. She told the Samaritan to go into the gardens, and then had a private conversation with the king.

So it was that Gomer was walking among the trees, drawing strength from their stolid, ancient life, forgetting her puzzlement because of the king's words in her new-found peace. The Lady might be savage and bloodthirsty with her enemies, but to her own she was kind and protective, and Gomer felt grateful for her guardianship. "Blessed be the Lady," she murmured, and the breeze echoed her soft sigh.

She saw the priestess walking out to her from the back door of the temple, and braced herself for she knew not what. But the old woman's first words were mild. "The king is gone—Ishtar protect and keep him. I will place you among the novitiates, and as you are already wearing their robe you may join them immediately at their supper. I will not see you again, except at the evening rites, until the day you join our sisterhood. You understand—you won't be a priestess like myself, for only the nobility may attain such an honor. But you will be among the sacred maidens to do the will of Ishtar, which is to love and serve men."

Gomer nodded, her eyes still dreamy from her walk. "It is good to serve others," she said, and wondered at the amusement in the other woman's eyes. "I have served all my life. First my parents, then my husband and children, then my king." She could speak unemotionally, for the part of her that had once belonged to her father's household was long dead. Even her love for Pekahiah was becoming a memory of unreality, filled with dreams and light. She was remote from all that had once touched her and wanted to keep it that way, for only then could her eyes forget their weeping and her heart its sorrow.

The priestess said quietly, "Service wears many guises. Ishtar is your whole world now, and disobedience to her means death by fire."

Gomer frowned slightly. "Why should I disobey? We have priests and priestesses in my land, and they took care of the poor and orphans—I think. At least, they were supposed to do that. I mean—or did we have priestesses? No, they were—they belonged to the evil one. My head—it hurts."

The priestess caught Gomer as she tottered and sank to the ground. Her old eyes glared at the white face as her clawlike hands grasped the slumped shoulders. The younger woman's obvious weakness exasperated her, and she slapped the white cheeks hard until the golden eyes opened.

"What . . . where am I?"

"You know where—the temple. Now sit up. I'm much too old to be supporting a great weight like you. What's wrong—the sun too hot for you?" She eased Gomer against a tree trunk, and then knelt beside her. *Lady help us,* she thought, *all we need is a sick one.*

"I lost my baby."

"What?" The priestess thought the girl was rambling again.

Gomer kept her unfocused eyes on the grass. The fragile peace of a few moments ago was gone, and she was remembering the agony of the desert crossing. "I lost my baby," she murmured, and the old woman bent over to hear. "I didn't tell Renin—he had enough to worry about. But the pains were cutting me in half as I walked, and the sun was so hot. I went behind some rocks when we stopped for the night."

The priestess shuddered, picturing the scene. The lonely girl with no one to help her, vomiting, moaning, seeing her own blood spread over the sand as she lay there, and finally the last shudder when the tiny formed shape came out.

No wonder the girl was so thin and weak. Lovely she might be, but no one who had just walked across the mountain and desert and managed to make it to Nineveh should faint the first time she came to a decent quiet oasis. She should have died on the road.

Gomer leaned her head back against the rough bark, hardly remembering the words she had just said. It was all so confusing, and she still wondered if the last couple of days were just one of the many dreams she had had in the desert nights. Renin had always awakened her from them, and her face would be streaked with tears. After the first month, when she lost Pekahiah's child, the dreams had been cruel, and she had feared sleep. Now this dream seemed quiet and peaceful, but the woman beside her hated her. She could sense it, and she was still afraid. She almost wished she had accepted the king's offer to join his harem. But he wasn't the king; Pekahiah was . . . *Pekahiah, Pekahiah, where are you? My beloved!*

She moaned, and opened her eyes to see the priestess peering into her face. She shuddered at the malice in those bleary eyes and turned away. *Gods, O gods, help me!*

"Are you strong enough to stand up and come to your meal now?" The quiet voice reached her mind, whirling in weak confusion. She looked up to see the priestess standing already, her gnarled hand stretched down to help.

"Yes—yes, I'll come."

She went inside the door and heard it shut behind her. For some reason, a nameless fear took hold of her heart.

TWENTY-EIGHT
Marriage of the Gods

The desert flowers were starting to bloom, and the first rain of the season had come and filled the Tigris once more with life-giving water. The birds and animals were mating in the fields around the farms. The inhabitants of Nineveh saw all these signs and rejoiced, for these meant that any day now the priests would proclaim the *akitû*—the festival that heralded the arrival of a new year.

Soon the farmer would sow his crop and the merchant would send out his first caravan. But first the gods must give their blessing, and first the people must go to them in supplication and gratitude and expectancy.

Tiglath-pileser, returning to Nineveh for the festival from Kalakh, looked at the temple of Ishtar as his barge swept past. It stood back from the river, surrounded by trees, protected from marauders by the innate fear of the Lady all Assyrians felt. Outside the protective walls of the city of Nineveh proper, it yet seemed the focal point of power and authority. The king smiled, thinking of the festival ahead, and remembering just how special this one would be.

Within the temple, the usual peace was disrupted by much running to and fro by the slaves. Each carried an armful of spices or boughs to decorate the presence chamber, where the last ceremonies of the festival would be held. It was capable of holding over 500 people if they were crammed into every corner, and they would be, one week hence. Every wealthy merchant who could afford to buy a place would be there, as well as the nobility who had privileged seats. Even the Sargonids, in disgrace, ventured out of their hiding place in the north for this festival. In tribute to their great ancestor, Sargon I, they were given choice seats near the platform. Tiglath-pileser wanted no rebellions in his own domain caused by slighted feelings.

Within the city, the people were pulling out their best garments, packed away in myrrh, and shaking out streamers that hadn't been used since last year. The women were jubilant. They could wander the town and buy what they pleased, for the keynote of this festival was pleasure and happiness, and no husband dared displease the Lady and her divine consort by refusing his wife anything. The children were screaming with glee, for school wouldn't be in session for the full week, and they were also free to wander and play as they willed.

The men were not as happy, for many were firmly convinced that the whole week had been planned in the beginning by greedy women under the directions of the Lady, though none dared say this aloud. Still, their stalls would know brisk business, for the rural population would descend upon Nineveh in the next week ready to buy whatever was offered.

The priests were always glad to see the *akitû,* for many bulls and goats were bought and slaughtered to please the gods. There were over 1,000 altars in the city, and many small temples. The scent of burning flesh would rise from the city to the nostrils of the deities, and they would smile and not disturb the affairs of men for another year.

But the Lady, they thought, *she was another matter.*

The Lady Ishtar was the source of all life that flowed from a man through his woman to produce children. She it was who blessed or cursed the womb, as she blessed or cursed the seed of the fields. At this time of the year, especially, she had to be appeased or consoled, so that her bounty would once again cover her people, the children of Ashur. So the men murmured, as they gathered their merchandise together; so the farmers prayed, as they plowed their fields, readying them to receive the seed presently stored in the granaries.

When the great day came, after five days of feasting and sacrifice, the people of Nineveh and all the surrounding area swarmed into the sacred park of Ishtar, dressed in wedding garments and carrying cymbals. Singing, shouting, they danced around every tree they passed; but even the most foolhardy of boys dared not grab a branch to climb up.

The priestess, veiled in black, stood on the terrace above the main doorway, surrounded by her maidens, and watched the noisy arrival of the mobs. She smiled slightly, for always at such a time she felt the surge of power within her, and it was sweet.

The maidens were also dressed in black, a gauzy film that fluttered in every breeze, so they looked like large black birds come to perch above the temple doors. Gomer, in the back row, was still able to see everything because of her height. Indeed, the Assyrian women were even smaller than her own countrywomen, and they seemed to resent her tallness.

The priestess stepped forward, and a great silence fell upon the crowd. They lifted their eyes to her in expectancy.

The only sound was the soft chatter of a few birds among the trees, for even the wind had died down. Gomer shivered. The holy grove that had seemed so peaceful now seemed almost sinister, filled with silent watchful faces raised in dark eagerness to her mistress.

The priestess lifted her arms, and the black sleeves fell back to her shoulders so that her skinny arms were bared in the sunlight. "Ishtar!" she cried, her voice clear and high. "Ishtar, attend to us and hear us! Ishtar, Lady of our land, hear us!"

The echoes died away, and slowly the priestess sank to the floor, her head bowed, and none present doubted that the Lady's holy presence was weighing her down. The maidens swayed back, afraid. Only Gomer stood still, fascinated.

A sudden cry from above made her look up quickly. A man stood on the uppermost pinnacle, naked. He was black and slim, his hair long, for he had been dedicated a year less a day ago, and his hour had come. He called again, a formless call, and when the people had knelt, he cried, "In the beginning were the waters, the sweet water and the salt, and they flowed and moved under the wind waiting, always waiting. And Tiamat was the bitter waters holding within herself the seeds of life."

Gomer watched him and wondered at the exalted

glow of his face. He looked into the sun with wide eyes and never blinked. *He is in a trance,* she thought. *The goddess holds him in her hands.*

His call went on, a lilting liturgy of life: "Then it was that the gods were formed within them. Lahmu and Lahamu were brought forth, by name they were called."

The generations of gods were described at length. Yet not a person stirred under the heat of the sun. To do so would mean instant death at the hands of the gods through the Temple guards, who were watching intently for any such blasphemy.

The story was familiar to Gomer: how the gods disturbed Tiamat, how she fought with Enlil and was defeated, and her body used to form the heavens and the earth. The details were gruesome and horrid, but all listened openmouthed, for this was the way the gods did things. Then Enlil made man to serve the gods, to be flesh to their spirit and do their bidding.

Here the people stood and cheered themselves hoarse, to assure the gods that they were yet willing and eager to serve them. And then the youth cried out, "Let the gods come among us. Let Ishtar and Tammuz bless our land with their presence! Let the loving touch of Ishtar raise her husband from the shades, that he may once again and forever rule in our skies! Let Enlil and Esharra and Ninib come with Ashur to our city and once more be our comfort and protection!" The people were crying with him in joy, cheering and calling, their hands reaching to the sky. Just as the tension mounted to a breaking point, the youth flung up his hands and gave a last great cry, and cast himself from the pinnacle.

Gomer stood there immobile, her ears ringing from the sound, and she gave a dry sob. He had been a good man; yet he had been the Lady's, and she had called to him and he had gone to his death. She covered her face with trembling hands to shut out the sight of his smashed body, not yet surrounded with faggots for the sacrificial burning.

A touch on her arm roused her. The priestess was beside her, her face still veiled. The quiet voice said, "Come with me. It is your time now."

Wondering, Gomer followed her into a small room off the balcony, where a slave girl awaited them. A pile of shimmering garments lay across a chair, and several pots of paint were lined up before a mirror.

The slave took off Gomer's dark dress, revealing the white shift underneath. The priestess smiled, and Gomer was suddenly afraid. She had thought that it was now time for her to enter the sisterhood, for she had learned all the liturgies and the words for the offerings. But at the gleam in the old woman's eyes, she was filled with doubt. The priestess was once more just an old, jealous woman.

The slave girl ceremoniously tore the white shift in half, and Gomer was naked. Swiftly, though, she was covered with a long red robe that was belted with gold. She knew she had never seen one of the sacred maidens dressed like this. What was going on?

The noise outside had died down, but Gomer could hear the crackling of the bonfire and smell burning flesh. She gagged, for she had fasted all day with the sisterhood. The priestess noticed and laughed. "You'll get used to it," she said caustically, as she directed the slave about her work.

Gomer was pushed toward the now empty chair, and she sat gratefully, the heavy headdress pulling her neck back. She had only caught a glimpse of it before they had fastened it upon her hair, but she had noticed a large golden snake emerging from the crown.

The slave girl was well-skilled. Her fingers dipped into pot after pot, and she smeared paint onto Gomer's face until the skin was packed. Finally Gomer felt like a stiff doll, and glancing into the mirror found she looked one as well. Her face was chalk white, her eyes surrounded by kohl and green powder, her mouth touched with red. She saw a stranger.

"Stand up." The priestess led her to the door, where the shadowed arches protected them from the gaze of the mob. The fire was just dying down, and low chants could be heard rising from hundreds of mouths.

"Ishtar, Ishtar, Ishtar, come to us, come . . ."

"They are going into the presence chamber now—those who can fit in. We will go along the high stairs." She motioned to the slave girl to pick up Gomer's train, for the red robe trailed behind a fair length. They turned into the dark hallway.

At the other end of the temple, the king was lying upon a golden bier, his body covered with white linen. Around him his attendants, the priests of Tammuz, were chanting a low dirge, their heads and shoulders covered with ashes. Tammuz was dead, and only the touch of Ishtar could bring him back to their needy land.

A knock at the door stopped the dirge. "Enter," the high priest called out.

The door swung open, and several of the nobility stood there, dressed in gorgeous wedding clothes, their faces alight with joy. "Come with us, Tammuz!" they cried. "Come where your Lady and wife awaits you!"

The priests rose, brushed off the ashes, and let their dark robes drop to the ground like discarded feathers. Then, clad only in loincloths, they arranged themselves around the heavy bier and lifted it, groaning and panting.

The nobles moved back from the door to allow the bier and its burden through and then, singing and banging their cymbals, followed as it wound through the halls of the temple, heading for the presence chamber.

Gomer stood trembling in the dark hall, hearing the singing within the chamber. She couldn't understand what was going on, for of all the ceremonies she had learned, the priestess had never assigned to her the *akitû*. Now she felt lost and frightened, and the insane desire to see her mother flashed through her mind. But what could Shana have done against Ishtar?

A sudden great shout shattered the stuffy quietness of the hall, and the priestess gave a satisfied sigh. "He is here," she said to Gomer, who could not nod or smile. She felt paralyzed beneath her splendor and paint.

"Tammuz! Tammuz! Awake and be our king! Awake at the touch of Ishtar!" Then the people cried even louder, *"Ishtar! Ishtar! Come among us! Come!"* The last roar burst into her ears, and Gomer nearly screamed with fear.

The doors before them swung open, and she was looking at the priestess' platform. The throne had been removed, and in its place was the golden bier. She recognized Tiglath-pileser lying there, and wondered frantically if he was dead. Before she could think further, the priestess had taken her hand and was leading her forward.

The frenzy of the mob doubled at her appearance,

and their cheering vibrated the air around her. Step by step she paced forward, holding her neck erect so that the headdress wouldn't slip. Step by step she went, with the slave girl proudly holding up the long red train that slithered like blood over the pavement.

The priestess stopped her so that she was facing the crowd from behind the bier. The noise resolved itself into shouting again. "Ishtar! Ishtar! Bring us life, bring us joy. Ishtar! Give life to your lord!"

The priestess held Gomer's hand over the king's heart, and left it there. As if she were watching a dream, Gomer saw the king's eyes open and look into hers with a smile. Then he sat up and taking her hand, kissed it.

The rest was a blur. She vaguely heard the words of a ceremony in which Ishtar and Tammuz were reunited to give life to Nineveh forever. Then she was led away again, into a dark chamber that seemed to stretch on forever. Her headdress was removed, her face wiped off and washed. Once she saw the slave girl's face close to hers, and wondered at the awe in the black eyes. But she couldn't think, and so let it slide past.

Finally she was alone. Looking around, she saw that she was in a large bedchamber dimly lit with two oil lamps. A huge bed dominated one half, hung with silks that shimmered softly in the dim light. With a sigh of relief, she slid off her sandals and walked over to the bed.

A low voice halted her. "Ishtar."

She whirled around. The door was closing behind the king. He stood there tall and proud, his eyes smiling at her, his long blue robe sweeping the floor as he approached her.

Finally she spoke, her voice cracking in her dry throat. "Why do you call me Ishtar?"

"I am Tammuz, Lady. Don't you know what we did today?" When she mutely shook her head, he smiled again, his tanned skin wrinkling in amusement around his eyes. "It is *akitû*, Lady. It is the day the gods descend and become man—and woman. Each year one of the sacred maidens is chosen to be Ishtar, as the king is always Tammuz, for is he not one of the gods himself? And when I saw you, I knew you would be the best—the best Ishtar I would ever wed."

"Wed?" she whispered, clutching her throat in panic. He came closer, unbuckling his belt. She retreated to the window.

"But you were dedicated to Ishtar by Pekahiah. Surely you understand that her maidens are meant only for the service of men?" He threw his robe into a corner and stood before her, his arrogant nakedness seeming to fill the room.

She understood. She wondered what had taken her so long. This, then, was the true worship of Ishtar. She wanted to die.

TWENTY-NINE
The Beloved

The quiet green of the forest enclosed Hosea as he wandered along the path toward Samaria. He had just spent six months on another tour of Israel and was heading home at last, footsore and weary from weeks on the road, heartsick from the reception he had received. Everyone knew him by sight now, and he no longer needed to wait until the people heard his message before they were mocking him or throwing dung in his face. Yet no matter how frustrated or angry he became, he could never bring himself to call down the curse of God upon them as Elisha had. Two bears had come to that prophet's assistance and mauled his opponents, for they had mocked the man of God. But Hosea never felt that this was the way God wished him to act at this time. He was to call the people to repentance, yes, but demonstrations of power were not to be involved. For some reason, God had limited him to the spoken word, and Hosea obeyed without question.

The trees sighed in the spring wind, and a breath of sweetness came to his nostrils. He stopped walking and inhaled deeply, filling his lungs with the smell of newborn leaves and sodden ferns. It was a great country God had given his people, fertile and rich. Some parts were becoming eroded, it was true, because Israel was disobeying the Law commanding the land to lie fallow one year out of seven. In her greed, the country was ruining her soil, and Hosea dreaded the day when the desert started moving across the Jordan. It was all part of their general attitude, he thought, ignoring God and his good laws, and so destroying themselves and the land along with them.

He sighed again, hating his gloominess, yet seeing no way out of it. Then he remembered the latest letter from Isaiah that he carried in his pack, and smiled faintly to himself. Yes, that would certainly help—God had been good to give him such a friend, who always seemed to write at the times his encouragement was most needed.

Looking around for a place to sit down, Hosea saw a pair of bright eyes watching him from the cover of a clump of ferns. His smile broadened, and he crouched down, clucking softly to the little animal. But fear held it motionless, and when he stood up again it vanished, only a rapidly disappearing bushy tail showing him its progress among the undergrowth. It was a fox, he saw, and ruefully he laughed at himself for his futile attempt at making friends. He must be lonelier than he had realized.

Finding a dry spot not soaked by the last rains, Hosea settled himself under a spreading sycamore, and drew the scroll out of his pack. *Might as well eat while I'm at it,* he thought, and broke off a chunk of bread from a loaf he had bought in the last town. The baker had been surly, but willing to sell even to a hated prophet if he had money. Hosea sent up a prayer of thankfulness for Diblaim, who always let him take as much money as he needed from the family jar for his frequent trips.

The thought of Diblaim reminded Hosea of home, and he brooded a while on his life the past few years. His children were growing well, for Shana and Diblaim had been more than delighted to train the two boys, having only had girls themselves, and with Rachel dead and Gomer worse than dead, their grandchildren kept their lives full and their minds from bitter memories.

Munching his bread, the forgotten letter clasped in his hand, Hosea raised his eyes to the sky and watched the clouds scurry across the sun. Jezreel was a man now, having reached his maturity just before his father left on this journey. It had been a grand feast, with all the relatives from the valley joining in. Jezreel had stood tall and proud beside his grandfather as he had read the Scriptures the way Hosea had taught him. Shana had cried quietly into her shawl, hugging Ruhamah and Ammi to her as they jumped about in excitement.

Hosea remembered his joy on that day, part and parcel with his pride in the son who already topped him by an inch. He had his father's coloring, the boy did, with his brilliant dark eyes and lean face that apparently was already causing a few young girls to go in whispers to their mothers. But he had his mother's build, for his slim body and long legs could have come from no one else.

His mother... As always when the thought of Gomer crossed his mind, Hosea made an involuntary movement, clutching his hand over his heart where the pain had once centered. Too often in the past year, for no reason, the image of her came unbidden to his eyes and it seemed she was running toward him, her arms outstretched and her eyes shining with love.

But I dream like a child, he chided himself, sitting bolt upright and frowning. *I haven't seen her for seven years, and I'll never see her again. She has had her wish. She lives with those idol-worshipers who will fill her with dark pleasures and wild stories of immoral gods. She is gone from me, and well rid I am of a woman who always secretly yearned toward Ashtaroth.*

Thus he brusquely dismissed Gomer from his mind, as he had done since the day she went to Pekahiah. She was evil, wayward; she was indeed the harlot her father had always feared, and a man of God could only know sorrow and evil with her. That he had once loved her more than anything in his life except God he now doubted, deeming that love to be only the dreamings of a youth. After all, he was thirty-three now, an elder in the tiny Samaritan synagogue he had finally been able to set up, composed of the few remaining believers in that city and valley. A couple of the men had been drawn back to the worship of the one true God by his urgent pleading, and he rejoiced in such evidence of God's blessing upon his mission. The rest were either relatives or old friends of Diblaim's and Dan's. Diblaim had been rendered speechless by tears during the first Shabbat celebrated in his home, which Hosea had chosen to be the headquarters of the new group. The old man's joy made all the pain and frustration of the previous ten years worthwhile.

That had been four years ago, and since then three other small, struggling groups had been set up, in Dan,

Shiloh, and Megiddo. Untaught at all in the old Laws, barely able to read, these handfuls of devout men were the faint but steady light in what Hosea saw as the evil darkness of the land. They struggled through the Torah while he was away, and spent intense days of learning while he was with them. But they were afraid of their neighbors and didn't spread their new faith. Hosea was still alone, except when a letter from Isaiah arrived along with the latest goods from Jerusalem. Uneasy peace between the neighboring countries allowed caravans across the border of Israel and Judea. But all knew that sooner or later war was bound to come, for the Assyrian overlord had been insulted; and though he had waited so far five years, all knew that one day his armies would appear like locusts in the northern mountain passes.

Dragging his mind away from memories, Hosea opened the scroll in his hand and read the familiar words of greeting. Isaiah, being an impatient and impetuous man, found the formal addressing of a friend very tedious. So he would hastily rid himself of such a necessity with a few well-chosen words and then plunge right into whatever he had on his mind.

"You are very unhappy, my friend. I can read this in your stilted words, and so can my good wife. She sends her prayers to you, realizing how lonely you are now, and wishes you to know our joy that she will bear a child in the spring."

The babe must be here by now, Hosea mused, for the letter had been written two months before he began his journey, and now the summer drought was almost upon the land. How blessed was Isaiah, with a good woman beside him to calm his nerves and mix honey and herbs for his headaches. Once again Gomer was before him, bending over with a gentle smile on her mouth, holding a steaming cup in her hands.

"No!" He jumped up and clenched his fists, his teeth grinding with anguish. *Why is she so real these days? Why?* For years he had managed to keep all thoughts of her away, at first because the intolerable pain had made him weep. Then repugnance had set in, and the thought of her in Pekahiah's arms had brought anger instead of sorrow. But now . . . It had started when he set out on this last trip. She had met him at every turn of the road; her voice whispered to him when he lay down to sleep. He had each time banished her, and for a while had been at peace, but always she returned. *I dream,* he told himself. *I but dream.*

But could a dream come in broad daylight? Could the uprush of yearning in his heart be caused by a memory? He knew he had left all hope of her return behind; indeed, he feared it because her death would have to follow. But still she came to him, a part of the sweetness and fresh light green of the countryside, not a ghost, but the memory of his love made new by some power he couldn't understand.

Slowly he relaxed as the impression of Gomer's nearness faded, and his hands fell to his sides. Suddenly a thought struck him, and his heavy black brows furrowed his forehead. Could it be that Gomer was thinking about him, reaching out to him? No, no, she had made it plain that he meant nothing to her, and it was this that had made his love so painful that in the end he had buried it.

Hoping once again to banish her from his mind, Hosea picked up Isaiah's letter where it had fallen among the wild flowers and started to read again.

"You have told me how unresponsive your people are to the message of God, and I must agree. Sometimes, in the power of God's Spirit, we are blessed beyond most men with the vision of his glory and might. It is then that words of adoration and praise pour from our depths, and those who listen are moved to repentance, fear, and sometimes worship of our most holy God. But mostly we walk heavily, do we not, bound by our inadequacies, knowing deeply the humiliation of our humanity. We are but men, called to a work that only God can do: to cause the wicked to repent, to call the erring back to his ways, to show that man without God is not really man.

"Someday God will tear away the veil that separates men from him, and will expose our world to the full glory of his majesty, but that day is not yet. When I saw him, I fell to the ground and wished to die, and I had lived all my life following his laws. What will be the fate of those who have spurned him so long? This is my nightmare and my horror, and it is this we warn our people against: the blackness of separation from God."

Hosea lifted his head from the papyrus sheet, tears rolling slowly into his beard that now brushed his chest with graying locks. *I am but a man,* he prayed, lifting heavy hands to the gentle blue sky above the waving treetops. *I am but a man.*

"I am here." The quiet voice seemed a part of the breeze that filled the forest, but the joy that ran through every nerve of Hosea's body told him differently. Slowly he turned, fearful yet exultant.

The Man was smiling, his eyes twinkling, and his hand reached out to beckon Hosea closer. "Come and sit beside me, my son, and let's talk."

It was the most deeply real encounter Hosea had ever

known. The birds flew overhead and occasionally alighted upon the Man's hands, chirping and flashing their brilliant plumage. The fox had returned, his bright eyes fixed upon the Man's face, his tail swishing through last year's leaves that lay in drifts under the ferns. Hosea sat there at peace, looking at this One who was totally there, totally alive, and who spread joy with the touch of his hand.

Feeling that he should kneel, Hosea yet responded to the friendly gesture and sat facing the Man, with the fox panting between them. The sharp jaws of the animal gleamed and his black nostrils quivered with life. Hosea could see his ribs moving under the thick ruddy coat of fur. *I have never felt so alive,* he thought with wonder, and realized that all the torments of his heart had vanished with the close presence of this Man.

"I wish you were always here," he said suddenly, and then flushed. He had sounded like a child crying for his father.

The Man smiled, amused. "I *am* your father, my son."

Hosea bowed his head. It was all too much for him, even trained in the Law as he was. That God should come thus to him . . . And Isaiah only knew him as blazing glory.

"Isaiah's message to my people is different, my son, for he has a different evil to fight. Here in Israel the people must come to know me as they never have— and it's up to you to take me to them, in your words."

Hosea groaned, and his littleness seemed unbearable. "Adonai, I do as you ask. But they don't listen to my words; they hate the very sight of me now. Just last week a mob threatened me with death unless I left their town, and this has happened time without number."

Silence fell, so that only the fox's quick breathing was heard. Yet the silence was a heavy and sorrowful one, and Hosea looked up from his clasped hands to the face opposite him. The eyes looked directly into his, and a shock went through him. Ageless sorrow was there, compared to which his own was but a shadow. But something else was there too. He wasn't sure just what it was.

"Hosea." Hearing his name brought deep comfort to his heart. He sighed quickly, involuntarily, as though a huge weight had just melted from his chest. He straightened his bowed shoulders and listened. "You've been close to death, yes, but I have protected you, for your time is not yet come and I have need of you. Your mission, my son, is just beginning."

"Just—just beginning? But, Adonai, you met me more than fourteen years ago, and I have spoken the words you gave me ever since!"

The Man smiled, deep wrinkles shadowing the corners of his mouth. His eyes were laughing. "Yes, it seems long to you, doesn't it? But you've only been learning so far."

Hosea was stunned. Had all this work been for nothing?

"No, you've done well, my son." It always disconcerted Hosea, the way this Man picked out his innermost thoughts. But then God always knows a man's heart, as the ancient wise man once said. "Recently you've been coming to the new part of the work that I have for you, but you've been drawing back in fear. Yes, Hosea, that's why I came for this talk today, to help you take the next step along the road I have laid for you to walk."

"Yes, Adonai," Hosea said humbly, his head once

more bowed. Who was he to question God, or to wonder at his ways?

"Hosea, think now, and remember the Torah. Why have I sent you out among my people?"

"Why—why, because they have turned from you, Adonai, and despise your holy Name. They worship other gods, and Moses warned us that if we weakened ourselves by forsaking your ways and forfeiting your protection, other nations would swallow us up. We who were to tell other nations about you will instead be ground under their heel, as has happened to us so often. And I—I fear this will be the last time, for Assyria is stronger than any other country that has come against us, even Egypt, and they treat the conquered differently. They—they scatter them like chaff among other nations that are under their sceptre, and once Israel has been scattered, can she come together again?"

The Man had listened intently, disappointment in his expressive dark eyes. When Hosea finished, the Man sat quietly for a moment, thinking, his dark face wearing a brooding frown. Then he said, "All that you say is true, Hosea, and your fears are right. Assyria will scatter Israel among the nations. But I have sent you out with a message of repentance, which you have spoken; but more than this, you have warned the people of their evil ways. And," he added gently, "it seems to me that you gain pleasure from the last more than you do from a response to the first."

Hosea hung his head, ashamed. "But—but they *hate* you, Adonai. They delight in their wickedness, and so few repent!"

The Man nodded. "You hate *them* too, don't you, for their ways? And they know it, Hosea! They know it!

They see you and hear you, and know my wrath and anguish from your words, but that only pushes them further away into their fear. All they know of me is what you tell them, so that I seem like a raging thunderstorm striking down all who stand in my way." He paused, his intense eyes searching Hosea's forlorn face. "Tell me, my son, is that all I am to you?"

"No, oh no," Hosea whispered, tears blinding his eyes. "You—you are filled with wrath for the evildoer, but to me, who least deserves it, you have shown love."

And suddenly, like a blinding flash of lightning, the truth of what he had just said illuminated Hosea. *Yes, God loved me! God responded to that earlier search with love and compassion before he sent me out among his people! And I, blinded by my zeal to the true intent of my mission, saw only God's rejection by his people and fought against it. I failed to see that they are searching too, and finding in their wealth and orgies a fulfillment I found in my God. It is this he seeks to destroy, not them but that empty fulfillment, so that his people will see the hollowness of their alcohol and their idols. All I spoke of was their waywardness. I totally failed to show God's ardent desire for their return. How blind, how blind! And what a fool I've been!*

"No, my son, not a fool. The fool has said in his heart that there is no God, and you have never said that. But my people have. They have fled from my Laws and my worship and embraced other gods whose rites fulfill their desire for pleasure, as Gomer did."

Gomer! Hosea felt numb. She was there again, filling his awareness, and he knew that she wept.

"Your wife fled my worship for that of Ashtaroth and

found happiness with Pekahiah. She forsook my laws, and she is a whore." The Man spoke with infinite sadness, and his words seemed to plunge to the very depths of Gomer's sin. Hosea shuddered, still unwilling to think about her. "Hosea, you must listen, for this is the next step that I am showing you now. You put Gomer behind you. You shut your love for her out of your heart, and even the mention of her name makes you cringe. Think, Hosea, think. I ask you why I sent you to Israel and you told me that I was angry with her, that I wished to warn her of her coming destruction. Yes, I am angry, but why am I angry? Think, Hosea. It has been years since you let yourself be angry with Gomer. Now you shrink with distaste from her. Do I shrink from Israel? Have I not more reason to let her go her own way than you do with Gomer?"

Hosea was weeping, the tears running in rivulets down his cheeks. He had stopped struggling against the words that pounded against his ears. He had stopped fighting what he now saw all too clearly was the will of God. He went limp, his hands dragging on the ground, his shoulders sagging in defeat.

The Man waited a few moments, his eyes resting tenderly upon the bowed head before him. Yet a tremor shook his mouth as he felt the anguish Hosea was feeling, and bright tears stood in his own eyes.

Finally Hosea looked up, gulping for air, his dusty robe soaked down the front with salt tears. "I—I hear, Adonai. I hear."

The Man reached out and laid his hand against Hosea's wet cheek in a gesture of deep compassion. "My son . . ."

When Hosea was calm again, he felt surprised that all

his fear and distaste had vanished, as had the consciousness of Gomer's presence. The Man stood up and wandered toward the path, his head bowed. Hosea hastily got to his feet and joined him. The fox had disappeared again.

"Hosea, I will ask you once again." The Man drew a deep breath, his eyes lifted to the branch above his head. "Why am I sending you to my people?"

Hosea bit his lip, and whispered painfully, "Because—because you love them, Adonai."

"Hosea, how can you show my people how I love them?" The Man was smiling gently again, and his eyes returned to Hosea's wretched face.

"Adonai, I think—I think you wish me to—to go and bring Gomer back to my home. As—as you have loved Israel through her infidelity and warn her away from coming destruction, so—must I treat the woman you gave me. But—" Hosea stood there twisting his hands in his girdle, tugging at the material anxiously.

"But what, my son?" The Man still smiled; yet the sorrow was still in his eyes.

"Adonai. I have put aside my love for—this woman, as you never did for—for your people. It is gone from me. How can I bring her back into my household as if nothing ever happened? Her father—he will command the death penalty. And I can't go against the Law—your Law, Adonai."

"The Law will be fulfilled." His voice had a quiet finality in it, and Hosea looked quickly into his eyes. The sorrow and love in them quieted all questions, including the meaning of the words he had just spoken. "Gomer will be your wife again, and you will know what to do with her when the time comes, for after today you will find that it will be easier to hear my voice, now that you know your hate is wrong. As for your love for Gomer"— his voice softened to a humorous chuckle—"you'll find that it's not as dead as you suppose."

Hosea had more questions that started to swarm about in his mind, but suddenly the Man's face started to shine with the inner radiance of his love. Hosea stepped back a pace, frightened, and sank to his knees, for suddenly the friend who had conversed so intimately with him for the past hour was becoming the God who had revealed his glory to Moses on Mount Sinai, the God who had blazed in the Temple before Isaiah. And he reached out a hand in blessing to the prophet who knelt in awestruck worship before him, as the glory grew too bright for men's eyes to behold.

When Hosea opened his eyes again, he was alone. Yet the lingering memory of that glory still held him enthralled, and he stayed on his knees for a long time, watching the clouds as they gathered to the west for a storm. *He was here,* he thought, *he was here with me, his creature, as he once was with Adam, and Abraham. How am I blessed, my Adonai, my Beloved, how am I blessed! And how can my puny words tell of your great love?*

Then he remembered: Now he must act out God's love, as God had ordered him. He must bring back to himself a woman black with adultery, and forgive her as God so yearned to forgive his people—if only they would repent and come to him.

But what if Gomer doesn't repent? What if she laughs at me and turns away—again? Can I live through another rejection? But God has lived in his eternity through countless rejections, and still he comes to men and calls for their love. *I must call for her love,* he thought helplessly, *the love she has never known for me.*

O my God, my God, it is impossible. She will never return, as Israel will never return. But I will do your will.

He stood up and walked slowly back to the sycamore where he had left his pack. Stuffing the neglected letter into it, crumbling up the leftover bread into bits for the birds, he shouldered his pack, his mind still brooding over his new task.

He lifted his head and looked at the path before his feet, leading toward the distant mound of Samaria hidden by the crowded trees. Then, setting his jaw, he turned and started back the way he had just come that morning.

THIRTY
Reawakening

Gomer leaned against the parapet, letting the cool morning wind from the desert lift her heavy hair from her forehead. She had spent countless mornings here watching the low profile of the mountains to the south-west, straining her eyes across the golden dunes and gray rock piles to see if anything moved along the winding road on the other side of the Tigris River. The water flowed sluggishly this time of year, for the drought was on in full force and it hadn't rained in Nineveh for more than two months. Even the temple reservoir was getting low, and the priestess mumbled incantations as she went about her work.

Here above the temple Gomer could be alone, and nowhere else. No one seemed to mind her early morning absence from the second floor, for the only escape from the roof was 400 feet straight down. The priestess marked this sign of discontent in one of her maidens, but kept silent. No harm could come of it.

Gomer didn't really try to understand this longing to watch the shadows lighten to the west each dawn. She always gave in to it, and each sunrise found her hands clasped upon the stone railing and her eyes searching the horizon for she knew not what. *Maybe I do know,* she thought, *and I'm too afraid to tell myself.*

It had started two years before, when the priestess had assigned her to a cleaning job in the temple archives, not knowing that Gomer could read and might find more to do than dust the ancient jars. The room below the presence chamber was dark and smelled of mold, for the reservoir occasionally leaked water into it. Gomer had fastened her torch to the wall bracket and proceeded about her task, thankful that she was alone. The rest of the sacred maidens were working elsewhere in the huge temple on this mammoth job of a yearly cleaning.

Sweeping cobwebs and dust piles into her bag as she went, Gomer occasionally lifted the lid of a jar to peer inside at the tablets jammed to the top. Most of them seemed to be written in a language she hadn't learned in Pekahiah's library, perhaps a tongue even older than the city that was beginning to spread outside the nearby walls.

Finished at last, Gomer tied up the cloth bag and headed for her torch when she caught a glimpse of a small jar pushed to the back of one of the shelves. Curious, she lifted it down, careful not to get the mold that coated the shelf onto her hands. It was a simple jar, poignantly reminiscent of the several in which her mother had kept her herbs. Taking off the lid, she saw only one tablet inside, and her wonder grew.

Putting her bag down on the floor under the torch, she

took out the tablet and held it in her hands. Examining the script closely, she gasped with delight—it was Hebrew! What was a Hebrew tablet doing in Nineveh?

It will take me too long to read it now, she thought. *It's been too long since I've read anything. I wonder . . . could I take it to my room? No one will ever know—it's been years since that jar was touched.*

Making up her mind, she put the lid back on the jar and carefully replaced it on the shelf. Then, glancing at the stairs to make sure no one was coming, she flipped up her skirts and tucked the tablet into the undergirdle that belted her shift. *There,* she smiled to herself, *I've got something that's all my own—a joy I haven't had since I came to this wretched place.* Hastily grabbing the torch, she held up her skirts and the dust bag in one hand while she dashed up the stairs.

Standing on the roof, feeling the hot sun on her back as it rose above the roofs of Nineveh, Gomer remembered her initial shock when she finally read the tablet. It had been written by a man of her own country, a man touched by God, as Hosea had been. Only this Jonah had disobeyed God's express order to go to Nineveh and warn the people of coming destruction unless they repented.

She had dropped the tablet and stared out her window, anger and fury making her whole body shake. *Even here, he pursues me,* she thought, *even in far-off Nineveh! What God is this that is not content with one people but must go to all?*

She had continued reading, amazed at Jonah's reluctance to obey God, for Hosea had always stressed that a man of God must always put God first. It had been that very insistence that had stopped all her internal efforts to love him. How can one love a man possessed by an invisible God, a man who disappeared for months at a time on God's business?

Jonah had finally come to Nineveh after several strange adventures. He had been shipwrecked on the Great Sea going west instead of east; he had been swallowed alive by a great fish and thrown up three days later on dry land. Gomer didn't find that hard to believe. After all, this was the same God whom her father claimed had drowned the whole world except one family! Securing one fish to chastise a runaway prophet would present no problem to him.

Gomer was never sure afterwards how it happened, but that simple story gripped her whole mind for weeks. She kept remembering details at the oddest times: during a ritual burning before the tall statue of Ishtar (surely the old temple had been there when Jonah came, the temple that had burned in the first year of Tiglath-pileser's reign and been rebuilt with his money); or when a man would enter her door for a paid night of sporting with one of Ishtar's maidens of dark pleasure (was this part of the wickedness God had abhorred in Nineveh, the selling of a woman to the Lady for the service of any man who chose her?); or when the cry came every evening from the highest parapet of the temple for all within to kneel and offer prayer to the Lady (did this daily ritual fail during the years of Jonah's ministry here?).

For some reason, the little story obsessed her, although she had never heard anyone refer to the events within it. But wait—hadn't Tiglath-pileser mentioned once that he had had to order a priest executed for refusing to return to the old ways? And he had been amused the one time she had answered his questions about her husband and had remarked that the God of her people was weaker than they supposed, for Nineveh had killed him. She had thought he meant his proposed attempt to defeat Pekah, but now she wasn't so sure.

Jonah had fought against God—and had finally given in. She had fought against God, too, she remembered, and she shivered. Now she was a part of the wickedness of Nineveh in the eyes of all who still followed the God of Moses—and just as deserving of punishment as Jonah had felt Nineveh was.

She had figured out the reason for the prophet's reluctance to warn Nineveh. He had known that if they repented, God would forgive them, and he hated the city so much that he *wanted* it to perish. *If he had seen me,* she thought, *he would have recoiled with righteous fury and called a curse upon one who painted her face and laid with any man who wished to be a god for the night. But that's not me, that's not me,* she wanted to cry passionately to the accusing prophet she could see quite vividly in her dreams, who sometimes looked uncannily like the husband she had deserted seven years before. *I don't worship Ishtar. I hate her, I hate her! She has enslaved me; she has degraded me into a mere thing to please the men who come through my door. I hate her!*

Once she woke up from such a dream sweating, and stared with revulsion at the snoring man beside her. He was one of those who loved to rape a woman, and would laugh when she cried out in pain. Gomer, an expert now at allowing a man to do the least to her that he possibly could, had quickly satisfied him, and he had gone off to sleep.

She had looked out the window, her nightmare still colorful in her mind, and had seen the first gray light of dawn stealing across the sky. It was that morning that the walks on the roof began. The men never missed her, for Ishtar in the morning was never the woman of darkness and passion she was at midnight.

Only the king wouldn't let her leave before he did. Tiglath-pileser came to her once a week without fail, and never went to any other room but hers. She had grown reluctantly to admire him, for he spent half the night talking to her about his growing empire, his weak advisors, his distaste for city life, and his yearning to be back with his army, leading it to war. "But that must wait," he always said, but would never explain why. Those times she could almost forget her slavery and feel like a person again, until the inevitable moment when he would stretch to his full height and walk over to her chair.

The morning walks were essential now. She could no more face a day without them than she could stop breathing. She found a certain clarity of thought on the roof, a certain yearning that went deep into the reawakened memory of what her life had once been, back in Israel. Reading the tablet of Jonah had brought back to her all Diblaim's teachings, successfully buried during her years with Pekahiah. An uncomfortable tremor always shook her when she thought of her parents, knowing how they would feel if they knew what had happened to her.

Then she would remember the last time she had seen Shana, when the small gray woman on the roof had reached out with a loving cry to her banished daughter. *She still loved me then, even though in her eyes I must have been a walking death. She still loved me.*

The greatest puzzle in Jonah's story was raised by God sending the prophet to Nineveh in the first place. They were, after all, not his people. Yet, look at all the trouble he went to in making sure they heard his message! Why did he do it? What kind of a God was he? The only reply she could give herself was a very unsettling one: Hosea would know.

Hosea . . . Once she let the first thought of her husband enter her mind, Gomer was never quite free of him after that. For two years now, ever since she had found the tablet, the old memories of her life with Hosea had been seeping back, and she almost welcomed them. He, at least, had loved her purely, as no other man ever had. Not even Pekahiah had taken her honorably, for no pious Israelite would have dared before his God to touch a married woman.

Calmly, with the detachment of time, Gomer thought on that roof about her former life, and forced herself to remember the steps that had brought her to Nineveh. *I saw with bright colors; I loved with all I had in me when I loved. The Egyptian, Pekahiah . . . they called to me with laughter and pleasure and colorful words, and so I loved in return. But Hosea . . . I lived with him, I bore his children, I cooked and sewed and slept with him, and grew weary of the never-changing days. It was so easy for me to leave a man like him who had cast no ties about my dreaming heart!*

Watching the road to the west, letting her eye run along the mountain range that stopped the desert sands, Gomer saw herself as she never had before. *Could it*

*have been any different if—if I had loved his God as
he had? At least we would have then worshiped
together! But why follow such a God when Ashtaroth
held out to me such happiness?*

*And look at you now, she told herself. Who are you
fooling? Here you are in the middle of the worship of
Ashtaroth, bitter, used up, well on your way to becoming the same miserable old crone as the priestess.* For Gomer had been told by the king about his
plans for her, and found herself shrinking from them. To
run the vast estates, to worship daily before a stone
statue that billowed with exaggerated womanly curves,
to cut up animals that still quivered with life and guess
the future by reading their entrails—she wanted no part
of it.

When the morning breeze ruffled her hair, she would
whisper with it, *Maybe . . . maybe, all along, I've been
wrong . . . about him. Hosea said he brought joy and
peace. . . . Surely the lights in Hosea's eyes weren't
reflections of our lamp. . . . Maybe, maybe I've been
wrong.*

And if I have been, I will die!

Only that morning did she really let that thought sink
into her heart. *I will die!* The mountains were the same,
the sun shone as bright, but sudden fear brought darkness to her mind. *If God is really as all-powerful as
Father claimed, if he really can reach into Nineveh as
he did with Jonah, then there is no place on earth for
me to escape him. I will die, for I broke his Laws.*

The fear grew and crushed her soul. She found herself
sinking to her knees, sobbing, clutching at the parapet
with trembling fingers. *I must die . . . No! No! God of
my fathers, let me not die! It is too sweet seeing the*

sunrise, and Sheol is so misty and gray. Help me! God, help me! I see you now. Jonah has brought me back to you with his reluctance and his obedience. I have been more reluctant. I have played the whore. She shuddered, although the sun was still warm on her back. *O God, can't you overthrow the power of Ishtar as you did once before in this city, and let me begin again? Let me come back and live a life that may somehow bring me the quiet joy my parents and my husband had, instead of the restlessness and eager folly that has brought me to this living death. God, God, are you there? Can you hear me?*

Once before she had sobbed on a rooftop, and she had flung away the waiting comfort of an invisible presence. She remembered that time now, and hated herself for her blindness. *What a fool to think I could mock him and never pay! A fool to walk away from a God who is before me and behind me, and could crush me with the merest thought! A fool . . .*

She stood up finally, drained, her face flushed with weeping, and dried her eyes. The sun was well up now, and she had missed the first meal of the day, but she didn't feel hungry. There was no answer to her plea in the warm air around her or in the bustle that had started along the river, the road of trade for Assyria. The boats sailed past with no knowledge of the woman who watched them from her height. She looked down and thought of the way the young men each year cast their bodies forth for the goddess, and wondered if Hosea's God would accept such an offering from her. *No, I am unclean,* she thought dully, and turned to go in.

THIRTY-ONE
Redemption

Another evening was throwing its dusky shadows over the temple of Ishtar, and Gomer laid down her comb to look at the long shadows on the floor of her room. A dread seized her, for any moment now the king would arrive with his guards posted outside in the hall, and he would want another evening of laughter and living. *I have played his game long enough,* she thought. *Surely he tires and will seek another of the girls!*

She remembered that one time Renin had come to her to give the message that Tiglath-pileser was ill and unable to attend to her, so he had sent his captain of the guards to make sure she spent the night with no other man. Renin had walked in, his face red with embarrassment, for he had never seen her in the temple, indeed not since the day they both had arrived at Kalakh and met the king. Now they faced each other, five years older, and he gave his message stiffly.

"Thank you, Renin. How does your king intend for you to make sure I stay alone?"

"I will stay outside the door all night, Lady," he had answered, falling into his old address for her. He had already noted that her hair had its old glory, and her eyes were as full of mystery and golden fire as they had been when she first caught Pekahiah's eye. Renin had never married, and when asked why he replied that his manhood was dedicated to the Lady. All thought he meant Ishtar.

Now he was seeing his heart's goddess again, and his simple loyal soul was overwhelmed. She was frowning slightly to herself as she absently plaited together a few locks of hair that fell over her bare shoulder. Feeling the intensity of the captain's gaze, Gomer had looked up and seen the suffering and longing in his eyes. Startled, she had instinctively drawn back a step.

"Renin! Why, I never knew you—you cared—like that." Her eyes softened. It had been too long since anyone showed such love for her. Unlike Pekahiah, this man was content to worship from afar. She understood immediately how the years had been for him, and her heart that had grown bitter was touched.

"Renin," she said again and gave him her hand.

This time it was he who was startled. Her hand was warm and friendly, and her eyes were smiling. He didn't know that it had been years since she had smiled. "Lady," he stammered, as a gladness started to fill his heart. "I—I must go out and guard the door now. Ishtar give you peace."

"No, there is no peace from Ishtar, Renin, only demands and empty promises." She saw that she had horrified him, for he firmly believed in the goodness of the gods, no matter how bloodthirsty they seemed to her. "Renin, must you leave? Can't we talk about——the other days?"

Unsure, he hesitated, but after a moment's thought put aside his shield. "They will all think the king visits you, I'm sure," he said, and she nodded.

They had talked about Samaria until the oil lamp finally gave a last spurt and went out. She hadn't realized how homesick she was, and now she didn't want this sympathetic man who loved her so tenderly to leave. She had given him her hand again when he stood up, and said, "Renin, please, I'm so lonely. Please stay with me."

Once again he had hesitated, but her sad face lifted up to his made it impossible for him to go. He had bent and kissed her lips, unable to believe that he held his Lady in his own unworthy arms at last. For a night, Renin was the god he had always yearned to be, lifted high by his goddess.

If it was Renin coming each week, Gomer thought, *I could stand it. But this king drains my heart and my soul each time he comes. Why do I wait? It has been three months since that healing night with Renin, a week since I begged for mercy from the God I left behind in childhood . . . for what do I wait? A miracle? There are no miracles. There is only death to release me.*

The thought was a welcome one for the first time, and she raised her head to stare at the sword that hung above her pillows. Tiglath-pileser had put it there and ordered it left, in case he was caught on one of his visits to her by assassins. The edge was sharp. He had laughingly tested it on a strand of her long hair. It would cut the veins in her wrists well, and no one would really care that she was gone, except Renin. Everyone back in Samaria probably thought she had died long ago.

She rose from her stool, her thin robe falling in draped folds about her graceful body. *Let it be,* she thought and crossed the room. Reaching out her hand, she was about to lift down the heavy iron sword when she froze. Had those been footsteps in the hall? But it was too early! It couldn't be the king yet. He never left the palace until the sun was well down, and it had just dipped below the horizon.

Dropping her hand, Gomer stared at the wall, listening intently. The footsteps were heavy and tired, but determined. *I have heard those sounds before,* she thought, and her heart was beating uncontrollably. She gasped for breath. She felt like she was choking.

She heard the door open behind her and wanted to turn, but couldn't. It closed and someone was with her. Someone was breathing heavily; someone took a step toward her and said in a low, hoarse voice, "Gomer."

She found the strength to turn and look. It was Hosea.

"God of our fathers," she moaned, "have you come to do the deed instead of letting me do it myself?"

His bewilderment showed in his furrowed brow. "What do you mean, Gomer?"

She gestured weakly toward the sword. "I—I was about to kill myself. The Law demands my death, doesn't it? I had reached the point where life was only a living death, where memories only served to show my wickedness up even more. So why not die in my shame?"

"Gomer . . ." His voice was gentle, as were his eyes. Her memory of his eyes was as nothing compared to the reality. "I haven't come to kill you. I've come to take you home."

The stillness in the room grew until Hosea felt he had to say something else. She was standing there dazed. Maybe she hadn't heard him. "Our beloved Adonai sent me here to get you, my wife. It's taken me two months to find you, but now I'm taking you back to Samaria."

"Home," she whispered. It had an unfamiliar sound. "And—Imma and Abba? They live yet?"

He realized that it was twenty years since she had used those words. "They live. They don't know I'm here, but I know they'll be glad to see you again. Your father has wept often over you."

She closed her eyes, shame and grief choking her. That such a man should weep over her, a man who had worked hard and never doubted his God. . . . She had met no such man as he in the nights in the temple, a man strong in all things and especially in his faith. The men here had been like worms in comparison, except for Tiglath-pileser—and Renin.

She opened her eyes and looked at Hosea, the twilight barely bright enough to see by. She saw a man still lean of face and body, but with lines of suffering around his mouth. His graying beard swept his chest. His straight back spoke of his never-ending courage in the face of all the opposition he must have faced these seven years, especially the mockery that came from her desertion. But his eyes were the same, dark in their tenderness. The two-month journey through the mountains and desert had washed all of the hate and bitterness away that she remembered, and only the gentleness remained, refined by meditation, suffering, and his last poignant meeting with God.

Hosea in his turn saw a woman who was a stranger, for he had never seen Gomer helpless and in despair. Always she had been defiant, her chin up and her eyes flashing, but in her voluntary thought of death she had admitted her defeat at last, a defeat brought about by her own passions and wishes. Her form was slim and seductive, her hair long enough to wrap himself in—as he knew Pekahiah surely had if he had loved her as the young Hosea once loved her. Only Pekahiah probably had done it, and the young Hosea had never dared. Her golden eyes were sad and empty and bewildered, but he sensed that her fire was still hidden inside somewhere.

"Hosea . . ." She tasted his name, loving the warmth it kindled within her desolate heart. "How did you find me?"

He stood gazing at her, remembering what the Man had told him, that his love for her wasn't as dead as it seemed. *He was so right,* Hosea thought, *for I love her more than I ever did in Samaria. And to see her again is bringing back all the joy I once thought God had taken away forever from my life.* "I knew from your parents that you had been sent to Nineveh with the exiled Assyrian soldiers, so I came straight here. When you were sent away I—I was ill, but some good people took care of me until I was well. When I returned to Samaria and found that Pekah had succeeded—but we won't speak of that," he said hastily, wondering if she still cared about Pekahiah, if the thought of his murder still hurt. But she stood there, patiently waiting for him to go on, and a great relief swept away the last of the jealousy and hurt that had crippled him for so long. "When I came to Nineveh, I asked the guards at the city gates if any of the soldiers sent back by Pekah were still around. I felt that if anyone knew where you had been sent, or if you were indeed still alive, those men would. They sent me to Kalakh to ask for Renin, the king's captain."

She gave a strangled sound. "Renin! Did he tell you?" How would the soldier have felt to see the man she had left behind, the man who had once so furiously denounced his master Pekahiah?

"Yes, he did tell me. He was most courteous. Indeed, he said that he hoped I would get you out of here quickly, before nightfall. Otherwise, the king will catch us and have us both killed. He was quite urgent about it, but I know our God will protect us. He brought me thus far, and he won't desert us now. He told me my time is but beginning. This, Gomer," he said hesitantly, "is our real beginning, for from here we go, both of us, with God, if—if you will come." For with dismay he realized that she might well not want to return to Samaria, even though she had already shown that she had no wish to remain here.

But Gomer was smiling, and a gentle light was in her eyes. For she was seeing again Hosea as he had been so long ago when they had romped as children through the meadows. He had been brave then, too, in his quiet way, not caring if the city bully had threatened to knock him over. She had thought him so wonderful then. . . .

"Hosea, how can I return? The Law must be fulfilled." The reality of what she said didn't make Gomer shudder as it once had, for she found she could face this calmly; for the first time in her life, in these past few weeks she knew she deserved to die.

Hosea frowned. "When I asked that question, our Adonai told me that the Law *would* be fulfilled, that I would know what to do when I brought you home. I—I think he means that you won't die, but that somehow someone else will pay your penalty."

"But who would die for me, Hosea?" she asked, her gaze on his face. *How could I ever have left this man?* she was thinking in quiet wonder. *Here is peace; here is love if I had but seen and not looked elsewhere; here is joy if I had but understood that source. Can he really have forgiven me?*

He had no answer. They looked at each other, the stillness holding them together. Then they heard footsteps in the hall.

Suddenly Tiglath-pileser flung the door open and glared at them. "I heard that a strange man had come up to your room, a man who didn't pay and moreover who told the priestess that she would die within the year for her sins. What sins would the highest worshiper of our Lady commit? And how dared you, a foreigner, show your face in this place?"

He shot his grim words at Hosea, who stood calmly before him. Gomer spoke quietly from the shadows. "He is my husband."

"Your *what?*" The king's roar must have disturbed all the occupants of the second floor. "This is the trouble-maker of Samaria? What do you here?"

"I have come to take my wife home."

Tiglath-pileser laughed, anger burning in his black eyes. The two soldiers behind him were trembling, for they had never seen their master so furious. "Listen, prophet, your wife, as you call her, has been devoted to Ishtar, and here she stays until she dies. Besides, how can a dark nomad like you claim such a fair woman? She's not one of your women!"

Hosea smiled, amused. "Pul, her grandfather was a Greek who became a proselyte of the faith of Moses and married Gomer's mother's mother. Our faith accepts foreigners and honors them, but yours degrades them as my wife has been degraded. I know about your temple," and his voice had grown grim, "where the unwanted girl babies born to wealthy families are sold, where tiny girls found on garbage heaps behind poor homes are brought. They are slaves, trained to wait upon men, and you have made my wife into a slave. This is a shame upon your nation, Pul, as are many other things."

The king was growing purple with rage, and the repetition of his despised surname brought him close to explosion. He spoke through his gritted teeth. "Yes, your wife is a slave, *my* slave, for *I* am Enlil, *I* am Ashur, *I* am Ninib, *I* am Tammuz—and all that is here is mine!"

"Beware, man, of calling yourself God," Hosea said softly. And the quiet assurance of his bearing halted the king's murderous tantrum, for he had been fumbling for his sword with trembling fingers. But now he paused, and a crafty look came into his eyes.

"A slave may be bought, prophet."

"Yes."

Gomer watched them, praying, hoping, wondering if she could reach the sword over the bed before the king reached Hosea. She was afraid that Hosea wouldn't be able to free her after all. But then she remembered her wild cries for mercy a week before, and realized that the answer was before her. God had, indeed, sent her a release much better than death: a new life lived with Hosea in the love she had once scorned. She relaxed and listened.

Tiglath-pileser was enjoying himself. He was sure that

the man before him had not managed to come all the way to Nineveh with any money, for robbers were plentiful and the man was unarmed. "The price for a slave is thirty pieces of silver, prophet. I'm sure a man of your means is well able . . ." His jaw dropped.

Hosea had calmly taken a purse out of his girdle and was counting silver discs into his palm. He raised his eyes and smiled at the king's stunned face. "I met no robbers on the way, O King, for my God protected me. I will give you fifteen pieces and this bag of barley I bought outside for the return trip, a homer and half again, for which I also paid fifteen pieces." He handed the money and a bag Gomer hadn't noticed by the door to one of the soldiers. "There. Now, my wife is my own again."

He didn't seem to notice that the king was still sputtering with rage like a huge dog balked by a mouse. He turned to Gomer and held out his hand. Smiling, her heart too full for words, Gomer reached out both hands to him, and he led her out of the room.

EPILOGUE — 721 B.C.

As soon as the Assyrian army had started its long trek home, leaving behind the smoldering ruins of Samaria, Prince Sargon sent for the commanding officer of the army. When Renin arrived, the prince spoke as he adjusted a strap on his horse's saddle. "My father, the king, has received disturbing reports concerning the guerrilla bands to the east, by the river Jordan. Apparently they are harrying our scouting parties and need a lesson." The prince was bent over his horse's neck as he talked, and Renin glanced over at him, a giant smirk of amusement on his lips. The whole army knew that Shalmaneser the king had spent the last two days too drunk to care about messengers. He had no doubt that the prince kept his father well supplied with the beer that was rapidly killing him.

"You wish a detachment sent then, my prince?" Just then Renin's horse shied slightly, and he gripped its broad ribcage with his knees. It felt the control of strength and subsided reluctantly.

Sargon had noticed, and chuckled. "We are all eager to leave this place. It's been a dreary three years, Renin."

"Successful" was all Renin answered.

Sargon looked at him with his clear, young eyes, and Renin felt all his usual mistrust. Most men were fooled by those eyes, but Renin had known the royal spawn since birth, and knew the twisted cunning in that brain, the brain that was masterminding the slow murder of his father so that he could take control of Nineveh as soon as he arrived. He probably had it timed to the day. And Renin could do nothing, nor did he wish to try; he had no use for kings anymore. Nor any use for war, but that he could not face, for then life itself would have no purpose. Purpose had departed with beauty, yet he maintained the fiction of its existence.

Sargon was speaking. "I don't want you to send a detachment, Renin. I want you to take a troop of your best men, preferably with some who know the area. I want you to patrol the area by the river as the army goes north, and then join us in three days where the falls become the river, up by Dan. I want any leaders of the bandits alive, if possible. I hear they have hidden hoards of great wealth."

The prince did not miss much, Renin thought. *And he is obviously aware of my suspicions concerning his father and wants me out of the way. So much the better,* the general mused. "Yes, my prince." Renin turned and rode back along the line.

The night came swiftly westward on silent wings over the wilderness of Moab as Renin and his chosen troops came up to the edge of the river. Rugged hills lay silent around them, a hint of menace in their seeming emptiness. Renin knew that watchers were waiting for them to make camp, and he intended to cross before he did so. He wanted any encounters to be by his choosing.

"We cross here," he said briefly, and he started to turn his horse into the sluggish brown water.

But one of his men said, "Adonai, what is that? Look across the river."

He looked and saw a mound of stones stacked hastily against the rise on the other bank. The stones were small and piled into the shape of a grave.

"Someone has died here," said the soldier who had stopped him. "Who knows what demon lives in these waters? Perhaps he does not know Assur. Perhaps we should cross elsewhere."

Just then another voice spoke. "General, if I may answer?"

Renin nodded, his eyes on the grave. He felt a sense of stillness, of waiting, of destiny. *Some god is here,* he thought.

"I am a man of this region, my general, and I joined your army as you came south three years ago because I hated Pekah, our king. Once when I served him, he had me whipped for no reason and—"

"I care not why you joined, man; speak of the grave."

"Yes, Adonai," said the voice behind him. "Three years ago a man, his wife, and family fled Samaria—did you speak, general?"

"Go on." Renin's back was stiff, his mouth tight from the sudden knowledge that pierced him. *Gomer. . . .*

"Well, the bandits we are hunting now were here then and saw this family as they came here to the Jordan and stopped them to demand their wealth. The man protested and said they had no money, and the woman—

Adonai, she was beautiful that one, although she looked old. She walked like a queen." The man's voice still held remembered awe, and Renin closed his eyes.

"Go on." There was tight fear in his voice. *Did she lie over there?*

"I was one of those bandits, Adonai. The man showed me his pack, and there were only scrolls in them. Then I recognized him: He was the holy man from Samaria. I told my leader, and we let him go. They crossed here, the man and woman and their three children. But one of our number was crazed; he hated holy men, and he lifted his spear and threw it. The woman saw it coming and shoved her children away—they were walking in file through the water—and her husband saw her danger and pushed her down too. It all happened so fast. . . . He lies there. The woman built the grave over him, for we had no tools for burial. She refused our help."

Renin felt his spine go slack with relief. It was not she. To what god should he offer sacrifice that this was so? He sat his horse a moment in the silence after the man finished, his head turned to the south already wrapped in darkness. He wanted to go south, to Judea, to see if she had come to a safe place. Or was there another grave lying hidden among those hills?

He heard the men behind him whispering, wondering. They thought he was afraid to cross with the grave over there. He was afraid, but not of him who lay under those stones. He recalled the one time he had seen the holy man, when he came to Nineveh to buy his wife back from Tiglath-pileser. The prophet had been gaunt and weary from the trek across the desert, but his eyes had held Renin's with their intensity and certainty. He remembered that so clearly. Her husband. . . .

Another few seconds passed in silent salute. Then: "On," he said. He turned his horse to the north, leaving the grave in its still isolation. The troop followed him into the dusk.

Other Living Books Bestsellers

THE MAN WHO COULD DO NO WRONG by Charles E. Blair with John and Elizabeth Sherrill. He built one of the largest churches in America . . . then he made a mistake. This is the incredible story of Pastor Charles E. Blair, accused of massive fraud. A book "for error-prone people in search of the Christian's secret for handling mistakes." 07–4002 $3.50.

GIVERS, TAKERS AND OTHER KINDS OF LOVERS by Josh Mc-Dowell. This book bypasses vague generalities about love and sex and gets right down to basic questions: Whatever happened to sexual freedom? What's true love like? What is your most important sex organ? Do men respond differently than women? If you're looking for straight answers about God's plan for love and sexuality then this book was written for you. 07–1031 $2.50.

MORE THAN A CARPENTER by Josh McDowell. This best selling author thought Christians must be "out of their minds." He put them down. He argued against their faith. But eventually he saw that his arguments wouldn't stand up. In this book, Josh focuses upon the person who changed his life—Jesus Christ. 07–4552 $2.50.

HIND'S FEET ON HIGH PLACES by Hannah Hurnard. A classic allegory which has sold more than a million copies! 07–1429 $3.50.

THE CATCH ME KILLER by Bob Erler with John Souter. Golden gloves, black bell, green beret, silver badge. Supercop Bob Erler had earned the colors of manhood. Now can he survive prison life? An incredible true story of forgiveness and hope. 07–0214 $3.50.

WHAT WIVES WISH THEIR HUSBANDS KNEW ABOUT WOMEN by Dr. James Dobson. By the best selling author of *DARE TO DIS-CIPLINE* and *THE STRONG-WILLED CHILD,* here's a vital book that speaks to the unique emotional needs and aspirations of today's woman. An immensely practical, interesting guide. 07–7896 $2.95.

PONTIUS PILATE by Dr. Paul Maier. This fascinating novel is about one of the most famous Romans in history—the man who declared Jesus innocent but who nevertheless sent him to the cross. This powerful biblical novel gives you a unique insight into the life and death of Jesus. 07–4852 $3.95.

LIFE IS TREMENDOUS by Charlie Jones. Believing that enthusiasm makes the difference, Jones shows how anyone can be happy, involved, relevant, productive, healthy, and secure in the midst of a high-pressure, commercialized, automated society. 07–2184 $2.50.

HOW TO BE HAPPY THOUGH MARRIED by Dr. Tim LaHaye. One of America's most successful marriage counselors gives practical, proven advice for marital happiness. 07–1499 $2.95.

The books listed are available at your bookstore. If unavailable, send check with order to cover retail price plus 10% for postage and handling to:

Tyndale House Publishers, Inc.
Box 80
Wheaton, Illinois 60189

Prices and availability subject to change without notice. Allow 4-6 weeks for delivery.